My Sister's Keeper

Also by the Author
ONE EASY PIECE

My Sister's Keeper

Don Merritt

Coward-McCann, Inc.
NEW YORK

Wilfred Owen, *Collected Poems of Wilfred Owen*. Copyright © 1963
Chatto & Windus Ltd. Reprinted by permission of New Directions
Publishing Corporation, the Author's Literary Estate, and Chatto &
Windus Ltd.

Library of Congress Cataloging in Publication Data

Merritt, Don, date.
  My sister's keeper.

  I. Title.
PS3563.E74538M9 1983   813'.54   82-22230
ISBN 0-698-11230-X

Printed in the United States of America

FOR PAMELA

and with appreciation to Dr. Clark Eldridge, who offered his psychological expertise but is in no way responsible for the uses made of it; also thanks for the aid and comfort— Dr. Eugenia Kos, Mark Felton, Michele Kubli, and my agent, Molly Friedrich.

Contents

Love automatically tends toward madness. Left to itself, it goes to utter extremes.
—José Ortega y Gasset

prolegomena

carl and claire

1

Carl Grant accepted his sister crawling into bed with him the night after he broke his ankle jumping from the garage roof with the same sense of beguiled confusion he accepted the dogmatic religious fervor that characterized his home—that is, with no more consciousness than he would suppose to debate the existence of Claire herself. Some things just were. Life had its necessities: to worship God, obey one's parents and all suitable elders, eat nutritionally balanced meals, avoid vice in all its devilish forms, respect the law, and this and that. To this list Carl added the name of his sister, Claire. Such was the state of things. He never did understand how Claire escaped it.

It was quite a deal, Claire's scooting in there next to him. He a good ten sheets to the wind on Demerol for the pain of a broken bone. "Mayday, Mayday!" his brain wanted to scream, but he turned silently toward her.

"Are you cold?" Claire asked. "You're shaking."

"I had a dream," came his incongruous answer.

"Why did you jump off the garage roof, dummy?"

"Don't call me dummy."

"And don't tell me that lie you told Mother either."

"I wanted to live with Daddy, I guess."

"True? You dumb little shit."

Her mouth was already against his ear, the smell of her hair defining the limits of his world. Her fragrant, strawberry blond, silken, paradigmatic hair. He whispered, "Please don't say dirty words, Claire, because He hears them and gets mad." He did not like Claire's recent discovery of the power of "shit."

"Your breath tickles my ear," she said, touching his nose with her fingertips. "Promise me here and now you'll never do anything like that again." Carl nodded easily, for it was not in his plans. "Dying isn't the whizbang deal Mommy tells you it is. So don't do anything stupid, thinking you'll get to see Daddy. Is that an okay?"

"It's okay."

She turned his head up to get his breath out of her ticklish ear. Her nose touched his nose.

"And if you ever want to talk about Daddy, ask me, not her, okay? I know more, okay? Promise?"

His nose rubbed hers when he nodded.

"You dumb little shit."

"Oh, Claire."

She was to him the smell of her hair, the pungent warmth of her breath, and her luxuriously manipulating thin fingers.

Claire was ten then, three years older than her brother.

2

Nothing made sense to Claire. She was a scoffer, a creator of mockeries. But that was all right. No law said the world had to make sense. Events were capricious, chaos ruled, random the law. Such an attitude made her difficult.

Claire was born, so her mother often said, with the devil's imagination. Among other curses. A child of many curses, not the least of which was extraordinary beauty. She was conceived in godless lust on the banks of Keosaqua Creek during the Assembly of the Brethren picnic on a hot, mosquito-filled summer night; Coreen soon-to-be-Grant's interior spawned Claire. And Claire *was* beautiful from the moment of her birth, an evil rivaling her unfettered and ambitious imagination in that household. Doomed to lust, her mother said. Not that they didn't try, Coreen and Charles Grant, to save her. But no amount of force-fed Bible verses, no amount of whacking with a good-sized belt, no way of dressing her—nothing overcame the power of the devil in that child. Conceived in the only instant of pleasure Coreen Grant ever knew.

Maybe if Claire had only been beautiful. If it were only that. Then the effect she had on others, though still awesome, might have been less devastating. But her voice came out low, lilting, sensually raw, making her the point of too much unhealthy attention. Maybe if her eyes had been a little less full and round and dynamically blue. If not the totally disarming smile. If not so bright and quick-witted. But Claire was all those things. She staggered men; she terrified women.

Everything existed for and around Claire, the child of sin, as if she did not have the ability to distinguish fully between herself and others, everything, rather, coexisting within her. It seemed an odd sort of inner life, she always acting as if she were directly in the center of everything because the world was only a projection of herself in it. She lived in the midst of her own subjectivity and explained it, when called upon, as the way things go. Or, in her mother's words, an example of the devil's power on earth.

Her mother tried to save her, and her father tried to love her, both with moot success. Claire noticed both attempts. Surreptitiously Claire watched her father. Coreen Grant disapproved of open looks, for they could be mistaken as wanton, she said plainly and without a trace of sarcasm. So it was a secret viewing, private and wondrous. Claire compared her beauty with his, as though to confirm her source, to find a place for herself within the family. Charles Grant was a handsome man; all red and Nordic, all tall and firm, all form and fashion. A banker by trade, a Christian by necessity, a father by desire, a husband by default. Claire watched him eat, drink, cough, wink, wash, walk, nap, read. How did he frown? Smile? Laugh? Knife in right hand, fork in left. No switching. And thus she ate. Did the peas bleed into the potatoes? Okay. Then neither would hers. Did he cross his ankles when napping on the couch?

Okay, hers would, too. A cow and calf, even if wrong gender. It never confused Claire.

When she could get away with it, Claire peeked through the bathroom door's keyhole to watch her father shaving: the pat of warm water on his face, the squirt and application of salty-fragrant lather, the gentle run of the razor. She knelt in the hall, cautiously attentive to the sounds of her mother in the kitchen below. Daddy standing at the sink in his off-white boxer shorts. Eye to the keyhole those special mornings, Claire studied him. Down on both knees, one ear attuned to the sounds in the kitchen and the other to the door of Carl's bedroom, she spied on her father, aching for his touch. His long-lost, neglected, abandoned touch. "Claire's getting too big for that now," Coreen warned solemnly. "We cannot cater to her base instincts, aren't things bad enough?" So he stopped in favor of peace, which he craved with every breath; stopped the good-night and good-bye kisses, stopped the easy-chair television cuddles, stopped everything warmer and more significant than a handshake and a proud pat on the back. The only place left was church, where, as they were seated side by side, Claire's shoulder touched her father's arm.

Sometimes down there on the floor Claire watched his eyes watching his eyes in the mirror, wiping condensation with his off-white towel once or twice. In some awkward childish fashion she mourned his reflected sight. But some other times he quietly hummed playful tunes and seemed to want to whistle, although he never did. Claire wished he would whistle. The acrid smell of Old Spice drifted to her, funneled through the keyhole, reminding her of old still-bright good-bye kisses. In those safer, innocent days she watched him through the living room's bay windows until he strolled out of sight, into the sanctuary beyond the house. She could see him for almost three blocks down the straight elm-shaded street. The elms, drooping with disease, died the same year her father did; Claire believed, from the loss.

Light from the bathroom window sparkled through the fine, light hairs stretching in a line from his chest down his flat, freckled stomach to disappear beneath the waistband of his shorts, where the bump was. Only once had Claire seen the bump exposed. Once, that time, he stood by the window, peeking through the slit in the curtains and absentmindedly, it seemed, pushed his shorts down until they clumped on the floor. The bump, visible then as some odd appendage more like a limp, chubby thumb than anything other, drew his absentminded fingers. He pulled it, probed, withdrew, and stared out the window. His mouth slack. Almost to drool. She watched it grow to fill his hand and beyond and thought it a miracle of transfiguration, in her way. That like a lizard with its tail, Daddy could revitalize a limp, shrunken piece of his body and make it beautifully strong. Claire assumed a personal deficiency in the absence of her own bump.

She would stay there, always waiting for another miracle, until her mother called, "Claire! Come and set the table." And reluctantly she would pull herself away from the keyhole to plod downstairs, mimicking the journey from heaven to hell. She never saw him perform another miracle. A year later, or maybe it was two, he died: a frenzied seizure at the public water fountain in the bank lobby. Claire was ten.

Carl was seven. Sometimes he saw Claire on her knees at the altar of the bathroom door. When he investigated, she jumped up on wobbly, asleep knees and pushed him back into his room, her hand over his mouth before he could ask, ordered never to tell on penalty of death by drowning head down in the toilet bowl. It was another year before Carl discovered to his amazement that one could actually *see* into a room through a door's keyhole.

The day they buried Charles Grant, after the neighbors, friends, relatives, and curious had finally left, Claire awakened to the sound of ominous mumbling from downstairs. In a grog she waited until curiosity overcame her before getting up. The clock chimed its methodical announcement of midnight as she padded softly down the stairs.

The living room was a shrine, Mother kneeling before the coffee table, on which were intricately placed the family's fat red-leather Bible, four skinny candles at the corners, an ornately framed, black-bordered photograph of Father surrounded by dry sprigs of fern from the funeral arrangement, and the bright, sparkling blade of a meat carving knife. Mother's hands were held to her face in prayer. Like a Catholic thing, Claire thought. But Mommy hates Catholics. So Claire perched herself curiously at the bottom of the stairs to peer into the living room and wait for ghosts or something. Mother mumbled.

Claire watched for a long time, occasionally rubbing her eyes with tight fists. She wanted to cry again, Mommy's mourning was so terribly sad. But how much could a small heart bleed before it was dry? she wondered.

Her mother's voice raised in prayer.

"My dear God, savior and protector, maker of all things, holy father of the Brethren, God of the universe, I call to you in humble adoration, in fear and trembling. Please hear my submission, O God."

Claire scooted down two more steps to the floor and crouched by the corner banister, holding her breath to save each word intact.

"Infinite, merciful God, I believe. In the name of your only begotten son, Jesus, leader of the Brethren, I do believe.

"My spirit is trembling, and my heart does beat in absolute agony. My Charles has left this earth. May his soul fly to your side, O God. Let him shine now and forever in your reflected light, your eternal glow.

"I ask . . . I beg, please do not send him to the eternal fiery furnaces for the sins of our youth. If someone must pay your exacting price for our sin, let it be me. I pray thee.

"We accepted the child of that lust, the devil's own child, and called her Claire, she conceived in the devil's grip in the darkness of the devil's night. And we tried to save her for you. Have I not tried to give her your holy light? Will you punish us for the power that lurks within her?

"Did you not give us a son, Carl, whom we dedicated to your name and service?

"Allow the balance, O God, in your infinite wisdom and mercy. I beg you to have mercy on my dear Charles, whose ways were your ways.

"I make this vow in your name and his memory: I will raise my son in your name and offer this oath."

Claire watched her mother raise the knife into the air, light popping off its bright blade like sparks shot through a prism and dancing off the walls.

"This I pledge: You, dear God, will be the last man to see my body, to lust after me will no man, to envy me will no woman, nor will any man ever touch me or desire me carnally . . ."

Claire watched in horror as her mother pulled open her robe, exposing herself to the flickering light. The robe fell back to the floor like an abandoned scrap of cloth.

"I will mark myself with your sign, and all will know that I belong only to my Lord and Master and our son. The remainder of my gift of days will be devoted to your service."

Claire watched the knife blade lower in her mother's steady hand until the sparkling tip of it was against the skin on the upper rise of her right breast. Slowly, deliberately, she carved the mark of a cross in the skin there, stretching over the mound to the nipple. Blood dripped in a double line encircling the breast. Then she carved a second cross in the skin of her left breast. Bleeding from both sides, targeted breasts and tracks on her stomach, she leaned back almost ecstatically, stretched out her legs, and carved a third mark in the skin below her pubic hair. The blood disappeared between her legs. Then came a joyful moan.

Pushing backward with her hands, Claire crept up the stairs without turning around until she reached the bend at the top. Then she went quickly to her bedroom and hid beneath the covers, afraid she was next for the knife. "I am my father's child," she cried into the pillow, "not the devil's." Soon she slept in anguish and exhaustion.

Some days later, when Carl noticed a neighborhood boy had gotten a new father, he asked Claire if they were ever going to get a new father. "Not a chance," Claire told him. So Carl decided to go see his old one.

3

Carl had never been certain about the first time Claire came to his bed. In a Demerol stupor and soundly asleep, he could have had an evil, perverse dream. She did not come again for years.

Carl knew more about the Bible than any other book, of which there were no others on public display in his house. It did not occur to Carl that being called by the other kids in the neighborhood the littlest disciple was not intended to honor him for an obvious piety. Youth was a time for lessons. Every story had a moral; every action, a religious meaning and consequence. Every word spoken, every thought imagined were noted meticulously in a book in heaven carrying his name on its cover. Everyone had such a book. At the moment of death Carl, like everyone, would stand before the tribunal of angels while his words, thoughts, and deeds were read back for all to hear. Then God would judge. Death, then, was the alpha of mankind's most glorious moment—an eternal moment. Or maybe not so glorious. Only those who led the good and holy life, the life of the Brethren, would be bathed forever in the benevolent light of the Maker. Others, those who lived persistently in sin, who entertained sacrilegious thoughts, who did not receive God's son as Lord and Savior, who did not *believe*—for them, a vengeful and malevolently omnipotent God, the one with the angry eyes and wild white hair Carl saw in his nightmares, would cast the offender into the horrible ovens of hell without blinking an eye.

Why, Carl wondered, was everyone so sad and mournful at his father's funeral? Was Daddy gone to hell? Heaven? If heaven, why the sadness? Was there a lie somewhere? He was spanked for such blasphemous logic.

It was not long after when Carl jumped from the garage roof to find out where Daddy went. And Claire did come to him that night.

The next time, Carl was twelve years old and Claire was fifteen. There had been that day another in the *ad infinitum* series of arguments between Claire and their mother, only that one, as some did, degenerated into violence, ending when Coreen chased Claire out the back door with a mad broom handle.

Carl rushed to the sanctuary of his bedroom directly after supper—a solemn, even pathetic affair those battlefield evenings—and listened to the portable radio his mother had bought for him as a reward for filling his five-year gold star book for perfect Sunday school attendance. He tried to block out the hatred he felt for his mother. Honor thy father and thy mother. Not being able to love her scared him to death. But all he could produce was a little bit of fearful respect.

Coreen awakened him when she turned off the radio; she made him stand before her to rebuke him for falling asleep with the radio on. Waste was an abomination. It was cold standing there in his underwear, but he was afraid to ask if he could close the window or cover himself with a robe. She riveted him in place with her hard eyes.

Rhetorically she asked if he deserved to be spanked.

"Yes, ma'am," Carl answered, shivering.

"Waste not, want not."

"No, ma'am."

"I am waiting for you to say it."

"I'm sorry."

"And to ask the Lord's forgiveness."

"What for?"

Rubbing the sting left by the slap across his face, he said, "Forgive me, Lord," adding silently, *I know not what I have done.*

"Good boy. Now turn around, and let go your underwear."

"Oh, Mom."

"Do it."

Carl turned around, facing the bed, and pulled down his pants. Chill bumps covered the pale skin below. It was the waiting that destroyed him each time. She bent him by pushing down on his neck, then slapped his thin buttocks once with the palm of her hand.

"Rise up," she commanded.

Carl did, waiting, embarrassed by his nakedness.

"Turn around."

"Oh, Mom."

He did, closing his eyes.

"Have you been touching yourself down here again?" Roughly she raised his scrotum and inspected him. "Tell me the truth, son."

"No, ma'am," Carl lied.

She pulled at it, tugged and let it droop. In spite of himself, blood filled it.

"What is this bump here? Is this a wart? Don't lie to me, son. It feels warm to the touch. Did you abuse yourself tonight?"

"No, ma'am, I promise." The truth of it raised his voice.

She let go of him and said, "Cover yourself."

Carl quickly retrieved his pants. "May I get back in bed now, Mommy?" She nodded, and he pulled the quilt up to his neck.

"Do you love your mother and honor the memory of your father?"

"Yes, ma'am."

"And you did say your prayers before bed?"

"Yes, ma'am."

Her lips were cool and waxy against his. When she had gone, Carl thought about the slap of her hand on his hips and wondered how much different it was when Claire was beaten with a strap. He needed to go to the bathroom but was afraid to get up.

Carl had not been sleeping very long when movement on the bed awakened him. Claire's smell stirred him. "Huh!" he cried out.

"Ssssh," Claire whispered, putting her hand over his mouth. "It's just me."

Carl opened his eyes and saw Claire leaning over him, she in her nightgown, the yellow one with lace on the bodice, her hair tied back in a ponytail, smelling freshly washed.

"It's snowing. I thought you might be cold," Claire said, climbing beneath the quilt to lie beside him. Her head rested on the pillow next to his.

Carl winced at her touch, yet snuggled next to her, contented with the warmth and smell of her.

"It isn't sticking to the streets yet," she said.

"It's snowing?"

"I said that."

"I wish you and Mom didn't fight so much."

"Hmmm," Claire murmured distractedly. "Do you know where I went tonight?"

"How would I know that?"

"Well, aren't you going to guess?"

Carl rubbed his eyes, then looked at her again. She smiled cryptically. He propped his head on a bent arm and curled a lock of her ponytail around his index finger, as he often did. Their knees bumped together and stayed. He felt horribly wonderful.

"Katy Unger's house?" he guessed.

"Jeez, are you kidding?"

"She's your best friend."

"Used to be. Come on, guess again."

"What did Katy do?"

"Nothing, nothing. She's a liar, all right? Forget it. Come on."

"Is this my first or second? How many do I get?"

"Three, dummy. Everybody gets three."

"Who made that rule?"

"Don't talk so loud."

"Hey, and don't call me dummy," he whispered. "This is just my first since I didn't know we were counting only to three."

"What? What kind of BS line is that? Everybody knows you only get three wishes. Jee-sus!"

"You better be quiet, too."

"All right, so this is your first, okay? Suit you? I'll give you a hint."

"No, not yet. Wait and see if I get it this time. You can give me a hint if I don't get it after the second try."

"This really *is* the second try."

Carl turned over, away from her.

"Hey, all right. It's the first. Jeez, you're a pill sometimes."

Carl turned smugly back toward her and said, for he had been thinking, "The Lumberjack."

"Wrong-o, kiddo."

Carl frowned, furrowed his brow, closed his eyes, and five seconds later said, "I don't even care."

"Is that supposed to be a guess? Let me give you a hint since you'll never get it anyhow."

"Okay, but not a big one."

"It starts with *H,* the letter *H.*"

"*H?*"

Claire waited awhile until her patience ran out. She knew he wouldn't get it in a million tries. "Give up?"

"No! Wait, I'm still thinking. *H?*"

"Well, you better think quieter, kiddo, or we'll be invaded by the Wicked Witch of the West."

"You be quiet while I'm thinking."

She didn't wait. "Hennepin Avenue," smugly announced.

"Where's Hennepin Avenue? Is that the answer?"

"You are an absolute cretin."

"A what?"

"A dumb-ass."

"Don't cuss."

"'Ass' is in the Bible, kiddo."

"Not the way you say it, it isn't."

"Do you want to know about Hennepin Avenue, or what?"

"Yeah, I gues so."

"Hennepin Avenue is only the wildest street in Minneapolis."

"Wild?"

"Jee-sus, you know! Dirty bookstores, dirty movies, bars, hookers . . . like whores, the whole thing. That's where *I* was tonight."

"Gosh." Carl felt a twinge of awe, but fear quickly replaced it. "Mom will kill you."

"She's been trying for fifteen years and hasn't done it yet. Besides, what she doesn't know won't hurt me. You better not tell."

"I won't. What did you do?" He feared to ask.

"Want three guesses?"

"Just tell me, all right?"

Claire put her hand on the slope of Carl's hip. It felt hot enough to leave an imprint.

"Well, for one thing, I went to a bar."

"You can't. You're not old enough."

"Maybe I look old enough. I didn't get carded. Besides"—she paused for what seemed like a minute—"I went with a man."

"What man?" Carl sat up, and Claire's hand fell off his hip. Noticing its absence intensified its previous presence. "What do you mean, 'a man'?"

"A man man. How many other kinds do you know about? Come on, Carl—jeez!"

"You're teasing."

"Wanta bet?" She touched a fingertip to his lips as a warning to keep his voice down.

Carl felt the flush of jealousy in his throat and face, feeling like nausea. A car's tires squished through the slush in the street outside. He studied her face while she let her hand find its way back to his hip. It lay expectantly, trembling on the line where his underwear met his right thigh. Carl felt her fingertips tapping on his thigh like a curious spider. He said, "Did you *really* go to a bar with a man?"

Claire nodded. "And that's not all. I drank three glasses of Tom Collinses. Big, tall glasses. A Tom Collins is like gin and lemonade, in case you didn't know. Smell." She exhaled into his face.

All Carl noticed was the sourness, which he took to be the smell of gin. "Ugh," he said, turning his head away.

"Well, they sure tasted good. I mean, *good!* I could have drank a dozen if I wanted to. But I didn't have any money, and the *man*"—she emphasized excessively—"had other ideas."

"You don't even know his name. You're teasing, Claire."

"Yeah? His name's Bill Carter, and I do too know. Plus he's a senior at U of M, and he's studying prelaw."

"College?"

"So?"

"So nothing. I don't believe you anyway. Mom will kill you."

"Shit."

"Claire!"

"Ssssh."

Her two fingers tugged at the elastic around the legband. A finger dropped down to search.

"Oh, well," she said absentmindedly, "I don't have that old virginity crap hanging around my neck anymore."

Carl was lost in the anticipation of her fingertip but caught his breath. There was some delay before her statement registered. He gulped and scooted up against the headboard. Claire's hand passed over his crotch while falling away.

"You didn't!" Carl said too loudly.

"For chrissakes, kiddo. Ssssh! If you don't keep your voice down, we'll both be dead ducks." She moved her hand up to rest on his stomach. "I swear, you're so dense sometimes."

"Claire!"

Her hand covered his mouth, his lips moving beneath her palm. "If you don't be quiet, I'm going to leave. Do you want to hear about it, or what?"

Carl shook his head; her hand stayed over his mouth.

"Suit yourself." Claire moved both hands—from his mouth and stomach—and lay on her back, staring at the shadows on the ceiling. Blinking her eyes rapidly made bird images appear in hyperkinetic flight.

Carl slid down and lay next to her, looking where she looked, trying to destroy the pictures in his mind by thinking of going on a picnic, and tacitly awaited the return of her fingers. When, in a minute, her fingers were back, he felt himself stirring there. It flooded and grew, like when he anxiously abused himself. The loss of control sickened him. Lost in the devil's grip. Claire's hand threatened to sneak beneath his pants, threatening to infest. Jealousy burned like rising bile in his throat. They both stared at the ceiling as her fingers snugly wrapped him, her thumb resting on the head of it.

"It wasn't really the big deal you think," she said quietly, suddenly, reflectively.

"Did you really do it?" Carl's tone matched hers.

"Uh-huh."

"What did it feel like?"

"Pretty good, mostly. *He* sure liked it. It's quicker than you think it's going to be. Of course, we were in his car, and anybody could have seen us, maybe. That's why we had to hurry, he said."

"It's a terrible sin, and you know it. I'm afraid for you."

"Oh, Carl. Isn't one in the house plenty? I think if there is such thing as sin, and I'm pretty doubtful about the whole idea, it's not what *she* says it is. How does she know anyway? Don't let her fill you up with that stuff, too."

Her fingers stroked him faster, and Carl moved his hips to the spontaneous rhythm she established. It provoked a concentrated silence, a focusing of attention. It lasted until Carl had to ask, "Did you touch him this same way?"

"Sure."

"Then I don't want you doing it to me." He stopped moving

and tried to sit up. Claire let go. "Just leave me alone," he said in an angry whisper.

"Carl, why, I do believe you're jealous."

"Am not. Go away." He would punish her by punishing himself.

"Carl. Jee-sus."

"Just go away . . . and don't ever come back either."

"Don't act like a dumb-ass."

"I hate you." He cried softly; tears formed.

"You *are* jealous. That's sweet."

"And God hates you, too." The tears fell. "And God will punish you. So go away. I don't want Him to get me, too."

"He won't *get* you, Carl, ssssh, don't talk anymore." She urged him to lie down, and he let her. Her fingers stopped a tear. "Don't cry, Carlie. Don't cry." She kissed the track of a tear and licked it. "I love you," she whispered. "Together, we're all we've got."

"You don't love me."

"I do," said very softly. "I really, really do."

"Sure," trying for sarcasm but failing as his voice trembled.

"I love you," she whispered, insistent that he believe her. She licked his salty cheeks again.

"Ugh!" Carl groaned.

"You taste good."

"Ugh, ugh, ugh!"

"Let me show you. Will you let me do that? Teach you? Let me. Okay?"

For a long time Carl refused to cooperate with her in any way, lying flat and still, arms rigidly by his sides. She kissed his eyes and licked his nearest ear. He opened his eyes when she stopped and saw the nightgown leave her body and float to the floor. Her breasts were warm when she put them against his arm. "Let me show you," she said, sliding onto his chest, her tongue licking around his lips, showing him what she had just learned, what she liked. He let her tug down his underwear after only a halfhearted attempt to stop her. For he was already condemned, he already wanted her. He waited for God—wild-haired and angry—to jerk him from the bed and fling him straight to hell.

"Let's try it, I'll show you." Her tongue pushed his aside as it entered his mouth. And he wanted that, too. She cupped him softly, and he grew against her warm, soft stomach.

They did try, but it didn't work. He shrank from the door again and again.

"That's all right. Let's do this." Claire pushed herself up until her breasts smothered his face. "This feels good, too." She guided a nipple to his lips. Feeling awkward and childish and embarrassed, he accepted it. At her warm, heavy breast, he fell asleep. He did not dream about God that night.

Carl never knew when Claire left him; only that morning found him alone and needing to urinate. His attempt to scrub the yellow sticky nocturnal fluid out of the sheet with a washcloth made it only larger and more distinct. When his mother came for the bedding, she spanked him, then inspected him for signs of Onan's curse. He was ordered to spend the entire day in his room studying appropriate Bible verses. Carl found one:

For the lips of a loose woman drip honey, and her speech is smoother than oil; but in the end she is bitter as wormwood, sharp as a two-edged sword. Her feet go down to death. . . .

Carl prayed, but it had the feel of futility: that nothing he could ever do in his ambiguous future would remove the taint. He was madly in love with his sister.

4

Claire returned to him now and then. She was very random about things. When she did come, it was always around midnight, after their mother had been asleep alongside her ornately framed picture of Jesus for at least an hour. Claire woke Carl with the gentle probing of her fingers.

Sometimes Claire would come each night for three or four in a row, then not return for weeks. Carl never went to her during those three years. But on the nights she did not come, Carl would awaken just after midnight, as if some biological alarm had gone off, and reach across the empty side of the bed. He had very little understanding of his need for Claire in those days. Puberty was making him a wreckage all by itself. Sometimes he wanted other girls, but his fumbling attempts to attract them were silly and unsuccessful, although he did manage an occasional kiss and quick feel during neighborhood mixed parties. There was just Claire. When his arm discovered the empty bed, he would roll over and dig his fingernails into the palms of his hands, his insides burning with revulsion and desire. Then he would sleep again. God was fading from his dreams fast, replaced by Claire.

Claire taught Carl in the dark and sheltered hours of those nights together how to use his hands on a woman, how to move his fingers, what could be done to bring pleasure with his lips, how to kiss using his tongue. She taught him about himself, directing him like a puppet. When she wanted him to touch her, she had to place his hand. She initiated the kisses. If she wanted him to suck at her breasts, she had to guide his head and mouth. When she wanted to feel him inside her, she had to direct him with her fingers. He shivered when coming. Claire held him tightly and listened to him breathe in her ear.

Claire had another life, one she led independently of Carl, although he did not. She was elected to things in high school. In defiance of her mother, she dated frequently and went to parties lasting all night. She started smoking cigarettes, and Carl made her open the window no matter how cold it was in his bedroom. He finally started smoking to impress her. But she got angry and made him stop. Sometimes she came to his bed drunk. Sometimes she passed out there and Carl had to carry her back to her own room. He was tall and very strong by the time he was fifteen. And becoming very handsome. Some of Claire's girlfriends teased him, but Claire knew they really wanted to go out with him. Fifteen or not. She told her best girlfriends that Carl was "better than you'll ever know," and they laughed at the joke.

Carl usually saw Claire only at home. Her high school and his junior high were in separate buildings. They rode the bus together in the mornings, but Claire found other ways home, and always an hour or two longer than it should have taken. On Saturdays, occasionally, Claire took Carl to a nearby park, where they went swimming and tanned themselves. Carl would lie in the sun and read the books she recommended for him, ones she had read and liked. When Claire entered the pool in her bikini, everyone fell silent until the water covered her. Lifeguards made fools of themselves in her presence. Carl lay on the concrete decking, reading and fuming with anger. But he liked watching her swim. Claire could throw herself out of the water like a dolphin—shiny, dark, lithe, erotic.

When their mother was away at the hospital, where she worked the evening shift as a licensed practical nurse, Claire brought her boyfriends home. The boys were nice to Carl and talked to him about cars and homework and football. But only for half an hour at the most. Then they wanted him gone. Claire would take Carl up to his room and ask him to be nice and stay out of the living room for an hour. Carl watched them fucking from the bottom of the stairs.

Then their mother came home early from work and found Claire naked on the couch in the living room with a boy's head buried between her legs. A marijuana cigarette burned in the ashtray. And Claire was kicked out.

When Claire left the house, a single large suitcase in one hand and the other hand in her back pocket, their mother standing on the front porch shouting Bible warnings and yelling "whore," Carl expected to see Claire turn the corner and come back to apologize.

It was ten o'clock the morning of Independence Day 1967; Claire was one day into her eighteenth year and a still-fresh high school graduate. She declared her independence with a final gesture when she was less than thirty feet from the house, turning toward her mother with her free arm raised, the middle finger thrust defiantly skyward.

Watching her from the bay window in the living room, Carl saw the gesture. It was not until then that he realized she might not turn back—not an hour later, not a day later, maybe never. He shuddered and began to sweat. His mother's voice was still piercingly loud. "God will curse you for this," Coreen screamed. "You will endure the horrible burden of God's hatred for as long as He lets you live in suffering!"

Carl ran to the door, but his mother's body stopped him from getting outside. "Claire, Claire," he cried. Coreen pushed him back, and Carl struggled against her. "Let me go," he yelled. But she shoved him back inside and slammed the door.

"Leave her to the devil," Coreen said. "She is cursed."

"Get out of my way," Carl cried out in tears. "You did this!"

"Leave her go."

"God damn you!" he screamed.

Coreen Grant picked up a vase filled with daisies and smashed it across Carl's head, splitting open his forehead and knocking him unconscious.

5

Claire had no trouble at all getting out of Minneapolis. It was only five miles from the Grant house to Interstate 35. Claire got a ride with a man who had just been going to the grocery store but knew a good thing when he stumbled upon it. He took her over to the interstate and let her out at a truck plaza.

Claire didn't even have to ask for a ride. She was barely out of the car before two drivers asked if she wanted one. She stayed at the truck stop for an hour, trying to decide among her options. She had rides offered to New York, Miami, Chicago, Seattle, Phoenix, and Los Angeles. She considered each one, all sounding pretty good. She considered going to San Francisco so she could see the Haight-Ashbury and maybe get to see the Jefferson Airplane in concert. She wanted to put flowers in her hair and smoke dope. But nobody was going to San Francisco.

While she was eating a hamburger and drinking a Coke bought for her by the Seattle-bound driver, a man offered to take her to Corpus Christi. While the cowboy-looking driver explained his route—Des Moines, Kansas City, Oklahoma City, Dallas, San Antonio, Corpus Christi—trying to induce her with tales of each town, it occurred to Claire that Corpus Christi meant "the body of Christ." It seemed utterly appropriate.

"Corpus Christi sounds just fine to me," she told the driver. "When are you leaving? I mean, do I have time to finish lunch?"

"Take all the time you want, sugar," he said, smiling so

widely that she could see the fillings in his molars.

Claire left the Minneapolis truck plaza with her suitcase and a $20 bill she had stolen from her mother's purse. She arrived in Corpus Christi three days later with the suitcase and $120, the $100 a thank-you present from the driver. He was so thankful he wanted to marry her.

6

Four days after Claire left home, Carl received a postcard from her. There was a picture of an Indian on it, and across the top in slashing white letters it said: "HOWDY FROM OKLA-HOMA." Carl got the mail first by watching out the window. He hid the postcard in his pants, then took the bills, brochures, and letters in to his mother. She wanted to inspect his stitches, and Carl could feel his sweat against the postcard. When Co-reen finally let him go, Carl rushed up to his room and sat at his desk to read the card.

Hiya kiddo, hope you can read this writing cause I'm trying to make it small enough to fit on this little card and I'm writing it in a truck too. I haven't seen any Indians of any kind in OK yet, except the one on this card. Ha! Hope you're not P-O'd at me for taking off w/o a proper good-bye, but what else could I do? I know where I'm going but can't tell you on this card in case the bitch gets hold of it and calls the cops or whatever. Keep your eyes on the mailbox cause I'll write some real letters and tell you everything. Love ya and miss ya . . . Claire

After Carl had read the card a half dozen times, he put it in his bottom desk drawer beneath a pile of school papers and a dictionary. It lay with the other treasures he had gotten from Claire: an earring; a photograph of Claire in a bikini; a baby picture of her; a picture of Claire at the age of two in her father's arms; a cutting from her hair in an envelope; Claire's hospital wrist ID bracelet from when she had pneumonia; a manila envelope of old school papers Claire wrote in high school with titles like "Summer Explorations," "United States Justice," "The Faustian Image," "What About Vietnam?"; and finally an unopened package of Trojan prophylactics one of Claire's boyfriends had left on the floor a few months earlier.

That afternoon Carl unfolded a United States map that had come inside his civics book and tacked it to the wall next to his desk. When Claire finally told him where she was, he could mark it on the map. He decided to make just a pinhole in the map in case his mother might notice a pushpin stuck there. By the time Carl would see Claire again there would be so many holes in the map that a light shining through it would create a constellation of spots on the wall.

Otherwise, life went on. Coreen prayed in his bedroom at night, asking God to forgive her for cracking open Carl's head. Carl wasn't much interested. He was too big to spank, and Coreen was too afraid to challenge him. Carl just tried to be polite. When she asked him to pray, too, Carl turned over and quietly pretended to sleep. He had more or less lost interest in God.

But later, when he really tried to sleep, thoughts of Claire brought tears to his eyes.

7

Claire wasn't about to marry anybody, but the cowboy driver was hard to convince. Getting the $100 from him made her feel a little like a Hennepin Avenue hooker. The money was nice to have, even necessary given her situation, but she didn't like having it associated with sex. She liked the cowboy and would have slept with him regardless. She liked the slogan "Free Love"; it sounded sensible. Pocketing the five twenties, she decided to think of it as a fee for being co-driver. Like a wage. He had let her drive the truck around the parking lot at the Holiday Inn in Oklahoma City, and sometimes she shifted gears for him on the road. Claire was very proud of the fact that she had never driven a car in her life but could push that big truck around the parking lot without banging into anything.

"When you marry me," the cowboy said, beginning most of his statements that way after Oklahoma City, "I'll teach you to drive—cars and trucks. We'll make one helluva team."

He also gave Claire his cowboy hat, which was too big, but it had beautiful feathers on the crown and Claire had admired them. Claire wished she had something to give him, some kind of keepsake, but couldn't think of anything. The cowboy said she had already given him the best four days of his life. Finally Claire took his pocketknife and sliced off a thick strand of her long blond hair. He promised to weave it into a ring, which he would wear until they met again, when he would slip it onto her ring finger.

Leaving the cowboy at the truck plaza just outside Corpus Christi was difficult for Claire. He was a transition from the enslavement she felt in Minneapolis to the new life she imagined for herself, but being with him had given her a kind of security she hadn't felt since the death of her father. She could feel the cowboy watching her as she took her suitcase and walked out to the highway. She heard the diesel roar when he started the engine. When he blasted the air horn as he pulled out on the highway for Houston, she turned and waved good-bye. The truck was barely out of sight when a pickup truck stopped for her. An old man driving farm produce took her to downtown Corpus Christi. She gave the cowboy hat to the farmer when he admired it. Then she walked to the beach.

Claire's first sight of the ocean was exuberant; she felt delirious in its presence. She did not notice that the sand was more brown than white and littered with refuse, some of it human. The smell of salt, decaying fish, and car exhaust hung in the heated air, but she smelled only the salt. The silver-blue water stretched out to the horizon until it blended with the heat haze rising above it. At the limit of her vision, a giant ship passed with an imperceptible movement from west to east. Claire christened the spectral vision "The Flying Dutchman." She made a mental note to send Carl a postcard with the sea pictured on it, maybe one with a ghost ship, too.

Claire thought the beach was crowded for a Tuesday morning. Where did all the people come from? And such an odd assortment: Potbellied older men with baggy trunks and balding heads sat at the edge of the water where it could lap up over their feet and legs, children from infants to teenagers played in the cool water and the sand, mothers browned their bodies with one eye on the children, and there were dozens of people Claire's age.

It must be 100 degrees, Claire thought, realizing that everyone she saw wore a swimming suit except herself. She was dressed in jeans, tennis shoes, and a T-shirt with grease smudges on it. She felt like pulling off her clothes and running into the water. But would somebody steal her suitcase? Would bra and panties look enough like a bikini to keep her from being arrested? That was the last thing she needed.

Along Shoreline Drive behind her stretched one motel after another. She looked at them, realizing she would have to find some place to stay. She felt nervous but still excited. There was no one to tell her where to sleep, what to eat, what to wear, where to go, what friends to have. It was scary but glorious. How long could she stay in a motel with $120?

Standing by the Gulf of Mexico, Claire felt the weight of the vast bulk of the country separating her from Minnesota. She put the suitcase down on the sand and sat on it, facing the sea. An old man passed in front of her. He carried a metal detector, sweeping the beach in wide, serious arcs. Claire liked his hat. It seemed to be made of beer cans sewn together somehow. She wondered if the metal got hot in the sun. She was getting very hot. The sun stung her bare arms and face, making her skin feel as if it were frying. The old man passed her, eyes down to the sand, and Claire got up and moved her suitcase back to the seawall to sit in its shade. Twenty feet away, a human form slept on top of an empty cardboard refrigerator box with two ragged blankets pulled over its body. She could see the soles of old boots sticking out one end and a shock of wild, tangled, long hair sticking out the other. A bottle of Ripple rested in the sand near the hair end. Claire saw herself having to sleep that way when her money ran out. There was a moment of panic, but it was soon replaced by a confident feeling that she could survive anywhere. "I can always sell this," she said, referring to her body. She stared at the sleeping bum for a few minutes. She wondered if it was dead. She couldn't tell if it was male or female, but presumed male from the large boots. She would have to tell Carl all about this.

Claire noticed him walking toward her when he was still 100 feet away. He gave her quite a start at first, looking like Jesus Christ Himself. His wavy brown hair was long and wet, as if he might have walked right up out of the sea. He wore a dirty white robe and rope sandals, the robe stretching to his ankles. His beard was long enough to have tangles in it. The man could have been the model for the autographed picture of Jesus Claire's mother had ordered for $10 from a radio station in Del Rio, Texas, they could pick up in Minneapolis at night. The thought of that picture hanging over her mother's bed made Claire smile. A big fourteen-by-twenty-inch framed picture, a head shot of Jesus Christ, signed with a bold blue felt-tip pen across the bottom: "PEACE AND BEST WISHES, JESUS CHRIST." When her mother first opened the package containing the picture, Claire took one look at it and laughed out loud, saying, "You've got to be kidding!" Coreen knocked Claire to the floor with the back of her hand.

The incarnated Jesus model continued to walk in Claire's direction. She smiled at him once, then looked back out to sea. When his shadow fell over her face, she looked up at him again, smiling expectantly.

"Hi," he said, a deep, bass voice. "Coming in or going out?"

"Oh, the suitcase? Both, I guess."

"Coming and going, huh? Far-out. I like that." Jesus sat on his haunches next to her. He was so tall that when he squatted, he was only slightly lower than she was seated on the suitcase. "My name's Jess Noble, but my friends call me Rabbit."

"Claire Grant. Why do they call you Rabbit?"

"The way I hop back and forth across the border, I guess. Something like that. Could be other things I do, too."

"Pardon me for asking—"

"Where are you headed—"

They laughed for stepping over each other's words; then Rabbit told her to go first.

"I just wondered if you're some kind of religious freak?" Claire asked.

"Huh? Oh, this." Rabbit touched his robe. "No way. This is just an old beach robe, you know? For the sun. I've got delicate skin. Besides, I don't have on anything under it." He smiled.

"Must be hard to find a place to put your wallet," Claire observed, smiling with him. She liked his face, but particularly his friendly, casual attitude. The sound of his voice was melodic.

"Don't carry one."

Rabbit tired of squatting and let himself fall back until he was sitting on the sand, his arms stretched back for support.

"Do you live here?" Claire asked.

"Back that way about a mile"—Rabbit gestured to the east, along the beach—"on Lobo Street near the old Bayview Park."

"On the beach?" Claire asked.

"No, who can afford it?"

No wallet, dressed in a robe and nothing else, looking like a Haight-Ashbury hippie, Claire thought, he looked as if all he could afford would be the cardboard box the bum slept on.

"How about yourself?" Rabbit asked. "If you're coming and going, that must mean you're always here."

Claire didn't understand the logic, if any, but she liked the way he said things.

"The truth is, I just got here this morning. I'm from Minneapolis. That's in Minnesota."

"I know." Rabbit laughed. "Lumberjacks, ice, all that stuff, right?"

"Right."

"I've never been north of Dallas, but I've been from California to Florida. Always wanted to see some ice and snow."

"You haven't missed much."

"Smoke?" Rabbit asked, fishing a Baggie and papers from a previously hidden pocket in the robe.

"Sure," Claire said, surprised at the magical production of the marijuana from the folds of his robe. "But can you do it out here like this, in the open?"

"All the time. You hardly ever see a cop on this part of the beach." Rabbit shook some grass into two of the papers and expertly rolled a joint. "This is the family beach, you know? From all the hotels over there," he added, nodding his head toward the row of pastel-colored buildings behind the seawall and street. "A narc appears now and then, but they're so crude you can spot one a mile away. Nah, the cops hang out at Emerald Cove and Cole Park, down the beach another mile."

Rabbit lit the joint and sucked the smoke deep into his lungs, then passed it to Claire.

"Panama Red," he said as Claire inhaled. "Bet you don't see much of this in Minnesota."

"No shit," Claire muttered as she exhaled the smoke and coughed. "Gawd!"

"Gets right in there, doesn't it? This is really far-out dope."

They finished the joint quietly, concentrating on enjoying the ritual. Claire finished what remained in the roach clip after Rabbit waved it off. "Wonder how much good dope I'm not getting because I might set this mother on fire," he said, stroking his heavy beard and watching Claire suck on the remainder.

Claire handed him the clip and roach when she was finished, and Rabbit carefully pinched off the ember and shook the leftovers back into the Baggie in his lap. "Waste not, want not," he said. "How about another?"

Claire thought she was going to fall off her suitcase. Her head felt light and giddy. She wanted to slump down into the sand and have someone bury her. "Sure, why not?" she said, sliding off the suitcase and sitting next to Rabbit in the sand.

By the time they had finished the second joint Claire was lying back against the seawall, her eyes closed, watching the show of red and white sparklers on the inside of her eyelids. "Wow," she managed to say.

"This stuff's the top of the top, right out of the flowers. The next thing to hash," Rabbit told her. He sat lotus-style and looked at her. Beneath the robe he had an erection.

Claire did not realize she had been asleep until she felt Rabbit shaking her shoulders. "Severe munchies," he was saying. "Really bad. Severe munchies. Wake up."

"Was I asleep?"

"Zonked. Hungry?"

"Starving."

"I've got some Oreos and a frozen pizza at my place."

"Fantastic."

"Let's go then." Rabbit stood, pulling Claire up.

"Walk?"

"It's only a mile or so. I'll carry that," he said, picking up her suitcase.

"Oreos and pizza. Far-out."

Claire followed directly behind Rabbit—cautiously, but with loud giggles, stepping over the still-sleeping bum—until they reached Shoreline Drive. They walked parallel to the beach for half a mile, then cut up through alleys and backyards to Rabbit's place, an aging house subdivided into six apartments. Rabbit's was on the ground floor in the rear.

"Do you have a bathroom?" Claire asked as soon as they were inside.

"Straight back, turn left in the hall, door at the end of the hall. I'll start the pizza. Oh, there's just one bathroom for the three apartments on this floor, so if the door's locked, just pound on it until someone comes out. There's this chick across the hall that thinks she owns the place."

The door was standing open. Claire went in and closed it, dropping the hook into the latch. She pushed her pants down and sat on the toilet; just in time, she thought. There was a Day-Glo orange peace symbol on a black field covering the wall in front of her and a poster of a marijuana plant on the wall over the bathtub. The bathtub had hair in it and a thick ring around the sides. Two overflowing ashtrays sat on either side of the toilet back, and another on the edge of the tub. So this is how a hippie lives, she thought. It was exciting. But more, it looked free of all restraint. Her mother would be hysterical. A poster on the back of the door said that war is not healthy for children and other living things.

The doorknob turned, and something bumped against the door. Claire jumped. Quickly she spun off a length of toilet paper and hurried to clean herself. "Just a minute," she said. Someone pounded on the door so hard that Claire thought it would crack. "Okay," she called out, standing up and pulling her jeans on. She flushed the toilet, which gurgled embarrassingly loud, then opened the door.

A woman who looked like Cass Elliott of the Mamas and Papas squeezed by her. "Who are you?" the woman asked a little belligerently.

"I'm with Rabbit," Claire said, getting out of the way so the woman could force her bulk through the door.

"I'm fucking pregnant," the woman said by way of explanation. "Sorry to rush you." Then she closed the door behind her.

"That's all right . . ." Claire went back to Rabbit's door, wondering how anyone could tell if she was pregnant or not.

"I think I met the bathroom lady," Claire told Rabbit when she found him in the tiny kitchen.

"The bathroom lady, that's good," Rabbit said, laughing. "Her name's OP, for Owsley Pure; just call her Oop."

Claire didn't know then that Owsley Pure was a kind of LSD or that Oop got her name because she used more of it than anyone else. Rabbit put the pizza in the oven, then sat at the table and began rolling a joint. Claire wondered if Rabbit would try to make love to her and if she wanted him to. He looked so strange in that robe. It would be like screwing Jesus, she thought. A bag of Oreo cookies had been dumped on the table, and Rabbit shoved one in his mouth between rolling the joint and starting a fresh one. Claire picked up an Oreo, twisted it in half, and licked out the cream. They watched each other eat Oreos for a minute.

Then someone called Rabbit's name. It came from somewhere in the apartment, but Claire couldn't tell from where. It came again, a low, husky voice calling, "Rabbit."

"Didn't you hear that?" Claire asked, unsure since Rabbit had not shown any sign of hearing.

"Uh-huh," he said, concentrating on the next joint, lining each one up on the table in front of him.

"Rabbit . . . hey!" the voice called out again, insistently.

"All right. Gimme a minute," Rabbit said finally but didn't move.

A door behind Rabbit opened, and Claire saw a woman standing in the shadows, rubbing her eyes. She had long black hair hanging to her waist, a full, pouty mouth, and she was nude.

"I had a bad dream," the woman said.

Claire cleared her throat. Rabbit turned his head and then went back to the joint. Claire had never seen a live naked woman before, just pictures some boys had shown her. She was very pretty, although her breasts were small and her hips too wide. Claire noticed her crotch was shaved. She wondered if the woman was blind.

"Rabbit, damn it!"

"I'll be there in a minute; go back to bed," Rabbit said without turning around. The woman muttered something, then backed out of the opening without closing the door.

"That's Susie," Rabbit said, then licked the joint he'd just finished. "I'll be right back. Go ahead if you want." He handed Claire the joint in his hand.

Claire thought she should leave. She held the joint by its tip and stared blankly at it. She was still holding it a minute later when Rabbit returned.

"Can't find the matches?" he asked, pulling a kitchen match from the counter and handing it to her. Then he stuffed another Oreo in his mouth.

"Maybe I should go," Claire said.

"Why? You got someplace to stay?"

"Not yet, but—"

Rabbit took the match out of her hand and struck it. Then he took the joint and stuck it between his lips, lighting it. "You can stay here," he said, passing the joint to her.

"Ah, I . . ." Claire didn't know what to say, so she just puffed on the joint.

"Are you broke?"

Claire nodded her head and held the smoke in.

"Then crash here."

Claire held in the smoke, shook her head, and pointed toward the door behind Rabbit.

"Oh, Susie? Don't worry about her. She sort of lives with El Lobo, but he's in Mexico and she hates to sleep alone. He'll be back Friday. But I can go ahead and kick her butt back across the hall anytime."

Claire exhaled loudly and picked up an Oreo.

"People come and go, never speaking of Michelangelo; it's all right. Susie's just weird that way."

Claire munched the cookie and nodded her head. She smiled. She liked Rabbit. She was stoned.

Rabbit got up and took the pizza from the oven. Susie came out of the bedroom as if pulled by her nose, wearing panties and a man's T-shirt. "Pizza, far-fucking-out," she said, joining them at the table.

"Susie Creamcheese," Rabbit said, "this is Claire."

"Hmmm." Susie nodded, jamming two Oreos into her mouth and spitting crumbs when she spoke.

"You have to go home, Susie," Rabbit added.

8

Carl survived the rest of the summer of 1967 on Claire's letters and a growing hatred of his mother, whom he then fully blamed for Claire's absence. His emotions felt like a yo-yo on a string held by a madman. Claire's letters jerked him up, and his mother jerked him down.

He was a recluse that summer. Sometimes he would not leave his room for days except to use the bathroom and check the mail. He read novels secured during a weekly excursion six blocks down the street to the neighborhood library; he read and reread Claire's letters, added new holes to the map as she wrote from El Paso, Matamoros, Monterrey, Tampico, Veracruz, and Acapulco. He studied the contents of his "Claire drawer," staring for hours at her pictures, reading her old school papers. No puppy could have looked sadder.

Claire sent him a photograph from Veracruz, taken on a beach with grass huts or cabanas in the background, she wearing the bottom to a bikini and a bandanna halter top: barefooted, tanned, hair bleached out in the sun, the swell of her breasts rising above the halter. In one hand she held a bottle of José Cuervo, and in the other what looked like a toy pipe, the kind Carl once blew soap bubbles through. Carl sometimes fondled himself while staring at that picture, sometimes to a sweet, guilty release.

Claire's letters were never very long, never more than both sides of a single sheet of notebook paper, and more often just one side. But she packed them with information about her life. She introduced him to Rabbit in the second letter written from Corpus Christi. Claire never said exactly that she and Rabbit were lovers, and Carl decided to believe they were not. He could not conceive of Claire's loving anyone else the way she loved him.

Her letters also goaded him to work for peace in Vietnam, to "avoid Mother like a case of syph," to study hard but don't take it too seriously, to "knock the girls for a loop," and to wait for her to come "save him from God" one day.

But most of the time she talked about Rabbit and their friends—OP, Stoney, Leadhead, El Lobo, Susie Creamcheese, Juice, and Windy. Carl learned that OP was fat like Mama Cass, that Leadhead had dyslexia, that Stoney was stoned all the time, that El Lobo was just El Lobo, that Susie Creamcheese was a nympho, but when she wasn't screwing as if it were her last one she was a good cook, Juice was into beer, and Windy was the best gut singer in Texas. Rabbit? Rabbit was only the best acoustic guitar player in the world, a poet and a prophet, and a "barefoot vagabond."

Carl tried to think of special names for himself. When he wrote to Claire—he did not frequently have a current address—he signed himself varyingly as Ace, Lumberjack, and Main Man. He decided to be against the war and looked for magazine articles in the library to support his position. He lived between his bedroom and the library. There were still no books in his house except now those he brought in and took back. He studied *Ramparts, Rolling Stone, Nation, Time, Life,* and the *Mother Earth News.* He stopped going to church, and his mother got cancer, because of it, she said.

That fall Carl began the ninth grade. Claire's letters began to diminish. From one a week he began receiving two a month, then one a month. Carl added pinholes in San Francisco, Vancouver, Billings, Aspen, and Taos.

9

The next time Carl saw his sister was in 1970, nearly three years to the day after Claire had told their mother to fuck herself, then walked out, offering no good-byes. Claire was twenty-one and three months pregnant. Carl was eighteen.

Carl had received no mail from Claire since March, and it

was already the first of July. The last address he had for her was General Delivery, Carmel, California. He wrote to her four times in May but got no answer. He wanted her to know that their mother was sick, had cancer in her ovaries.

That summer, following his graduation from high school, Carl was working full time at McDonald's. His shift went from 11:00 A.M. until 7:30 P.M., with a half hour for lunch. From 8:00 to 9:00 each evening he sat in the hospital with Coreen. Then he went home to clean the house. His luxury was staying up late to watch movies on television, then sleeping late in the morning. He liked being alone in the house.

Carl was no longer much affected by his mother's zealotry. He had not been inside a church in two years. His personally-signed-by-the-preacher gift Bible was lost somewhere. God had given him nothing but loneliness and pain. He lived in a prison of loneliness and hated God for His part in it.

In the past three years Carl had tried three times to take his own life. Each time his courage failed. He swallowed two tins full of aspirin, then stuck his finger down his throat to vomit them up. He tried to cut his wrists with a razor but fainted at the first sight of blood. He climbed to the top of the tallest building in Minneapolis only to find the windows sealed and his courage gone with the climb. But if he could not die, if he had no courage for that loss, he could at least be strong in the face of pain. He held his hand over a candle flame until the skin charred and the smell of burning flesh filled his nostrils. He did that so often that he killed the nerve endings in each palm and knew to stop only when the skin started smoking. Carl prepared himself for the flames of hell even as he ceased believing in them.

Through all that, Carl managed to graduate from high school tenth in his class of 320, managed to save enough money to start at least the first year of college, and even acquired some popularity as an actor in school plays. He was very good with romantic leads, but maybe because he was so handsome and because he wasn't acting. But by the time he was graduated he had not had a sexual experience beyond furtive back-seat fondling with anyone other than Claire, whom he had not seen in three years.

When the phone rang that morning, Carl thought it was his mother. Sometimes she called very early to see if he was home. Sometimes she asked one of the nurses to call at midnight, when Coreen was in a drugged sleep, for the same reason. So when the persistent ringing pulled him from sleep, Carl answered angrily.

"Hello," he answered abruptly.

"Carl? Hi."

He knew her voice instantly. "Claire!"

"Is Mother there?"

"No. Is it really you?"

"Sure is. How you doing?"

"All right. Claire." He felt weak using her name, hearing her voice. "Where are you?"

"Down the street a ways."

"Here?"

"In the Hiawatha Motel on Twenty-eighth. Room one-twenty-seven. Can you get away and come over here? I'd love to see you."

"I can't believe you're here."

"Come see for yourself. We're going to be here only one day. I made Rabbit stop so I could see you and so you two could meet. Can you get away without Mom kicking your ass?"

"Didn't you get my letter?"

"Which one? I got one in February."

"But I've written five or six since then."

"Where to? I never got them."

"Carmel. General Delivery."

"Shit, I'm sorry, Carl. We left Carmel early in March. Didn't I write and tell you? Shit, probably not. It's been a little bit outrageous. Anyway . . ."

"Mom's in the hospital."

"What'd she do? Trip over her cross?"

"She's got cancer in her ovaries. She might die."

There was a pause. It seemed interminable to Carl, although it lasted only a few seconds. Just as he started to speak, Claire said, "I guess if you desert your womb, you have to expect something will take the place of the love that should be in it."

"Don't you feel anything, Claire?"

"I don't know. Let me think about it. How long will it take you to get here?"

"I have to walk. Twenty minutes maybe."

"Jeez, I can't wait to see you. You'll like Rabbit."

"I can't believe you're here."

"Well, then quit jabbering and get over here. Room one-twenty-seven, the Hiawatha."

She hung up. Carl looked at the phone as if he might be able to see her through it. Then he replaced the receiver and ran to his closet to find some clothes.

10

"Now be nice to him," Claire told Rabbit. "Don't give him any crap, all right?"

"All right for the fifth time. What do you think I'm going to do anyway?" Rabbit, dressed in faded, patched jeans, bare-footed, no shirt, and wearing a red bandanna tied around his head, found his cooking spoon, needle, and belt and started for the bathroom. "Just don't forget we've got to be in El Paso Friday at the latest."

"Do you have to do that now?"

"Yes, I have to do it now." Rabbit closed the bathroom door.

"Well, just don't fucking start nodding off while Carl's here."

"Tell him I was up all night, whatever," Rabbit said from the bathroom.

Claire stood in front of the dresser mirror and inspected herself. She wore blue jean cutoffs, a white peasant blouse with hand-sewn flowers around the bodice, was also barefooted, and had a garland of wild flowers woven into her hair. Her blond hair hung to her waist, and she had flowered braids hanging down each side from her temples. She bent toward the mirror and looked at her eyes. Not too bad, she thought. Her breasts, growing heavier with the pregnancy, hung loosely inside the blouse. Claire was still so beautiful that when she and Rabbit walked toward the room, the motel clerk touched himself and got a painful erection. The first bulge of her pregnancy was visible only to Claire, and she had not yet told Rabbit.

She was nervous. She straightened the flowers in her hair and checked her eyes again. The red streaks had faded slightly as the Murine took effect. She wondered if Rabbit had finished.

"I need this," she said to her reflection in the mirror as she fished inside her handbag for the cigarette package holding her rolled joints. Lighting one, she sat on the edge of the double bed and watched herself take the first deep drag. Rabbit came out of the bathroom, dazed and glassy-eyed, and fell across the bed.

"You didn't leave that shit out, did you?"

Rabbit only grunted.

Claire went to the bathroom and gathered the paraphernalia Rabbit had left on the counter and stuffed it inside his kit bag. Sometimes she got very tired of picking up after him. She went to the bed and crawled beside him, offering the joint. Rabbit shook his head and started to nod off.

She wondered why she loved him so much; he could be such a bastard at times. But she did love him, maybe more than in the beginning. He wasn't always a self-centered, doped-up son of a bitch. He had not been into the heroin for very long, two or three months. That frightened her. She tried it with him once, and it made her vomit.

"Don't fall asleep now," she told him, pushing his shoulder.

Rabbit only moaned and stared at the mirror on the dresser at the end of the bed.

Claire got up and took two whites from her bag. She swallowed one and brought the other back to Rabbit. "Here, take this," she said, stuffing it between his lips.

"Leave me alone," Rabbit said, but he swallowed the pill. His hands reached under her blouse and cupped her breasts.

"Jee-sus, not now!" She moved away from his hands. "And please put on a shirt."

She got out a shirt for him and helped him put it on, buttoning the long sleeves so he wouldn't push them up. The speed began to balance the heroin, and Rabbit sat up with his back against the wall for support. Claire lit another joint and stood by the bed with one hand on her hip in an imitation of Bette Davis and said, "What a dump this is."

"Come over here and sit on my face," Rabbit said with a smile.

"You incorrigible bastard." Claire laughed.

She went to the mirror and studied herself, fiddled with her hair, and watched Rabbit playfully stick his tongue out at her.

When someone knocked at the door, Rabbit started and told her to flush the joint.

"That's got to be Carl," Claire said, jumping up.

Before Carl could get a good look at Claire as she opened the door, she sucked him into her arms and squeezed the breath from him. Carl put his arms around her and held on.

"God, you've grown!" she said.

"You, too," Carl said, feeling the crushing of her breasts against his chest. His face flushed. There was a foul odor in her hair.

When she pulled away from him, Carl held on to her hands.

"You look like Dad. It's uncanny." Claire looked him over appreciatively. "I mean, it's unreal. You look so much like him."

"You look . . . beautiful, Claire."

"Well, let's not stand here in the doorway, being sloppy." She backed into the room, pulling Carl with her. "Rabbit, this is my brother, Carl." Claire stepped aside, and Carl could see the man sitting on the bed. His hair covered his ears and looked slept on. He had a full black beard and thick mustache. A cigarette smoldered lazily between his lips. Carl thought he looked awfully skinny, his skin had a gray tone, and around his face above the beard his skin looked as if it had been pulled back tight. Rabbit waved and said hello.

"Hi," Carl replied nervously. "I've read a lot about you in Claire's letters."

"Oh, yeah? Your name pops up a lot, too." Rabbit took a final drag from the cigarette, then reached over to the nightstand to put it out. "Kind of feels like we're related, doesn't it?"

"Yeah, sort of."

Carl wanted to like Rabbit. If Claire liked him enough to live with him, then there must be something special about him. Just the name alone made him sound appealing. But he looked like a leftover hippie or something. How could anyone get that skinny? Doesn't he comb his hair? Does Claire make love to him? Don't be stupid, he told himself. Carl didn't like Rabbit,

but what he didn't like most was the way his very presence
seemed to imply ownership of Claire.

Claire thought her nerves would explode. She regretted taking the speed, which wound her up and left her feeling agi-
tated. She wanted to do everything at once: clean the room,
make Rabbit's bed, kiss Carl, change clothes, make love to both
of them at once . . .

"You guys could sit down if you wanted to," Rabbit said.

"God, it's so good to see you," Claire said, hugging Carl
again. "Do you want something to drink? Some wine? Or
Coke?"

"No, nothing for me, thanks. But you go ahead if you want."

"Want a toke?" Rabbit asked.

"A what?"

"Rabbit!" Claire glared at him. "Here, sit down," she told
Carl and led him to a chair. She sat on the edge of the bed
across from him. "You are so good-looking. What happened to
you in the last three years?"

"I think she means you used to be ugly as an old dog," Rabbit
inserted.

"Rabbit! You know what I mean, Carl. You look so much like
Daddy."

Carl blushed. His mother told him often how much he looked
like his father. He was proud of it, yet annoyed. He didn't know
if he wanted to look like his father. When Claire leaned toward
him, as if she needed a closer look, as if to study him, her
breasts were exposed through the scoop neck of the blouse.

"I'm sorry about what I said about Mother." Claire interrupted Carl's gaze. He sat up straight. "I mean, maybe it's true,
what I said, but it was unnecessarily bitter. I don't actually
hate her anymore. In fact, I'm more or less ambivalent. I
hardly ever think of her, which might be its own kind of
hatred. I don't know. Is she really dying?"

"They don't tell me a lot. But I think she has maybe a year or
two. I guess she is."

"You can tell her I'm sorry, but I doubt she'd care."

"She cares, Claire. She just doesn't know . . ."

"Tell her anyway. I am sorry for her."

Carl glanced over at Rabbit. He was asleep. Carl nodded

toward the bed, and Claire turned around to look.

"He drove all night to get here," she explained, lying. "He's really zonked. It's not your company, I assure you."

Carl thought he preferred Rabbit asleep.

"Why don't we take a walk or something and let him rest?" Claire said, standing.

"Sure. Whatever you want to do. Are you really staying only one day?"

"Actually we need to leave tonight." Claire walked Carl toward the door.

"Tonight?" Carl's disappointment was evident.

"Yeah. I know it's the shits. But we have to be someplace on Friday. Want to walk down to Minnehaha Park? We could sit by the lake."

"The limit of Mom's reach," Carl remembered.

"Yeah, that's right. That's what she used to say, isn't it? 'I don't want you taking that boy outside the limit of my reach.' Then we'd take off for the park every time."

Claire grabbed her shoulder bag and walked out the door with Carl.

Walking beside her, Carl noticed that he was now as tall as she was. When she put her arm around his waist, he could easily put his arm around her shoulders. When they were on the street, a car full of high-school-age boys drove by and honked repeatedly. One of them hung halfway out the window and yelled, "Hey, mama . . . hey, good-looking, wanta go for a ride?"

Claire stopped and turned toward the car. "Fuck off, cracker-jack!" she said. Then they continued down the sidewalk to hoots and yells from the car as it circled the block three times. "Hope you're not into that kind of absurdity," she said to Carl.

"Of course not," he answered truthfully.

They reached the park and walked directly to an old elm tree on the bank of the lake where they had played as children. Claire sat against the tree and Carl sat in front of her, so he could look at her.

"Tell me everything, don't leave anything out," Claire said, smiling at him, devastating him with her face.

He laughed. "Sure, sure."

"What do you do with yourself? Are you making good

grades? You have a girl? Yeah, tell me about your girlfriends. They must fall on you like rain."

"I don't really have one . . . nobody special, I mean."

"Playing around, huh?"

"Well, yeah, sort of."

"Are you happy, Carl?"

"I miss you."

"Jesus Christ, I miss the hell out of you, too." She leaned toward him and put her arms around his neck. "Sometimes it really hurts to miss you so much."

Carl thought she was going to cry. He twisted around until his back was to her, then laid his head in her lap. Claire ran her fingers through his hair. "You ought to let your hair grow out longer," she said with a shaky voice.

"I might." Carl looked up at her.

"You have lovely hair."

"It's just like yours, only shorter."

"It's more like Dad's. You comb it the way he did."

"I don't remember."

"I guess you wouldn't."

"Are you in love with Rabbit?" Carl asked suddenly. The question had been in his mind since he entered the motel room.

"Yes. We've had some really good times together. Oh, it's not always super . . . sometimes we have to split for a while. But all in all, yes, I love him."

"Are you going to marry him?" Carl asked, his voice breaking.

"I doubt it. Rabbit doesn't believe in marriage. He says laws fuck up everything good."

"But would you if he asked you?"

"No."

Then there was hope, Carl thought.

"Does that bother you? The way I live."

"A little." A lot, he thought.

"My darling Carl, what you've been through here in Minneapolis is so alien to the rest of the world that you might as well be on another planet. Do you think because I'm in love with Rabbit that I no longer love you? Well, get that out of your head. You are my first and greatest love; you always will be. It's just . . . different with Rabbit. I still love you."

Carl could hardly stand to hear her talk about loving Rabbit, that skin-and-bones Jesus imitator.

After a long silence, during which Claire continued stroking Carl's head, she said, "I'm going to have a baby."

Carl's heart thudded violently against his chest wall, and he almost choked on his tongue. He rolled away from her lap and sat up on his knees.

"You can close your mouth now," Claire said, smiling.

"You mean, Rabbit's baby?" Carl said incredulously.

"Probably."

"Probably?"

"Most likely then."

"You mean you've . . . with other men besides Rabbit?"

"Sometimes. Carl, close your mouth and settle down. Don't give me that goddamn judgmental look of yours."

"Why did you come here? To tell me that? Did you come rushing through town to tell me you're a whore and you're going to have some stranger's baby?" Carl jumped to his feet.

"Jesus Christ, Carl! Grow fucking up!"

"'I *love* you, Carl,'" Carl said in a sarcastic, singsong voice. "'I *miss* you, Carl. You're my *greatest* love, Carl.' Damn you, Claire! Damn you, damn you, damn you!" He was crying by then, backing away from her. Claire started to stand. "Keep away from me! I don't ever want to see you again for as long as I live! Don't touch me!" he yelled, jumping out of her reach.

"Carl, for chrissakes."

"Go away, just *go away!*"

"Carl," Claire screamed after him, but he was already running away as fast as he could. Claire started after him, but she knew within a dozen feet that she would never catch up. He ran as though the force of a gale wind were pushing against his back.

"Carl, Carl." She sobbed in frustration and anger.

11

Carl ran for nearly a mile before exhaustion stopped him. He bent over, gasping for air, and rested his hands on his knees. A passerby stopped and asked if Carl was all right, and Carl shrugged him off. When he raised himself up, people were staring at him. He had not realized he was crying.

A young woman came up to him, offering a pamphlet. "I have the answer to your pain," she said when Carl looked up. "Would you take this and read it?"

Carl stared blankly at her.

"Do you know Jesus?" she continued. "Our Lord will walk with you if you only ask."

Carl ripped the pamphlet in two and threw it on the sidewalk. "I've had that bullshit up to here all my life," Carl screamed. "Fuck you, fuck Jesus, fuck everything!"

Then he ran. He ran to Hiawatha Avenue and north past Lake Street. He didn't stop until he ran into the campus of Augsburg College. He was hungry and bought candy and pop from vending machines in the Student Union. There were people like Claire and her friend Rabbit sitting on the grassy slope outside the union. Some of them smoked, some read, some talked, some napped. Carl felt like a child, a little boy, out of place in a world filled with people who could get along with others. He hated everybody.

Carl sat and watched them through a window for an hour. Then he went back to the street and walked as fast as he could, back to the Hiawatha Motel, back to apologize to Claire.

The VW bus that had been parked in front of the room was gone. Carl was out of breath from running the last block, as if by hurrying, he could make her be there. He knocked on the door, but no one answered. The curtains were slightly open, and he leaned against the glass to peek in. The bed was rumpled, and he could see a full ashtray on the night table. But the luggage was gone.

She had left again, abandoned him again. His last words to her had been "Go away." And she had. He felt his face flush and tears begin. Turning reluctantly away from the window, Carl ran blindly across the street, daring cars to hit him, and ran toward his house. Maybe Claire was waiting for him at home. Sure. Of course.

But she wasn't. The house was as empty as he had left it. He went up to his bedroom and lay down, rolling onto his side and looking at the yellowed United States map on the wall near his desk. Had Claire said where she was going? El Paso? So many holes had been punched into El Paso already that the spot looked torn. "No more holes," he said to himself, "no more following you all over the place with pins in a map." In a sudden burst of rage Carl jumped from the bed and ripped the map from the wall. Within a minute he regretted its loss. He knelt on the floor and carefully straightened out the map and taped the torn places. Then he tacked it back on the wall.

He guessed he might as well make himself a sandwich. It was a little after seven. On his way to the kitchen the phone rang. But it was his mother asking if he was coming to see her, telling him it was getting late.

"Yes, Mother, sorry I'm late. I'm leaving right now."

12

Rabbit was getting worse. The VW was getting worse. The weather was getting worse. Her headache was getting worse. The whole world's getting worse, Claire thought.

Driving all night, she reached Fort Worth and turned west toward El Paso at dawn, sustained by megadoses of speed and the desire to be moving. Rabbit came in and out in a random arrangement of lucidity and stupor. But most of the time he just slept in the back, sprawled on the floor between the bench seats and the icebox. He was covered with a serape Claire had tossed over him in Oklahoma. His junk was scattered all over the bus. If the police stopped them, Claire knew, it would be twenty to life in a federal prison. The bus was a rolling drugstore: heroin, cocaine, hashish, assorted pills, and a pound of marijuana.

Claire had been adjusting to the belief that she no longer had a family, that she was estranged even from Carl. It saddened her, but she could adjust. The distance between them was too great to close. She should have taken Carl with her when she left the first time. Maybe she could have salvaged him.

Claire's weight had dropped to 110 pounds from her regular 125. On a five-foot-ten-inch frame, she looked too skinny. Only the slight bulge in her lower abdomen gave away a hint of her pregnancy. She wondered how long she could keep losing weight and the fetus keep growing? She wanted the baby very much. But she couldn't force herself to eat when she had no appetite. Pretty soon she would have to tell Rabbit. It was probably his child. She wanted it to be his. There were only two other possibilities anyway. Sure, it's Rabbit's baby. Would the baby be born an addict? Pretty soon she was going to have to make Rabbit kick that stuff.

Rabbit woke up again just on the west side of Fort Worth, as Claire left Interstate 35 for Interstate 20. A Moody Blues tape played so loud through the stereo that Claire did not hear him stirring and finally crawling up toward her. When he put a hand on her shoulder, she screamed and nearly drove off the road.

"You shithead!" Claire screamed. "Don't do that!"

Rabbit crawled into the front seat. He woke up horny. After Claire got the bus straightened out, he leaned over and ran his hand under her peasant blouse and squeezed her breast.

"Oh, Rabbit, not now. I've been up all night."

"Looks like you're flying, too."

"Cut it out; you'll make us wreck. Can *you* talk your way out of the stuff in here?"

"Pull over then."

"We're on the freeway, for chrissakes!"

Rabbit leaned away from her and looked out the window. "Where are we?"

"Texas."

"Shit, I can tell it's Texas."

"A little west of Fort Worth."

"God, hours more."

She almost suggested that he drive for a while but was afraid he'd take her up on it.

It was as if he had read her mind. "Want me to drive? You must be dead."

"I'm all right. Just don't try to get me hot, okay?"

"You're so beautiful."

"Jee-sus."

"I love the hell out of you."

"Rabbit."

"The kid hurt you, didn't he?"

"Carl?"

"He's just a kid. He'll come around when he grows up a little."

"I guess I asked for it."

"Don't be so self-depreciating, Claire. It's not your fault."

Claire looked over at him. Rabbit was staring out the window. He looked as if he really did care how she felt. He seemed so sad.

"I love you," Claire said. She wanted then to tell him about the baby, but he scooted across the seat and pulled up her blouse until her breasts were exposed. It always excited him to think that passing drivers could see her that way. "Oh, Rabbit. Can't you wait?"

"You turn me on so much. You're the only woman I've never gotten tired of. With you it's just more, more, more, all the time." He put his mouth to one of her breasts, and Claire had to raise her arms to keep her hands on the wheel. "Nights in White Satin" played, and a passing truck sounded its air horn.

He was getting to her. How well he could do that. He knew everything she liked. His free hand dropped between her legs and rubbed vigorously. She would have to pull over. At the next exit she drove off the freeway and took the first dirt road they came to. Then she pulled off behind some mesquite trees and parked. They made love across the front seat.

Claire finished quickly, but as usual, Rabbit could not. He tried long beyond its usefulness. Claire tried to help him with her hand, but he fell limp and she couldn't hold him. "God damn, God damn!" he cried, then crawled over the seat and worked at packing a sticky black chunk of hash into his pipe. "Want some of this?" he asked after lighting it.

"Thought you wanted to get to El Paso." He's getting worse, she thought.

"What time is it?"

"About eight."

"Well, I guess you'd better drive then. Do you really feel all right?"

Claire took two pills from her bag and swallowed them dry. By the time she had driven back to the freeway her head was buzzing pleasantly. But her stomach hurt.

"We'll be rich in a week," Rabbit said. It was the last thing he said before falling asleep again.

Claire drove into the heat mirages and giggled as she toppled castles, camels, trees, and other cars.

13

Carl spent a week torturing himself. Although he no longer played with flames and burned his skin, the other tortures were severe enough. He had screaming, horrible nightmares, coupled with anxiety attacks that left him collapsed on the floor with a paper bag over his head, trying to regulate his breathing. In nightmares he saw himself—felt himself as well—tied to his bed while an army of worms squished over the bed, over his body, over his face, and finally into his ears to gnaw on his brain.

For a long time, as long as a year, he had been acutely frightened of dying. Before falling asleep at night, he would hum complicated melodies and try to think about anything pleasant to keep his mind from focusing all its energy on cancer. Carl had decided that cancer could be caused by thinking and worrying about it. Sometimes he was so sure he already had the disease that he could actually feel the cells going black and burning.

He knew he would never hear from Claire again. He had sent her away in anger, and she would never write to him, call, or ever come home. Not ever. He would die of the cancer, too, and nobody would know. Claire would never know. He fantasized a scene of Claire's coming to Minneapolis years after his death and asking if anyone knew what happened "to old Carl." Someone would answer, "Oh, didn't you know? Carl died twenty years ago. A horrible thing. His whole insides were black with cancer. Struck him just like that." Would she cry? Carl hoped it would kill her with grief.

For days Carl stayed in his bedroom and slept or daydreamed. He quit cleaning. He left food scraps on the floor, and when ants found the treats and formed a double line to and from it, Carl would spend hours lying on the floor, watching.

The ants and Carl shared the floor with articles of clothing, shoes, some magazines and newspapers, a few books, a moldy plastic drinking cup, and dozens of dust balls that roamed the room aimlessly whenever he opened the window. He had not made his bed or changed the sheets since the day before Claire phoned.

Eight days after Claire came and went, Carl's mother called from the hospital to say she was coming home. The Lord had cured her.

14

There was no moon. "Good night for it," Rabbit said.

They sat in the back of an old Ford pickup truck as it jolted its way south along the road from Juárez to the village of El Sueco, where they would cut off toward Flores Magón, in the high country of Sierra del Nido.

Waves of cramps rose and subsided in Claire's stomach. She had felt the pains for five days, since they reached El Paso and connected with Pancho, if that was his name. Rabbit called him Pancho, but Claire thought his name was something else, Pablo or Paco. Whatever his name was, she wished he would slow down and at least try to avoid running over the most obvious potholes.

As if sensing her pain, Rabbit banged on the rear window and yelled at the driver to slow down.

"Sí, sí." The man mouthed the words and nodded, his smile revealing the decayed stump of two front teeth amid a row of apparently healthy ones. Claire had wondered how only two could decay like that while the others remained normal. Pancho, if anything, sped up.

Claire wondered if cramps in the fourth month were normal. She had been sick for days, assuming it was morning sickness.

They turned off toward Flores Magón, and the road got worse. They went over bumps that tossed Claire and Rabbit a foot in the air.

"Hey, motherfucker!" Rabbit cried, banging on the rear window. "Slow your ass down!" Rabbit said in Spanish.

"Make him go slower," Claire pleaded.

"*¡Chinga tu madre!*" Rabbit banged on the window with his fists. "Put a goddamn Mexican in a pickup truck and he goes crazy—*loco!*"

Pancho chewed his cigar and drove happily into the mountains. Tex-Mex music cried through the static in the radio, barely audible in the back.

"Where did you find that guy?" Claire asked, trying to relax as the cramps eased. "I don't like any of this."

"Let's not start arguing again, for chrissakes. I'm not all that thrilled either."

"It's not worth this."

"Are you kidding? Just keep thinking of how much money we're going to have when this is done. No more Tinkertoy little runs for nickels and dimes. No more chances. We won't ever have to do this again. I spent a *year* trying to get together a deal like this."

"I don't feel very good."

"I know," Rabbit said sympathetically. He had been watching the pain in her face ever since they left El Paso that morning. "I'm sorry. You should have stayed."

"But I didn't want you to go alone."

"What's the difference?"

"Is that a put-down?"

"No. That's not what I meant. Don't be so touchy. I'm sorry you don't feel good. Why don't you see a doctor, or something?"

"I will when we get back."

"We're going to be rich, and we won't ever have to come down to this stink hole of a country again. No more VWs, no more dumpy apartments, no more bad junk, no more worries. Where do you want to go? Vancouver Island? You liked that. Maui? Just name it."

The truck jumped over a bump, and Claire banged her head against the back of the cab. It almost knocked her out.

It had not felt right to Claire from the beginning, when Rabbit was trying to raise the cash. Borrowing $10,000 from his straight brother on the pretext of paying off all his bad debts, cleaning out every penny of their savings, but especially taking $50,000 from "his friends" in Houston, friends she had never heard of or seen. Claire did not believe that running a few thousand dollars' worth of pills and marijuana across the border, regardless of how many times they had done it successfully, was adequate preparation for *this*. A hundred thousand dollars' worth of raw heroin they would convert through the Houston connection into $5 million—1 million for them. "All we have to do is pick up the stuff and get it to Houston," Rabbit had explained, "and we're millionaires."

"But we have all the risk," Claire complained.

"Houston has all the money."

What Claire knew was that Rabbit's fixes were costing them more than $40 a day and they could no longer support it dealing in a little marijuana and pills. They did need one big score. She was going to have a baby. They could go to Canada and get themselves straightened out. They could get a nice house, get clean, raise their baby, have good friends the way other people did. She thought of Rabbit's brother, living out in Ingleside, a good job with Amoco, a baby girl, a nice boat for fishing in the Gulf. Danny looked so much like Rabbit, but they were so different. Then she thought of Carl. So different.

"We ought to be there by now," Rabbit interrupted, trying to light a match to light a joint. "How long have we been going?"

"I don't know."

"I'm not feeling . . . this fucking truck. I need to get right, Claire."

"Should be soon. Rabbit, will you try . . ." No, she couldn't ask him to get off the junk now. But she would, she would as soon as they got back to Texas.

Suddenly Pancho swerved off to the right, and the truck bounced over a small ditch and over what looked like a cattle trail through the mesquite.

"Did we already go through Buenaventura?" Rabbit asked, sitting up nervously. "I don't remember seeing it."

"Neither do I. We haven't gone far enough."

"What's that fucker doing?" Rabbit banged on the window. "Hey, hey, *muchacho!*"

Claire looked around the side of the truck and saw a pair of headlights blink on and off. "There's somebody up there, Rabbit."

"What's this shit?"

"Are we there?"

"I don't know."

The truck stopped, and Rabbit jumped over the side and walked quickly around to the driver's door. He told Claire to stay in back until he found out what was happening. Claire told him to be careful.

Through the glare of the lights, Claire could see only the dark outlines of the men. Pancho got out of the truck and walked with Rabbit toward the headlights. There were at least six figures standing in the glare. She could hear feet crunching in the roadbed. The first voices were in Spanish, Pancho speaking first. Then, in broken English, someone said, "You breeng the moanee, señor?"

"Did you bring the heroin?" she heard Rabbit answer. She could recognize him by the skinny shape of his shadowed image.

"I will see the moanee?"

"When I see the stuff."

Then she heard Pancho tell the others in Spanish that the money was in the backpack Rabbit wore.

"What is this?" she heard Rabbit say, his voice rising with panic.

"Usted a las puertas de la muerte."

In less time than it took for Claire to translate Pancho's statement as "You at the door of death," she heard the shot and saw the muzzle flash. It cracked in the air like two boards being slapped together. Less than five seconds later another followed, but Claire did not hear it over her screams.

She continued screaming and tried to scramble over the side of the truck. But when she was half over the rail, her forehead bumped into the barrel of a pistol. She screamed Rabbit's name and tried to roll to the other side of the truck. A second man appeared there, a shotgun in his hands. A third man climbed over the tailgate and pushed her against the back of the cab. *"¡Puta!"* he yelled, and slapped her hard. She was still screaming when two of the men pulled her into the back of a camper truck, past Rabbit's body slumped over in the road in an expanding pool of dark blood. She tried to reach for him but was slapped again and pulled forward. She was thrown into the camper and landed on the feet of a smiling man, holding a rifle at her face.

15

The voices around her were in Spanish. Claire's understanding of the language was basic, she could understand more than she could speak, but she could catch only words and phrases.

Rabbit!

The picture coming into her mind was blurred and initially incoherent: Rabbit slumped on his side, curled in a fetal position, the black pool spreading around his head and chest like molasses in the sand. The darkness, the shouts, the shots. Rabbit was dead.

Claire tried to scream, but she choked. Her eyes opened to light, although it was a dim, dusty light. A rough hemp rope was tied around her ankles, to her wrists, and looped around her neck. It was just loose enough for her to breathe. When she pulled against it, the pain forced another choked scream. Her lips felt swollen, and her neck burned from the rope. Her stomach rolled with deep cramps.

She knew it had not been some horrible dream, a psychedelic nightmare. Rabbit was dead or dying out there alone. She sobbed.

A shadow fell across her eyes, and she looked for its source. She was lying on a dirt floor in a small adobe-wall room, like a storage shed. There were boxes and barrels against one wall, two tiny glassless windows were on the opposite wall, and some machinery parts and farm tools were strewn about. The door was out of balance and jerked open with a screech. A man stood in the doorway with the sun streaming in behind him, leaving only his form and his shadow across the floor. Claire remembered how the *bandidos* had looked backlighted in the high desert when she peeked around the truck. The man came into the room and jerked the door mostly closed. She could see him then and the automatic rifle in his crooked arm. It was Pancho.

"¿Qué te pasa, señorita?" he said, adding also in Spanish, "Are you sick again?"

"I don't . . . *Yo hablo* . . . No, I mean, *no yo hablo* . . ." She couldn't remember how to tell him she couldn't speak Spanish.

Pancho with the two bad teeth smiled at Claire's confusion. "Okay," he said, "I talk in Engless good. You are sick again?"

"I'm choking."

"I can take off the rope, maybe."

Pancho walked toward her, laying the rifle against the wall as he came, and bent down to untie the rope. He started at her ankles and worked slowly.

Claire looked down and saw that her blouse was torn and there was blood on the front of it. Her blood? Her lips did sting. Blood from her mouth? Her skirt was bunched up to her hips, and she noticed Pancho's eyes following the length of her legs to her waist as he toyed with the knot. He rubbed her leg. So this is where he rapes me, Claire thought.

"Did you leave Rabbit out there? Maybe he was still alive; maybe he was bleeding to death. Did you just leave him like that?"

"He very much dead, food already for the an-nee-mals."

Claire let out a cry, and Pancho slapped her.

"Make no sound to notice the others of you waking," he whispered angrily. "Some see you dead if they know."

"But why?" Claire whispered. "Why did you kill him? He didn't do anything to you. He would have given you the money if that's all you wanted."

"*Estúpido.* He was a stupid man. Emilio shoot him anyway, though. Stupid or no stupid." Pancho laughed. "Emilio shoot you, too, maybe. So you be quiet like the mouse." He loosened the knot at her wrists. Then the one around her neck. He put his hands on her breasts and squeezed them.

"Let him kill me," Claire cried. "Or you kill me. Let me die, too."

"No, no. You are very beautiful. No, no, señorita." Pancho let one hand roam up Claire's leg while the other smashed her breast. "To kill such a thing as you would be some sad, I think."

Claire closed her eyes and waited for his hands to kill her. She didn't care anymore what he did, what any of them did. As long as they would let her die. She let him roll her over onto her back, and when he jerked her legs apart, she did not struggle.

Pancho lapsed into Spanish again, telling her how beautiful she was.

Claire, her eyes still closed, did not see the woman come in the door, although she heard its screech. When she opened her eyes, the woman was beside them and Pancho was trying to pull up his pants at the same time he pulled down her skirt.

In Spanish the old woman said, "Son of a whore! Son of an old bitch dog! What are you doing? Get away from that girl."

"I just wanted a look," Pancho said sheepishly in Spanish. Claire did not understand them.

"Go now, or I will call Emilio."

"I'm going," Pancho said, scrambling to his feet.

"Go now!" She pushed him toward the door.

"I am, I am."

Pancho knew she would call Emilio and Emilio would feed his balls to the dog. Pancho grabbed his weapon on the way out and pushed the door shut. The old woman knelt next to Claire and touched her shoulder with tenderness. She told her in Spanish not to be afraid.

"Let him finish it now. Don't put it off," Claire said.

"There is nothing to finish," the old woman said. She pulled the loose rope away from Claire and helped her sit up. The woman was very large, stocky, and strong. She pulled Claire up and helped her lean back against the adobe wall. "Will you eat?" she asked.

Claire shook her head. She felt no hunger, although she couldn't remember when she had last eaten. "Who are you?" Claire asked.

"Luz María. You should eat."

Claire shook her head again. The woman, Luz María, sat on a box beside her.

"Pancho, he is a pig."

"They are killers," Claire said. "They killed my . . . man."

"Emilio is the killer. He is a very bad man. Loco in his head," Luz María said, spinning her finger around her temple. "The others, they are worms. They follow Emilio and take whatever braveness they find from him. But you and your man come to buy heroin. You are fools."

"It was supposed to be so simple . . ." Claire started crying.

The old woman let her cry until it was over. Then Claire asked how long she had been there.

"Just since they brought you last night."

"It is . . . ?"

"The middle of the afternoon. You were sick many times. I think you are . . . *embarazada*—how do you say?—bearing child?"

Claire nodded.

"I could tell. But not so long a time . . . you say?"

"Pregnant?"

"*Sí*, preg-a-nunt. *Embarazada*. Not so long, eh?"

"Three or four months. Who *are* you?"

"Emilio is my son. This is Emilio's camp."

"Where is this place?"

"This is no place. It has no name. In the hills between Flores Magón and Buenaventura. Just—how do you say?—a camp?"

"Why did they kill Rabbit? He would have given them the money if that's it. They could have kept the heroin, too. But to kill him."

"*¿Conejo?* You call him Rabbit?"

"My boyfriend. His name was Rabbit."

The old woman smiled. "*Conejo*, Rabbit, funny name for a man."

"Your son killed him, Pancho said. And for nothing."

"Emilio, he like to kill. It is his blood; it was his father's blood. It is the way. Emilio do not kill for the money. El General pay Emilio good. El General, he take the money and he keep the poppies, too, and that is the way. But Emilio do not kill for El General, no. Emilio kill because it is his blood, the . . . how do you say it? *Emoción*. For the . . . thrill?"

"But he is your son. Can't you . . . ?"

"*Espíritu maligno* . . . you say it like, the spirit of the devil. He is the son of the devil. He is a *maldito*."

"I don't understand."

"*Maldito*. My curse."

Claire thought of her mother. She was her mother's curse. Now she was to die at the hand of another mother's curse. It was pathetically comic. A rush of nausea rose in her throat, and she could not swallow it. She gagged and just managed to lean over before vomiting on the dirt floor. She felt Luz María's large hand rubbing her back. The sickness exhausted her and left her throat burning. The pains in her stomach intensified. Claire rolled to the floor, her dress lying in the vomited bile, and groaned loudly.

"Maybe you lose the child," Luz María said. "I cannot promise to keep the men away from you. You are a beautiful woman. But I will try until darkness. I think they will not have desire for a sick woman, even one of such beauty. They will wait. In darkness I will take you to the road and leave you in the sight of a car.

"Maybe they will let you live for many days or a week if they can have you, but they will kill you after. Emilio will kill you anyway, for he is not a lover of women. *Maricón.* Pablo I can keep away; he is the littlest worm of them all. But maybe not Pérez and maybe not José.

"If you can be sick, they will stay away until tomorrow. In the dark tonight, I will take you to the road."

Claire needed no inducements to be sick. She raised her head slightly and heaved. She gagged on the bile, for there was nothing else in her stomach. When it was over, she looked at Luz María and asked, "Why?"

"When I save one, *el Dios* gives me a . . . a mercy, He makes a good mark for me. If I can save one for each one Emilio kills, maybe I will be forgiven."

Claire was sick again. She thought her stomach would turn inside out. Luz María held her head for a moment, then got up. "I must go out now. Remember, be sick when they come. I will return at darkness."

Claire did not look up to watch her go. Rabbit could not be dead. It doesn't happen that way. He will get to a hospital, and then he will come get me, she thought. He will kill them all. He will cut their throats and kill them dead, dead, dead.

16

Only one of them came to molest her that afternoon. He came less than an hour after Luz María had left. Claire had managed to scoot herself into the farthest corner of the room and was lying on her side, unable to sit up because of the stomach pains. She needed something, anything. Where had they put her bag? She had not been able to find it in the room.

She heard a key in the lock and cringed against the wall. The one who came in she had not seen before. He was very young, certainly still in his teens, she figured. In the darkness of the room he looked a little like Rabbit; rather, he was shaped like Rabbit. Skinny, tall, lanky. Maybe he was bringing her some food. She had not eaten since the night before, and when she vomited, only bile came up.

If she had a weapon, she would kill him. He stood in the doorway and stared at her. But there was nothing, and she was weak. But the hatred in her was heavy and deep. She watched him move toward her a few steps. He seemed to be trying to figure out what had happened to the ropes.

He bent close to her. His face looked oddly puffy, as if he still had a lot of growing to do. When his shadow crossed her face, Claire tried to make herself sick. She concentrated on the most sickening foods she could imagine, but her stomach was completely empty. Before she could stick her finger down her throat, he was bending over her.

"Leave me alone," she whispered. "Go away."

He said something in Spanish and knelt beside her, dropping his hand onto her leg.

"I don't speak Spanish," she said in English.

Obviously he did not speak English. He said something else in Spanish and leered openly at her.

Claire closed her eyes, resigned to the inevitability of it, and felt him pulling, tugging at her dress. His hands rubbed roughly over her breasts as he made grunting noises. She wondered if Luz María would appear at any moment to save her again but doubted it. The air temperature in the room must have been 100 degrees, even shaded, but Claire had chills. Sweat had soaked through her dress. She felt his hands pulling at her dress. He was trying to turn her over. Claire realized that he intended to take her from behind. Maybe, with Emilio, it was all this boy knew. When he had rolled her onto her stomach, Claire put her finger down her throat as far as it would go and gagged herself. The bile came up and puddled around her face in the dirt. The boy made a groaning sound, and she felt his weight leave her back. More was said in Spanish, and she waited. The smell of her bile sickened her again. After a few moments she twisted her head around. He was gone, and she was alone again. She was able to move away from her own stench and curl up next to one of the barrels. There she passed out.

Claire was oblivious to any sounds or movements until Luz María shook her shoulders. It was black in the room.

"Come, wake yourself. We must go now," Luz María said. "Go while they sleep in drunkenness."

Claire let Luz María lift her.

"You must walk yourself. I am not able to carry you."

Claire had not been on her feet since she had been pulled from the back of the pickup truck. Her legs were unstable, but they supported her weight. When they were outside, Claire could see dim yellow glows from other adobe huts along a dirt pathway. There was an old army Jeep and four pickup trucks parked nearby. Luz María pulled Claire in the opposite direction, down a gentle slope. In the darkness Claire did not see the pickup truck until they were nearly upon it. She let Luz María help her into the passenger side.

After Luz María had climbed behind the wheel, she took it out of gear and let the truck start a slow roll down the incline. They rolled in the quiet darkness for nearly 100 yards, picking up speed, until finally Luz María jammed the gear lever into second and released the clutch. The truck lurched a couple of times; then the engine started. Claire was surprised at how quickly they reached the road. It seemed like only minutes, so they could not have been very far from it. She wanted to remember. If she survived . . . if . . . she would see them dead—the killers of Rabbit.

Luz María turned east on the road and drove very fast for twenty miles. They came to a village. It was dark. Claire had no idea what time it was.

Anticipating Claire's question, Luz María said, "Flores Magón. I will take you to El Sueco; there is the main highway north. You will be found quick there. It is only three hours north to Ciudad Juárez and El Paso."

"How can I thank you for this?" Claire said weakly. She felt her remaining strength ebbing as they drove.

"Tell your God I save you, I, Luz María, mother of the devil, save you."

Claire nodded in the darkness. Tell God, she thought. Tell my God? I have no God.

Luz María pulled the truck over and stopped. "We are on the south part of El Sueco," she said. "I must go back hurrying." She got out and went around to help Claire down. She told her to sit calmly and wait. Maybe it would be a long time, but someone would pass and stop for her. She was a beautiful woman after all.

Then Luz María kissed Claire's forehead and got back into the truck. Without a look back, she turned the truck and drove away.

Claire had been on the roadside for only half an hour when the first of the sharp, vicious pains came. It felt as if she were being stabbed in the stomach repeatedly. She fell back into the dirt and screamed. She was unconscious when the fetus aborted.

17

Less than three weeks after Carl had run away from Claire in the park, two men showed up, looking for her. They were dressed in business suits and pulled up in front of the house, driving a rented compact car. Carl saw them through the living room window and thought they were salesmen. But one of the men stayed by the car, leaning against the front fender, while the other came to the front door.

When the doorbell rang, Carl went to open it just as his mother yelled for him to "see who that is" from the kitchen. The man told Carl that he was a friend of Claire's who had lost touch and had something for her. When Carl persisted in telling the man, who called himself Mr. Walker, that he really had not seen or heard from Claire since earlier in July, Mr. Walker became angry. He pushed Carl aside and waved to the man by the car. The two of them began searching the house. When Coreen Grant came out of the kitchen, Mr. Walker grabbed her shoulders and started shaking her.

"Tell me where she is and we won't hurt the boy," Mr. Walker insisted.

"Carl, Carl!" Coreen screamed.

The other man pushed Carl to the floor and pulled out a gun.

"She's sick," Carl said impotently.

"And you're dead if you don't tell me where that bitch sister of yours is," the man with the gun said.

Coreen started praying.

Mr. Walker searched through the house while the other man held Carl and his mother at gunpoint. Whenever Carl tried to ask a question, the gunman told him to shut up unless he had something to say about his sister. Coreen was on her knees, praying in mumbles and sobs.

They stayed almost half an hour. As they were leaving, Mr. Walker turned and said, "Tell your sister and her freaked-out boyfriend that we *will* get our money back."

"Oh, oh," his mother cried after the men were gone, "we are reaping the foul harvest, O Lord. We must reap the harvest of the devil's seeds."

"Shut the fuck up!" Carl said as he went to phone the police.

"You will burn, you will burn, you will burn," Coreen repeated as Carl pulled the phone into the hall to get away from her.

18

There was no word from Claire, and she couldn't be found. The Nueces County sheriff's office sent a man around to Jess Noble's last known address and also interviewed his brother, Daniel. The only thing they could report was a high probability Noble and Claire Grant were in Mexico. Carl contacted the State Department on the advice of a police officer.

Nearly six weeks passed. It was mid-September, and a hint of early fall was in the Minnesota air. A few days before it had been more than ninety degrees. Now it was in the low sixties. Carl had been in school for two weeks, his first year at the University of Minnesota, but he didn't like it. There were too many people, all seeming to be going whatever way he went, crowds and crowds and everyone ignoring him. Around the lakes the leaves were starting to turn. Coreen Grant had gone back into the hospital right after the visit from Mr. Walker and friend, but her cancer remained in remission. Nervous exhaustion, the doctor decided. Carl couldn't afford the dorm, so he stayed at home and commuted across town in their old Ford. On Sundays he drove his mother to church, then waited for her in the café down the street before driving her home. He still worked evenings at McDonald's.

Then the registered letter came. Carl took it directly to his bedroom and tore open the envelope, careful not to destroy the State Department return address. It was from the American Embassy in Mexico City. "Regarding the whereabouts of Claire Grant," it began. The letter reported that Claire had been in a hospital in Chihuahua for four days in late July and had run away, leaving a substantial bill. She was reported to have a case of traumatic amnesia, be suffering from acute amphetamine addiction, and was treated for abrasions. She had also miscarried. Enclosed was a copy of the hospital's bill for $1,023 and a request for payment. The embassy had no further information concerning her present location.

Three weeks later Carl saw her. He was sure of it, although when he tried to catch her, she got onto a bus and disappeared. But he knew it was Claire. He was going crazy. He couldn't sit in class. He couldn't do anything but look for her. So he spent the next three days driving around Minneapolis, trying to see her again. He parked for four hours at the intersection downtown where he had seen her board the bus. She had seen him, too, that day, he knew. She looked right at him, then hurried onto the bus. It was Claire, he knew. Nobody looked like Claire. He cruised Hennepin Avenue at night after getting off work, staying out until three or four in the morning. He looked in the bars, watched people when they came out of the theaters, and talked to hookers. He showed her picture. A pimp offered Carl $5,000 cash for her.

The end of October came, and he had not seen her again. He had missed three weeks of classes.

19

Carl tossed in bed that night, unable to sleep soundly even though it was 4:00 A.M. and he had been trying for two hours. Coughing fits woke him every few minutes. He dreamed vaguely about Claire. Sometimes he could hear her voice. Once, he was sure, she had been in his room and kissed his neck. He thought she said his name aloud. He heard it.

Then he woke with a jolt. He couldn't breathe, as if someone were holding a pillow over his face. When he opened his eyes, he couldn't see. The room, his eyes, nose, throat were filled with dark smoke. He tumbled to the side of the bed and fell to the floor. He hit the rug before seeing it. Crawling to the window, he banged his right hand into a chair leg and cut his thumb on a splinter. When he was able to shove the window up, a ball of roaring flame exploded through the bedroom door and sucked the air from the room. Carl shoved his head through the opening and tried to get a breath. From his second-floor window he could see the dancing glow of the fire against the wall of the next-door house. Shadows and light made a strobe effect in the windblown tree branches. He pulled himself through the window and hung from the sill by his fingers. The blast from the rolling fire singed his hair, and he could smell it, like the smoldering flesh in his palms so many years ago. There was a comfort in its familiarity, and he almost didn't let go. Then a wide tongue of flame licked his face, and he dropped.

His impact with the damp earth stung but did not hurt as badly as when he had jumped from the garage roof. He bit his tongue.

By then the sirens were all over him, seeming to be so close they were inside his head. Carl got up and limped to the front, where a red car and two fire engines were screeching to a halt. Suddenly people were everywhere, and someone picked him up. Carl tried to look back at the house, but the front oak blocked his vision. He was dropped unceremoniously on the curb next to an ambulance, and someone pushed him to the ground and wiped at his face with a cold scratchy cloth.

"My mother," he managed to say.

"It's all right, be still," a voice replied.

An artificial dawn glowed over the machinery and the people. Ash fell on him. When he could, Carl turned his head and looked at the house in time to see the roof crash down in an explosion of flame and hot flying lavalike embers. Black smoke hovered over the neighborhood like a mushroom cloud. Scores of raincoated men wrestled hoses that looked like vicious, angry water snakes.

Later, when the uniformed police officer knelt next to where Carl sat on the curb with an oxygen mask over his face, Carl thought he was going to be taken to his mother.

"Son," the officer began, "your mother is . . ."

And Carl didn't need to hear the rest.

20

The Church of the Brethren made some production of Coreen Grant's funeral.

November 2 was crisp and crystal-clear. Carl shivered at the cemetery in spite of his borrowed wool coat. He did not own a coat nice enough for a funeral. Deacon Bacon gave Carl his.

And Carl thought about his mother as he stared at her closed coffin. "She was going to save you, son," a policeman said that day. "We found her body at the top of the stairs, her arm reaching toward your bedroom door." I did love you, Carl said to himself, to her coffin. Oh, I did love you. And I know you loved me somehow.

The fire was arson, he was told that day. No doubt. Two gallons of gasoline had been poured from a can throughout the living room. Mr. Walker, Carl thought, and told the police about his earlier visit and his threat. But, the police said, they suspected Claire. She had been seen hanging around in the hedgerows beside the house on three different occasions during the previous week. She had been seen by a neighbor walking his dog earlier that night. Carl told them they were crazy.

Carl did not see her arrive. His eyes were on the coffin, his thoughts inside it. Only when the minister stopped in mid-sentence and the wait became extended did Carl look up. He saw Claire running away, followed by two policemen, who had been hovering at the edge of the cemetery since the service began.

"Claire!" he screamed, jumping to his feet. The deacon and another man from the church held Carl's arms. "Claire!" he cried out when the policemen grabbed her and pulled her, struggling, to their car.

"Let them go; it's for the best," the deacon said, pinning Carl's shoulders to the chair.

Carl fought them and broke away, but not in time to catch the patrol car as it sped out of the cemetery. "Claire!" he screamed at the car.

part one

christmas 1970
fairbrook

one

Fairbrook State Hospital reminded Carl Grant of the Grand Hotel on Mackinac Island. Carl had never actually been to the Grand Hotel, although he had seen pictures of it. It seemed to him the kind of place a character like Jay Gatsby would pick to vacation.

Fairbrook was built in 1930, a couple of dozen miles southeast of metropolitan Minneapolis, on a wooded bluff that a hundred years before would have served well as the site for a fort guarding a strategic bend in the Mississippi River. It was a large, rambling white wooden building with red-topped cupolas on each corner. The look of it made Carl feel he was creeping up on the place.

"Creeping" was precisely the word that came to Carl's mind. It was suitable whether he was thinking of stealth, of moving timidly, or that other way—a sensation of the flesh, the experience of dis-ease—creepy.

Fairbrook was built as a private sanitarium, but growing expenses and a declining patient list plunged it into bankruptcy during the mid-1950's. Since then it was run by the state of Minnesota as an institution for the criminally insane. The first time Carl saw his sister, Claire, in Fairbrook, she called it the Alcatraz of mental health. Fairbrook sat up there on the high bluff like an island in a sea of deep, dark forests. There was only the one road in or out, and it had to circumnavigate the bluff in an ever-tightening spiral to make it passable. The only gate was guarded around the clock. The surrounding white brick wall was ten feet high and topped with concertina wire. As Carl approached the gate, he noticed that someone had had the bad taste to put strands of multi-colored lights around the gate bars.

It was Christmas Eve, and a thickly falling snow made the road precarious. Carl slowed to a stop just before the gate and lit a cigarette off the ember of the one he had just finished. When he rolled down the frosted window to let the guard see him, a rush of cold air froze the sweat-damp shirt to his sides. After he had signed in and driven to the far end of the parking lot, Carl made one last mental rehearsal of his plan before going inside.

"Come in, Carl. Julie, bring Carl and me some coffee, would you mind? I'll bet you could use something hot on a day like this?"

As Dr. Marshall Fields ushered Carl into his office, Carl said he would like two sugars in his coffee and thanked the doctor for being thoughtful, it was very cold. Dr. Fields, Carl thought, seeing him for only the third time, was Falstaffian in both size and humor. He reminded Carl of Orson Welles; not the Orson Welles of *Citizen Kane,* but the more recent parodies of himself Carl had seen on TV talk shows.

"Did you bring that for Claire?" Dr. Fields asked, nodding toward the gold-wrapped package in Carl's lap.

"Yes. It's a Christmas present. A jacket, cap, and mittens."

"I'm sorry, but you understand that we have to look it over first. I just hate this. Rules are rules. I'll have Julie look into it when she comes back with the coffee, and I'll tell her to be careful with the wrapping paper. If I know Julie, you won't even be able to tell it's been touched."

"If you have to."

"A warm jacket will be of great value for Claire this winter. It's so difficult to stay cooped up inside, and they do enjoy walks on the grounds."

They, Carl thought. Them. Claire is not one of *them.* "I hope she likes it," he said. "It's hard to know what to buy."

They were interrupted by the return of Dr. Fields's secretary, Julie, with the coffee tray. Dr. Fields asked Carl to give Julie the package; he did, and Julie left them alone again.

"We're all looking forward to the holidays around here," Dr. Fields said. "It's good therapy to have the families together this time of year, and we're glad you could come out."

"Thank you for inviting me to the party."

"It's standard, of course. But in this case Claire depends on you so much. You are her principal topic in group therapy, and all to your favor I should hasten to add."

"Is that why you wanted to see me first?" Carl asked, anxious to be out of the office and with Claire. Time was short.

"Oh, no. Were you worried that Claire was saying nasty things about you? Let me assure you to the contrary. Actually, did you get a copy of my report to the court?"

Carl nodded. He had received it in the mail three days before.

"You understand that it is just a preliminary thirty-day report and is required by the court?"

Carl nodded again.

"I supposed you might have some questions about it."

"I guess I don't. Not really. Well, I guess I don't know what 'anosognosia' means, but I could have looked it up."

"Well, Carl, you know the court likes it when we use jargon. More or less, it means that a patient refuses or fails to recognize the existence of illness. During Claire's month with us we've been completely unable to get her to recognize the fact that something's wrong with her."

Makes sense, since nothing is, Carl thought.

"By wrong, I mean that she is out of step with the norms of the society in which she lives or has tried to live. It's not just what she claims not to remember . . . the fire, her excursion into Mexico, but a whole range of threatening behaviors. There is quite a well of anger and violence in that young lady."

"You mean my sister."

"I'm sorry, yes, I mean Claire."

Dr. Fields produced a cigar from a humidor on his desk and made a production of cutting off its tip and lighting it. Then, after puffing lavishly, he continued. "Illness is a solution to a problem. Mental illness is one kind of malfeasible solution to an emotional problem or problems. We cannot successfully treat the symptoms without knowing the root of the problem causing them. In fact, the best we can do is attempt to mask the symptoms with certain drugs and therapies, which is not what we're here to do. We prefer to cure the problem rather than just treat the symptoms."

"So you electrocute her and pump her full of drugs to cure her of drugs."

"That's not what we're doing, Carl."

"Then what are you doing?" Don't get into an argument, he told himself; calm down.

"Right now? Right now all we *can* do is comply with the directives of the court that put Claire here. Let us not forget that Claire set fire to your house with you and your mother in it; she killed her mother. Nor should we forget that for years before that act she was living like a hippie, smuggling drugs, an addict herself."

"To tell me this? Is that why you wanted to see me?"

"I wish you wouldn't be so angry about it, Carl. It won't help your sister."

"I'm not angry."

"Claire had twenty-one years to get here. It will take a number of years for us to help her find the way out. But the longer she refuses to acknowledge the patterns in her behavior, the longer it will take. It is not going to be a quick cure, I'm afraid. She is withholding too much."

"I understand."

"If you think of mental illness as a kind of immensely complicated jigsaw puzzle," Dr. Fields continued, on a roll, "our job is to fit together all the pieces constituting a patient's entire life and find a recognizable, treatable pattern.

"Our central problem with Claire at this point is her refusal to cooperate. Only in the most perfunctory ways does she even acknowledge why she's here.

"Frankly, Carl, your sister is just making her situation worse by her attitude. And that is where I'm hoping you can help us."

"How would I do that?" Carl glanced at his wristwatch and nervously twitched his crossed leg.

"I would like to read something to you, a kind of sketch composed by a member of our staff who has spent the most time with Claire. Do you mind?"

"I guess it's all right. If you want to."

"I noticed you checking the time."

"Oh, I just wondered about the party."

"It doesn't start for another two hours. But don't worry, this won't take nearly that long."

Dr. Fields opened a file folder that had been lying on his desk. He puffed eagerly on the cigar, then placed it in a large glass ashtray.

"Don't expect all of this to make sense, Carl. Typical jargon. If you have any questions, feel free to ask. I would like for you to know that we have tested Claire quite carefully. Her Wechsler-Bellevue IQ test score was a combined one hundred thirty-six. That is awfully close to the genius level. She'd had the Minnesota Multiphasic Personality Inventory, which we like to call the MMPI, and such tests as Thematic Apperception, Word Association, Rorschach, Make-a-Picture-Story, and the like. Don't worry if those are meaningless terms."

"I know some of them."

"Good. I thought you were a bright boy. With your indulgence, I'll simply read this straight through. There is a page of addended test scores we won't bother with."

Carl shrugged, glanced at his watch again, and uncrossed his legs. He wanted a cigarette but had left them in the car.

Dr. Fields cleared his throat:

"'Patient, a female of 21.5 years and of normal physiological development, was in contact with reality at the time of testing. She showed a forced, almost severe sense of control during the testing as well as preceding and subsequent interviews' . . . I'll skip a few lines here. Let's see . . . 'There was an absence of extraordinarily bizarre or incoherent thought processes. She shows little evidence of being free of the amphetamine addiction. Her Wechsler-Bellevue is in the near-genius range. There appears no generalized impairment of her abstract reasoning ability, although memory functions appear sporadic; she suffers selective recall at near-severe levels.'

"I'm sorry, Carl. I should have mentally edited this a little bit beforehand. This is all mainly preliminary to the findings. Allow me to skip a bit, sort of scan the highlights.

"'Patient works efficiently and quickly when asked—does

not offer personal interpretations—pretends sleep when bored or angry, etc., etc. No signs of self-mutilation.'

"Ah, here we are. 'Patient clearly reveals an attitude of deep resentment toward mother, who is deceased at the hand of patient and possible incestual or misdirected Oedipal conflicts involving her only sibling, a brother three years younger. There is some possibility of incest or imagined incest involving the brother and a similar but less clear situation involving the deceased father. The personality inventory indicates feelings of estrangement, tendencies toward outer-directed violence, and severe personality disturbance. The picture is that of a young woman in the early to middle stages of a schizophrenic process of the manic type, with acute depression and acting-out tendencies which suggest a risk to others. Continued confinement is recommended at this time and patient should continue tricyclics and ECT for the psychodynamic depression.'

"There's a little more here, but I've covered the parts I wanted to bring to your attention for our discussion."

Carl was sitting on the edge of his chair. When Dr. Fields closed the folder, Carl leaned forward and whispered bitterly, "What kind of crap is that?"

"Well, I hoped for a better response from you, Carl."

"That was crap, pure crap!"

"Apparently you don't feel like discussing it," Dr. Fields said with a smile, attempting to defuse Carl's anger.

"You don't *ever* plan to let her out, do you?"

"Of course we do. Claire has no sentence here. Do I need to remind you that Claire is here instead of prison? I'm trying to get your attention, Carl. You are Claire's only relative and apparently her best friend as well. I'm trying to get you to help us help her."

Carl scooted back in his chair and fumed silently. All he wanted was to see Claire. It was almost dark. It was time.

"There, are you calmed down?"

"Can I go see Claire now?"

Dr. Fields picked up his cigar and relit it. "Yes. But first I'd like to ask you to think about what I just read. I can have a copy made of the report if you'd like to go over it again.

"We need you to help us get through to her, Carl. Until

Claire recognizes the depth of her sickness, we can't do anything but monitor her. I hoped that if you heard the report . . . oh, well, will you think about it?"

"I'll think about it," Carl said, trying to end the conversation. "If you want to give me a copy of the report, I'll study it."

"Fine, fine. That's all I wanted in the first place."

Dr. Fields stood, and Carl followed. "I guess you'd like to go up and see your sister now. I believe she's expecting you. The party's at seven. You may visit in her room until then if you'd like. Talk to her, Carl. Judge for yourself."

"Okay." Carl started walking toward the door. "Can I have her present back?"

"Julie will have it for you, I'm sure. She can escort you up."

"I didn't mean to blow up like that," Carl halfheartedly apologized.

"I know you didn't, Carl. I look forward to seeing you again."

Fat chance, Carl thought.

Claire Grant had a feeling of expectation that night but couldn't remember why. Was it important to remember? She didn't know.

Claire's room, with its single large window, was in the women's wing on the third floor of the building. The window was covered with a thin wire mesh, but through it she could see the Mississippi River and over into Wisconsin. When the days were very clear, as they were sometimes on crisp December days, she could see people fishing from the Wisconsin bank. The Minnesota bank was shrouded in trees. Claire enjoyed watching them—so patient, so contented, so free. Sometimes she watched them for hours. But looking out the window made her sleepy in a hypnotic way. It seemed that so many things made her sleepy, so that it seemed she was just about either to fall asleep or to explode with unfocused energy. She thought it was because of the Thorazine.

Claire was still in her robe. The persistent thought that she should be getting dressed for something was annoying. A few hazy pinpricks of light moving southward along the river caught her attention, and she watched the lights until they were gone. Snow piled up on the window ledge.

Claire had been given her eighth of the biweekly electroconvulsive therapy treatments that morning at ten o'clock. That they would do such a thing to her on Christmas Eve was offensive to Claire. Her jaw was still sore, and her teeth ached like from sinus pain. The Anectine had worn off quickly, as usual, and the paralysis was gone before they let her out of the recovery room; but she felt still dazed. She wondered if they were putting something in her water.

She wanted to see Carl very badly. His delay felt like betrayal. She felt like a caged wild animal, trapped in Fairbrook forever. She constantly feared that Carl would simply forget about her and stop coming to visit. Then she would be lost. She had written a note to herself earlier that morning, before the ECT, to remind herself to stop bothering Carl with pleas to get her out of Fairbrook. She told herself to stop being angry with him because he couldn't get her released. She hid the secret notes to herself under the mattress. The most recent one said simply: *"Stop bothering Carl so much or he might never come to see you again."*

It was dark then. Claire didn't have a watch but knew it must be late in the afternoon. Had she eaten dinner yet? Was dinner canceled or something? She couldn't remember. Why did she feel compelled to get dressed? Was Carl coming?

Claire pressed her fingertips to the thick glass and watched the redness gather beneath her nails. It was fascinating.

She could just hear music from a radio in the room below hers, a chorus of voices singing "Joy to the World." She found herself singing quietly along with the radio. She sang for a verse until terrible pictures came into her mind. Finally she had to stop singing, telling herself, "Stop!" And the pictures disappeared. She could still hear the music. When the next verse began, she was singing again. "Joy to the world, the Lord has come," she sang, then stopped suddenly and shivered. Floating through her mind went a picture of a young man who looked like Jesus Christ . . . who? She couldn't remember. Jesus masturbated himself to orgasm in her mind. *The Lord has come,* a voice inside her mind whispered playfully. In her mind, a rabbit hopped across the snowbanks and fell into the Mississippi River.

*   *   *

There was nothing in the hallway of Third West, the women's wing, to distinguish it from any first-class hotel, maybe like the halls in the Grand Hotel. Carl considered that as he walked along just behind Julie. Dr. Fields's secretary was overweight, a little frumpy-looking, and she walked ahead of Carl like a bellboy taking luggage up. Carl watched the Jell-O flesh wiggle inside her white dress and stifled an urge to grab a handful of her buttocks. He carried Claire's carefully rewrapped Christmas package in both hands.

When they came to room 320, Julie knocked lightly and stepped aside. "Call me when you're ready to come downstairs," she told Carl. Then she turned and walked away. The door swung open, and Claire's arms were around him.

"My God, Claire!" he cried. "You'll break me!"

"Oh, I'm sorry," Claire said, pulling back and kicking the door closed with her foot. "For some reason, I thought you might not come."

"How could you think that?"

"Is that for me?" Claire pointed to the package Carl had sat on her bed.

"No, it's for me, but I wanted to open it in front of you to make you mad," he said teasingly. Then: "Of course it is."

"May I open it now?" The excitement was evident in her voice.

Without waiting for an answer, she sat on the bed and began tearing away the paper. She was not very neat about it.

"Oh, look." Claire pulled out a tan down-filled jacket and shook the folds from it. "It's beautiful!"

"There's more," Carl said, "so don't throw out the tissue paper until you've looked through it."

"More?" Claire sorted through the paper and found a matching wool ski cap and mittens.

"Do you like it?"

"It's so light. I love it, Carl. Really." She stood quickly and kissed him on the cheek. "I'm going to put it on now," she said. Claire pushed her arms through the sleeves and tugged up the zipper. Carl thought she looked a little silly with the ski jacket over her yellow flannel robe. She put on the cap and mittens. "How do I look?"

"Like a ski bunny," Carl said, laughing.

She hugged him, then spun around the room in a dance.

"I have another surprise," Carl announced. "Can you get dressed now?"

"Dressed?" Claire stopped spinning and fell back to the bed. She landed spread-eagled, and her robe fell open, exposing her legs. Carl reached over and flipped it closed.

"Can't we go outside?" he asked.

"I don't think they'll let me. But you could ask. I don't know, Janie Lucas has been here for a goddamn year, and they won't let her go outside at all, even with her husband, unless an orderly goes with them. Why are we going outside?"

"That's where the surprise is."

"Why? Tell me. It's too big to bring in? Right?"

"It wouldn't be a surprise if I told you now."

"You can ask, I don't know."

"Why don't you get dressed anyway? I'll check with Dr. Fields."

Carl went to the intercom phone and dialed the office extension. Claire went to her closet and poked around for something to wear. The extension rang. Claire tossed her robe onto the bed and stood naked with her back to Carl. He looked down at the phone. "Don't turn around yet," Claire said as she fished some underwear from the bureau. She bent over and fitted her breasts into a bra, then pulled up her panties. "Okay," she said, then went to the closet to find a sweater.

"Wear panty hose, or something," Carl ordered. "It's really very cold out there." The extension rang for the eighth time. "Maybe nobody's home," he said to himself.

When Julie answered, Carl asked if he and Claire could go for a walk on the grounds. Claire wants a chance to wear her new jacket, he explained, and the snowfall is so beautiful in the darkness. Julie said she'd ask the doctor and call him back.

Claire sat on the edge of the bed and put on panty hose. Then she stood and tugged on her jeans. Carl wondered if the bra was hospital issue. It was white and bulky, not the kind Claire would choose, he thought. Claire's would have lace and be thin, gauzy. She pulled a sweater over her head and turned to face him.

"Well?"

"You're beautiful."

"No, I mean, can we get out?"

"She's going to call back."

The phone buzzed as his sentence ended. When he hung up, he told Claire that Julie was coming up to escort them downstairs. Dr. Fields thought it would be nice for them to have a little walk together before the party.

"Party?" Claire tried to remember.

"Never mind. Do you have any boots?"

"Uh-huh."

"Wear them, too."

"Boy, you're sure bossy tonight."

"I'm sorry. Could you hurry? I think Julie's coming right up."

"Must be some surprise," Claire said, getting her boots from the closet.

Julie left them at the door with orders to stay in the mall area where the lights were so they wouldn't chance getting lost in the snow. Fairbrook sat on ten acres of land within the walls.

The first thing Claire did when they were outside was hit Carl in the back with a snowball. Halfheartedly Carl tossed one back at her. "Come on," he said, "let me show you the surprise first."

He took Claire straight across to the parking lot.

"It's in the car?" she asked.

"Yes."

"Whose car is this?" she asked when they stopped beside a rented Pontiac.

"I rented it." Carl kept glancing back at the windows.

"What happened to the Ford?"

"Nothing happened to the Ford. I just sold it."

"This is the big surprise? A rented car?"

Snowflakes landed on Claire's face and somehow made her even more beautiful. Carl ached for her. He sweated through his shirt.

"I bought a Jeep Wagoneer," he told her.

"Really? Why didn't you bring it for me to see?"

Carl checked the windows behind them again, then took the car keys from his pocket. He led Claire around to the back of the car. He looked back at the building again.

"Claire, I want you to listen to me very carefully. I'm going to ask you to climb inside the trunk and—"

"You want me to what?"

"To get into the trunk. Then I'm going to close it. Now it will be dark in there when the lid comes down. There's a blanket for you to lie on. I don't want you to be afraid because you won't be in there very long. Ten minutes at most. Then I'll let you out."

"But—"

"Do you trust me, Claire?" He glanced back at the amber windows.

"Of course I do."

"Then just get in the trunk. We can't stand out here right now discussing it. Just trust me."

Suddenly Claire's face showed the recognition. "You're taking me out of here, aren't you?"

"Yes." Carl nodded. He let the trunk lid go up, then pushed her toward it with his hand on the back of her neck. Claire climbed over the bumper and curled up on the blanket. "Don't be afraid," Carl said. Claire was smiling when he closed the trunk.

Carl rushed around to the driver's door and got in. There was no point in looking back at the windows again. They were committed. He started driving toward the gate, wishing he could have picked a day with better weather. If they were stopped at the gate or chased afterward, he didn't trust his ability to control the car in the snow at high speeds. Now he could only drive forward and hope for the best.

Approaching the gate, Carl blinked his lights twice to alert the guard, hoping the signal would cause him to open the gate before he had to stop the car fully. The guard came out of the gatehouse and waved at Carl. Carl blinked his lights again. The guard crossed the drive and waited for Carl to stop, his hand on the gate button but not pushing it. Carl slowed to a stop at the gate, the tires squishing in the slush, and rolled down his window. The other guard was visible through the gatehouse window. He was reading a magazine and occasionally glancing at the flickering glow of a television set. Carl wondered if he could get enough traction from that point to bust through the gate without wrecking the car. The guard came to the window.

"Just wanted to let you know," the guard said, "that the weather report sounds pretty bad. They've announced some road closings."

"Yeah, thanks. That's why I decided to start home early."

"This could sure ruin the doc's party plans, huh?"

"Probably so."

"Hell, it's always party time in there, if you know what I mean?"

"Yeah."

"Well, take her easy going down the hill. I'd keep her in low gear if'n it was me," the guard said, walking over to push the gate button.

"Thanks, I will."

The gate slid slowly back, and Carl eased the car forward. In spite of the cold air coming through the open window, he could still feel sweat soaking through his flannel shirt. "Good night," Carl called out, and waved at the guard.

"Take her easy now," the guard called back as Carl drove past.

Carl glanced in the rearview mirror and saw the other guard pick up a phone. Carl pushed on the accelerator and nearly spun through the first turn. The gate closed. His headlights arced through bare stick trees as Carl straightened the car and started down the spiral. His lights appeared to expose packs of bloodhounds, men with rifles, snow ghosts. He had not counted on the whiteouts and ice. It took fifteen minutes to get to the bottom of the bluff.

After reaching the highway, Carl drove west for a mile until coming to a lane leading into a public park. A snowplow had been by on the highway, and the lane was blocked with a two-foot snowbank. Carl accelerated and pushed through it. A hundred feet up the lane the Jeep was parked. It was covered in snow.

Carl stopped next to the Jeep, jumped out, and ran back to the trunk.

"I'm sorry, Claire. It took longer than I thought," he cried as she started climbing out.

"Apparently we made it," she said. "Is that hump of snow your new Jeep Wagoneer?"

"That's it. And we better get the hell out of here."

Lights flashed through the trees and settled on them. Carl realized a car was coming up the lane.

"Damn! Claire, here take the keys and get in the Jeep. Quick! Get down on the seat, and don't look up."

He put the keys in her hand, and Claire went around behind the Jeep. She had not seen the lights turn in, and his urgency confused her. By the time Claire got the door opened and climbed inside, the approaching car was less than fifty feet away. Carl stood by the Pontiac and waited. The car stopped, and when the door opened, the dome light illuminated the face of the guard who had opened the gate. Carl walked toward the guard's car to increase the distance to Claire.

"Grant?"

"What's the problem?" Carl stopped next to the driver's door and waited for the guard to get out. The open car door was between them.

"It was very simple to track you up this lane, you know?"

"Track me?"

"Seems someone reported seeing you put your sister into the trunk of that there car. I'll need to have a look."

"That's stupid."

"Yep, I'd say it was. Now I'll have to have a look-see."

"Be my guest," Carl said, immediately taking a step back and kicking the car door shut, knocking the guard back against the side. Before the man could get up, Carl rushed around and punched him in the face. The guard's head hit the edge of the door opening, and he tumbled backward across the front seat. His glasses hung from one ear, and a trickle of blood seeped from his nose. Carl lifted his legs and shoved him inside; then he took the pistol from the guard's belt. He slammed the door and jogged back to the Jeep.

It took him five minutes to clean the snow off the glass; then he knocked on the window until Claire raised herself up and unlocked the door. When Carl got in and started the engine, Claire asked, "What did you do to him?"

"Just knocked him out."

Carl drove around the guard's car and followed the tracks back to the highway.

"Where are we going?" Claire asked.

"I don't know. Someplace warm, I guess. Warm and free."

"You look so tired, Carl." Claire reached over and rubbed his neck. "I owe you, forever and ever."

"You don't owe me."

"I'll help you drive."

"That's all right. I can do it."

"Well, I'll stay awake. We can talk."

"Okay. But just let me concentrate on getting us the hell away from here right now."

He looked over at her, thinking, My beautiful, beautiful Claire. She sparkled. Was this the woman who needed her psyche fixed? There was nothing wrong with his sister that a little love, attention, and freedom wouldn't fix. He would make up everything to her. Being with her again, alone together, she belonging to him now, consumed him with happy passion. He was building a monument to desire.

"I knew you'd get me out," Claire said after a while.

"So did I. I'm just sorry you had to stay in there for a month."

"But you're really in trouble now, little brother. Do you understand that?"

"Trouble?"

"That was illegal as hell. You could go to jail for taking me out of Fairbrook."

"Only if they catch us. And they won't."

two

After insisting that she would stay awake all night to keep Carl company while he drove, Claire kept leaning over by degrees until she was fast asleep with her head in his lap. She was gone thirty minutes after they had started south on Interstate 35.

Carl was wide-awake and jittery. Each time a pair of headlights appeared in the rearview mirror, his body tensed. He had no way of calculating what the people at Fairbrook would do once they found the guard. He half expected the highway patrol to stop them at any moment. He hoped the snowstorm would work in their favor, that the police would be too busy to go out hunting for Claire and him. Anyway, they had no way of knowing he had sold the Ford and bought a new car under an assumed name.

It wasn't too difficult maneuvering with the four-wheel-drive Jeep as long as the snow remained soft. He wanted to turn on the radio for a weather forecast but was afraid the noise would waken Claire. Her hair had fallen over the side of her face, and he couldn't see her. Her face was so warm against his right thigh that he could feel sweat forming there. She was still wearing the new jacket, but the mittens and cap had fallen to the floorboard. Her knees were bent so she could fit into the space between Carl's legs and the passenger door. Carl wondered if she was too warm with the jacket on. He turned down the heater just in case.

It had been dark for more than two hours. Carl held his

wristwatch up to the dash lights to see what time it was. A quarter to seven. He could see no farther ahead than fifty or sixty yards and kept his speed down to forty miles an hour. Twice earlier he had run right up on the rear of slower-moving cars before the washed-out red patches of their taillights became visible. Then he had been driving at fifty. He figured that at forty, the usual six- or seven-hour drive to Des Moines would take ten or eleven hours. He wished he had brought a thermos of coffee.

Claire really shouldn't be lying there, he thought, glancing down at her again. The driving conditions were too precarious, and if they should happen to run into something, Claire's head would be crushed between his body and the steering wheel. But there was no way to move her without waking her up. He would just have to be particularly careful. She looked so fragile.

Not able to see her face, Carl thought that Claire looked like a little girl the way she was lying on the seat. She was curled into a fetal position, on her side, her arms bent at the elbows and her hands held in loose fists in front of her mouth. He wanted to stroke her hair but was afraid that, too, would awaken her. Even above the continual squish of the tires and rumble of the engine, he could hear her breathing through her mouth. It was not the sound of snoring, just the loud, steady intake and exhale of air. He lit a cigarette and pushed open the side wing vent so the smoke would escape. The wind's roar then covered the sound of Claire's deep breathing.

He could not keep from glancing down at her. One thing the hospital, the terrible things in Mexico, and all the drugs had not harmed was Claire's irreproachable, startling beauty. She was still the most beautiful woman Carl had ever seen.

Carl wondered how so much violence could come from such beauty. He had considered that Claire could not separate the doing of violence to others from the doing of it to herself. The first time Carl spoke with Dr. Fields, he suggested to the doctor that Claire might be expressing a hatred of herself when she hurt others. Dr. Fields replied that maybe Carl was just trying to find another way to forgive Claire, that "maybe you've forgiven her too much already."

Carl put his hand lightly on Claire's arm and felt her warmth. No matter what happens or what you do, he thought, I will always love and protect you.

Claire slept all the way through Minnesota and into Iowa. Carl had to pull off the interstate on the northern edge of Mason City to fill the gas tank. It was still snowing but had diminished to flurries within the past half hour. A combination of the bright service station lights and the cessation of motion caused Claire to stir.

"Wake up," Carl whispered softly, rubbing Claire's shoulder.

Claire started to stretch but bumped into the car door with both feet. For a couple of seconds she seemed confused, pushing against the door with her feet and pushing against the dash with her outstretched hands. She turned her head and looked up at Carl. The return of consciousness to her eyes was so deliberate that Carl could monitor it step by step.

"Where am I?" she asked, starting to sit up. "I've got a crick in my neck," she added, rubbing the back of her neck with one hand. "How did I get outside?" A look of fright came into her eyes. "Where am I? Whose car is this? Carl!"

Carl touched her cheek and told her it was all right. "Mason City, Iowa, is where we are," he told her. "Buying gas."

Panic rose from Claire's stomach into her throat and started to gag her. She thought she had gone to sleep in the hospital, but here she was somewhere in the outside world in a strange car in a town she had never been to before. She sat up straight and closed her eyes, trying to make herself remember how she came to be in such a place, in such a condition. She looked out the window on her side and saw a young man in a college letter jacket standing behind a wide expanse of glass in the station office. He stared at her, and it made her afraid. Carl was saying something to her. She recognized his voice.

"I'll gas her up. Do you need to use the bathroom or anything?"

She did. Oh, how she did. Suddenly the most important thing in the world was to find a toilet. She understood then that the ache in her side came from the need to urinate.

"I hope they have a coffee machine in there," Carl said.

"I've got to go to the bathroom really bad," Claire said as she jumped out of the Jeep.

"Wait a minute and I'll come with you," Carl said, but Claire was already halfway to the office.

"I can't wait," she called back to him.

"Be careful," Carl warned, then got out and went back to the self-service pumps. He inserted the nozzle into the gas tank and set the automatic lever, wondering if he ought to check the oil. He could see Claire taking a key from the attendant, then walking out of his view toward the side of the office. The attendant's eyes followed her.

Claire fumbled with the key in the lock for ten seconds before getting it to turn. The frustration of the lock made her feel like screaming at it. She had already forgotten why it was so important to get that door open. She felt dizzy, her body ached, and her fingers tingled as if they were numb. Her jaw was so sore that it hurt to bring her teeth together. Where was she? Had she been down to ECT? Of course not, there was nothing like this at Fairbrook. She pushed the door open and rushed inside, still unable to remember why she felt so compelled to go in. She found herself in a bathroom. The walls were institutional green, and the paint was flaking in places. Scraps of toilet paper were on the floor, along with grease spots and cigarette butts. Claire closed the door and locked it unconsciously by pushing in the button on the knob. She looked to one side and was startled by the sight of a face in the mirror, a face she did not immediately recognize as her own. Then she said, "That's you," to the mirror. "I mean, you're me." She laughed. The agony in her side eased, and she felt a warm moisture spreading down her thighs. It felt wonderful. She felt light-headed, almost stunned, and like being in a void. Empty, she thought. It was a familiar feeling. She sat on the closed toilet lid and rested her arms on her knees.

She was attracted to the sight of paint flaking off the wall. One spot was diamond-shaped; behind it the concrete block wall was bumpy. Claire felt her body expanding as it grew out toward the wall, the bare spot coming closer until it seemed to be directly in front of her eyes. The bumps on the concrete looked like pimples on pale gray skin.

Like the ones that kept appearing on the skin of Rabbit's thighs. She saw Rabbit's face, his body, but did not recognize him. She cried softly without knowing why.

She noticed the warmth between her legs and the stickiness on her thighs. Like sperm, or blood, she thought. Or like evil seeping from her womb.

She dreamed of the ECT recovery room, dreaming and watching herself lying there dreaming, paralyzed by the curare so she could not move a single muscle at will.

She liked the feeling of being in and out of her body at the same time, its being somehow familiar.

Outside, Carl finished filling the Jeep's tank and went into the office to ask the attendant if they had a coffee machine.

"Back there," the boy said, motioning to the rear.

"Bathroom that way, too?" Carl asked.

"Right next to the ladies' room," the attendant said.

"Do I need a key?" Carl asked, counting out cash for the gas.

"Nah. Just the women's is locked. You know?"

Carl took his change and wondered if he should wait for Claire to come back before he went into the bathroom. He found the coffee machine and the two snack machines next to it. One offered potato chips, Fritos, crackers, and taco chips. The other had gum and candy. Farther down was a cigarette machine. Carl decided to use the bathroom first, then get the coffee.

When he came out, there was no sign of Claire. He looked out at the Jeep, but she wasn't in it, nor was she anywhere in the office. He wondered what the hell was taking her so long. He bought two cups of coffee, two candy bars, two packages of gum, two bags of potato chips, and a package of cigarettes. Still no sign of Claire. He stuffed the food into his coat pocket and sat the coffee cups on top of the machine.

"Did you see the lady come out?" he asked the attendant, who was sitting behind the desk, watching a portable television.

"Nope," the boy said without looking away from the movie.

Carl walked back to the bathroom and knocked lightly on the door. "Claire?" He waited a few seconds, then repeated her name. No response. "You didn't fall in, did you?" He hoped the attendant couldn't hear him over the television noise. He knocked once more and called her name. Then he leaned his ear to the door and tried the handle. It was locked. "Claire?" He pressed his ear closer to the door. "Are you all right? Answer me!" Maybe she had come out already, he thought. But where would she go? Would she just walk away? Carl felt a rush of panic. "Claire, damn it! Don't play games with me. This is not funny!" He rattled the door handle.

Carl went back to the attendant to ask if he had another key. How in hell do you explain something like this? he wondered.

"Excuse me," Carl said. The attendant looked up grudgingly from the movie. "Would you happen to have an extra key to the ladies' room?" Carl decided it would be better to offer no explanations.

"She locked in?" the boy asked, standing and pulling a ring of keys from his belt.

"She's not feeling very well. Would you just let me borrow your key?"

"Don't worry. We'll get it opened up."

They stopped in front of the door, and the attendant found the right key.

"Maybe you oughter open it . . . in case." He pulled the key from the ring, handed it to Carl, then stepped to one side.

"Thank you." Of course, she has to be in there, Carl thought; else how could it be locked? He inserted the key and opened the door.

Claire, fully dressed even to her jacket, was sitting on the toilet seat, staring at the wall in front of her. Her hands were primly folded in her lap, her feet were close together, and her back was straight. Carl started in, then remembered the attendant. He handed him the key, thanked him, then closed the door as he went inside. He knelt on the cold concrete floor beside Claire and put his hands on hers.

"Oh, Claire, what did they do to you in there? Don't you know everything is all right now? You're not in that place anymore. You're with me. Don't even think about that place. You're safe. They won't ever find us; you won't ever go back to a place like that. Claire, look at me." Carl reached up and turned her face toward his. "Claire, come on, darling." He rubbed her cheeks with his thumbs. "We've just got to get all the drugs out of your system and everything will be fine. Look at me, Claire." Her eyes were wide open and facing him, but he could tell she didn't see him. "Claire, don't start this stuff again."

Carl put one of his hands on her leg, then quickly lifted it back. Her jeans were wet. He looked down and noticed that both thighs were wet to the knees. "Damn," he muttered. He pulled her up and opened the bathroom door, putting his arm around her to move her outside. The wetness on her legs didn't show up too clearly on the new blue denim.

"Thank you," Carl said to the attendant, and hustled Claire out the door and to the Jeep. He fixed Claire on the passenger side, then got in and started the engine. He noticed that the attendant was watching them curiously.

Claire sat as she had in the bathroom: primly, her back straight, hands in her lap, and staring straight ahead. Carl pulled back onto the interstate and picked up speed. He hadn't gone a mile when he remembered the coffee left sitting on top of the machine. "Shit," he said, banging his hand on the steering wheel.

They had reached the southern edge of Mason City when a sign announced a rest stop ahead. There were two trucks parked in the lot and a wooden building with rest rooms. A few benches dotted each side of the park house. Carl stopped the Jeep in a dimly lit spot between two of the tall light poles that washed the park in a yellowish light. He left the engine and heater running.

"Claire, we have to get your clothes changed. Don't worry about it, okay? It's not your fault. You've just got to get the junk out of your system, and you'll be fine again. Just don't scare me this way. All right?"

Claire did not acknowledge him. Carl touched her shoulder tenderly, as if to let her know he would return, then climbed over the seat into the back. He reached into the cargo compartment and moved pieces of luggage around. He found the blue suitcase he was looking for and pulled it over. He hoped everything he needed would be in the one bag. He couldn't see without the dome light and hoped turning it on wouldn't attract any attention from the parked trucks. He fished around in the carefully packed suitcase and came up with a pair of nylon panties, a pair of navy blue slacks, and a pair of her old ragged tennis shoes. It took him another couple of minutes to find a pair of anklet socks. He put the clothing into the front seat, then climbed back over.

They had been in the park for ten minutes, and only one car had passed out on the interstate. The snow had stopped. Carl unzipped Claire's boots and pulled them off, pitching them into the back seat. Then he unzipped and pulled off her new jacket, which followed the boots over. "Claire?" She did not respond. "This would go a lot easier if you helped a little." He tried to sound relaxed but was far from it. How was he going to undress her? He unsnapped the jeans and slowly pulled down the zipper. The noise of it was startling. He had never before noticed how loud a zipper could be. Claire neither resisted nor aided him; she was pliable yet stiff, moving when he moved her, stopping rigidly when he stopped. Her eyes were closed, and her mind was completely unreactive.

Carl pushed and pulled at her jeans until they were down to her ankles. He bent her knees and released one leg from the jeans, then the other. He rolled down the window and threw the jeans out. Then he encountered the panty hose and began urging them down in a rolling motion. When he noticed that she was not wearing panties, he reached up and turned off the dome light. The hose followed the jeans out the window. Carl smiled as he wondered what someone would make of a pile of women's clothes in the parking lot. This is going to drive some guy crazy with envy, he thought.

The tails of her flannel shirt were damp. Carl reached over the seat and found a white cowl-neck sweater in the suitcase. He unbuttoned her shirt and pulled it free of her arms. The shirt went out the window. Claire sat stiffly in the seat, wearing only her bra. Working quickly and purposely, Carl pulled the sweater over her head and fitted her arms through the sleeves. He had started to put on a fresh pair of panties when he felt the sour stickiness on her thighs. "Damn," he said aloud, feeling exhausted from the struggle to undress and dress her in such cramped quarters. He took a handkerchief from his back pocket and started wiping her thighs, but it didn't help much. He laid the blue slacks over Claire's legs, jumped out of the Jeep, and jogged over to the rest room to wet the handkerchief in the sink.

He finished cleaning her thighs and gently between her legs, then pulled up the panties. The handkerchief went out the window with everything else. The slacks went on easily. He added socks and put on her shoes. Then he retrieved the new jacket and put it on her, zipping up the front. He turned the heater back to low and drove out of the park, trying to light a cigarette as he merged with the interstate. It was almost midnight.

Carl had been on the road for ten minutes when he began worrying about the way Claire sat. He feared she would become stiff, and her muscles cramp, if she stayed in that position too long. He pulled onto the shoulder, got out, went around to the passenger side, lifted out Claire, and laid her in the back seat with his jacket for a pillow.

Not everything was working the way he planned it. He thought they would get all the way to Kansas City the first night. With that comfortable distance from Minneapolis, they could decide what to do next, but it was becoming clear he would run out of steam by Des Moines. He ripped open a bag of potato chips and shook some from the sack directly into his mouth, crumbs falling down the front of his shirt. The next large town was Ames, two hours away, if they didn't hit another snowstorm, and Des Moines looked like an hour beyond that. He decided he could make it to Des Moines all right.

Claire did not awaken when Carl stopped at a Best Western motel just off the loop around the western edge of Des Moines. He parked away from the brightly lit office and locked the Jeep before going in to register. He signed the card "Mr. and Mrs. Charles Granger." He listed his occupation as "student," and their address as 100 Lakeview Drive, Minneapolis, which was the address of a suburban 7-11 store and also the address on his brand-new forged driver's license. He paid cash for one night and took the key from a distracted female clerk, who returned immediately to her paperback of *Magister Ludi*.

Carl drove around to their first-floor room and parked in front. Then he reached over the seat and woke Claire, touching her arm and softly speaking her name. She made a protesting sound but did not open her eyes. Carl shook her again. "Wake up so you can go back to sleep," he kidded. Claire came out of sleep the same way she had at the gas station, stretching and blinking her eyes, but it was quickly apparent that she knew she wasn't in the hospital. She pushed herself up on one arm and looked out the window. "We're at a motel in Des Moines, Iowa," Carl said by way of explanation.

Claire raised herself all the way up, smiling sleepily, and put both hands on Carl's shoulders. "Did you drive all night?" she asked.

"Not all night. It's a little after four. I'm sorry to have to wake you up just so you can go back to sleep, but I think you'll find a bed more comfortable. I will."

"Poor baby." Claire teased him, making a kissing motion.

"How do you feel?" Carl asked, getting out of the Jeep.

"Sore. Buzzed. Better, though."

Claire scooted over and got out of the Jeep. She followed Carl around back to get their luggage. When Carl unloaded three suitcases, leaving two others, Claire asked if he had packed for her, too.

"Probably just the essentials, what I could still find from the house. And I bought some stuff."

"How very efficient." Claire followed him into the room.

"Which bed do you want?" Carl asked after finding the light switch. He put the suitcases on the floor by a round table.

"Isn't this deliciously evil?" Claire said, inspecting the room.

"Don't get too awake. I want to leave around noon."

Claire spun herself onto the far bed, and Carl took her suitcase to it.

"You might want to check this stuff in the morning to make sure I got the right things. I tried to think of everything."

"I'm sure you did."

Claire lay spread-eagled on the wide bed with a contented smile on her face while Carl went back to search for his pajama bottoms in his suitcase.

Claire sat up and opened her suitcase to sort through it like a child looking for hidden presents. She pulled out a long white nightgown and tossed it over her head; it fluttered down over the pillows.

"It was the warmest one I could find," Carl explained without being asked.

Claire poked around, pulling out one thing and another. "Look at this! I haven't seen some of this stuff in years." She held up a pair of yellow silk panties with an index finger through a leg opening and smirked at Carl. "Did *you* pack this, too?"

"Get serious, Claire."

"Where did you find these things?"

"In boxes in the garage. Before the . . . house burned, Mom was going to throw it all away. I put your stuff in boxes in the garage."

Carl knew immediately that he should not have mentioned the fire. Claire's face sobered, and she stared at the wall. He walked over and touched her shoulder.

"I didn't do it," she whispered.

"I know, Claire. I know."

Then he went into the bathroom to undress and put on his pajama bottoms.

Claire plucked the nightgown from the pillows and put it over a chair back; then she began undressing. As she started reaching for the buttons she expected to find, she stopped and moved in front of the mirror. "Hey! Carl?"

"What?" he answered from inside the bathroom.

"I don't want to sound crazy or anything, but these aren't the clothes I had on last night—are they?"

There was an evident tone of caution in her voice.

"Just a minute," he said, quickly putting on his pajamas. He came out of the bathroom with his dirty clothes in his arms. He pitched the clothes on the floor by his bed. "You had an accident at the gas station," he said almost casually.

"An accident?"

"Don't worry about it, okay? All those drugs . . ."

"What kind of accident?"

"In the bathroom."

Claire's face reddened, and she looked away from him. "I

don't remember," she said quietly, more to herself. "I can't remember!"

"Just don't worry about it. Let's get their junk out of your system." Carl put his arms around her shoulders and held her. He could feel the frustration radiating from her body.

"I pissed on myself, didn't I?"

Carl held her and didn't say anything.

"Jee-sus! I can't even remember changing my clothes. Carl, I can't remember! What's happening to me?"

"It's all right, Claire. Don't cry. I changed you."

She sniffed away the tears and looked at him. "You did? But, oh, hell . . . I don't even remember *that!*" Carl backed her up until they were sitting on the bed.

"It's all right. I'll take care of you now," he said, stroking her hair. He kissed her cheek, tasting her tears. "Do you remember how you used to lick my face when I cried?" He licked her cheek.

"Oh, Carl, I love you." She cried deeply into his shoulder.

Finally Carl pulled away and said, "We really should be trying to get some sleep." He got up and went to his own bed, turning down the covers and keeping his back to her to hide his erection.

Claire pretended to pout for a moment, then said, "But I'm not sleepy now."

"That's no surprise. You slept all the way." Carl turned off the ceiling light, then got into bed. "But I hope you'll try."

Claire took her suitcase into the dressing area and turned on the mirror light. "Did you pack a toothbrush?"

"In that green vinyl bag."

Claire found the green bag and, unzipping it, found at the top a small box of tampons. "That's my Carl, never misses a thing." She held them out for him to see.

"Why? You think I don't know anything?"

"Sometimes, brother of mine, I suspect that you know everything."

Claire smiled, then took her bag and nightgown into the bathroom. Carl lay back in bed, frustrated that he was beginning to feel his second wind. It was five-thirty in the morning, he hadn't slept in almost twenty-four hours, he had driven for more than twelve hours—most of it during a blinding snow-storm—and here he was becoming wide-awake. He couldn't shake the nagging fear that the police were tracking them down. He heard the toilet flush and water start running in the shower.

Claire opened the bathroom door a crack and stuck her head out. "Did you pack a razor?" she asked. "I can't find one."

"Use mine. I'll get it for you." He started to get up, but Claire came out of the bathroom with a small towel barely covering her. "No, don't get up. Just tell me where to look."

"In the pouch inside the suitcase lid."

When Claire bent over to search for the razor, the towel rode up and exposed the lower curve of her hips. Carl turned over and closed his eyes. Why does she keep doing that to me? he asked himself. He heard the bathroom door close again and buried his erection in the mattress.

Carl had almost fallen asleep when Claire came out of the shower. He heard her somewhere in the recesses of his mind but did not turn over or open his eyes. If he had, he would have seen Claire standing between the two beds, nude, and running her hands over the skin of her stomach and thighs. He was so close to sleep that he did not hear her get into her own bed and pound the pillow into submission.

Claire could feel her body growing, blowing up like a balloon, getting so full and fat that she thought she might burst all over the room. Her skin felt prickly and heavy. She thought she would sink through the mattress. She grabbed the sides of her head and pushed. She felt herself losing weight then, seeming to float up to the ceiling, where she could look down on her shell still in the bed.

Sometime later she went to sleep.

Where was the smell of coffee coming from? Carl worked at opening his eyes. There was bright light and the smell of coffee all around him. One eyelid rose halfway; the other soon managed a slit. His face was pointed toward the large picture window, and daylight brightened the thin curtains. Coming into focus between his eyes and the window was a styrofoam coffee cup with steam rising from it. "You still wake up like an old dog," someone said.

Carl rolled over and looked toward the sound. Claire was there, seated in the desk chair, her legs crossed, a sly smile on her face, engrossed in watching him.

"I brought you some coffee," she said, pointing to the steaming cup on the nightstand.

"Thank you. What time is it?" Carl tried to finish waking himself. He felt bloated, full, foggy.

"About nine, give or take a little. I don't have a watch." Claire looked strangely pleased with herself.

"Nine? Really? Why did you wake me up so early?" He lay back down and covered his head with the blanket. But the urge to piss, he knew, would make him get up anyway.

"Nine Saturday morning," Claire said nonchalantly.

Carl tried to connect the word "Saturday" to something meaningful. Nine o'clock was plenty clear. It meant he had slept less than four hours. He might as well have not heard her add "Saturday." He realized that not only was Claire awake and dressed, but she had been out somewhere to get the coffee. Carl sat up and reached for the cup. "Where did you find this?" he asked.

"I went to the coffee shop and got it. It felt good to wander around. Oh, I took some money from your wallet. Just five dollars."

Carl was almost awake. He took two quick sips from the coffee and concentrated on getting the fog out of his brain.

"The Jeep is filthy, by the way. I think we ought to wash it before getting on the road again. I can't even tell what color it is."

"Black, with red trim."

"That's why. Black really shows dirt. Well, we'll just get it washed. We shouldn't have too much trouble finding a car wash open on *Saturday*." She pronounced the last word slowly and distinctly.

Carl picked up his wristwatch—a Christmas gift from his mother—and looked at it. Ten after nine. The calendar window showed "SAT/26." And then it struck him. Saturday, December 26. "It's Saturday!" he cried with some astonishment. "What happened to Friday?"

"Apparently we both slept right through it," Claire said. She was very impressed that they could have slept more than twenty-four hours.

"Shit. Now we owe for another day." Carl threw back the covers and headed for the bathroom. "You better start packing," he said.

"I'm already packed. You were sleeping like a log. I've been up for over an hour already. I made all kinds of noise, but you didn't budge once." She stood by the closed bathroom door and talked while he urinated. "I got cleaned up, pulled the tangles out of my hair, got dressed, packed, went to the coffee shop, and everything." She smiled. "I kept moving the coffee cup closer and closer to your nose until finally your mouth started twitching. It was really cute."

"I'll bet it was," Carl said, coming out of the bathroom. "I think I'll take a shower." He got his shaving kit and went back inside.

When he finished and came out, Claire had packed his suitcase and placed fresh clothes on the bed for him. Carl, with a towel wrapped around his waist and the back of his blond hair still dripping water, noticed that she had put out a pair of old jeans, a denim shirt, his belt, his boots, a pair of white socks, underwear, and a T-shirt. Their suitcases were by the door.

"Some service," Carl said.

Claire giggled, watching him look for a place to dress.

"If you'll turn around for a moment, I'll get dressed," Carl said.

"Well, aren't we the shy ones. I suppose you changed my clothes the other night with your eyes closed." Claire scooted around on the bed and looked away, toward the dressing area.

"I did. I kept my eyes shut the whole time," he said teasingly. "No tricks now."

"What a bullshitter you are," Claire said, but kept her eyes turned away.

Carl waited a couple of seconds, then looked back, trying to catch her watching. He remembered Claire on her knees at the keyhole those mornings. Finally he tossed the towel on the bed and picked up his underwear. After he had pulled on the jeans, Claire turned around and said, "Boy, you sure have a cute tush."

When Carl turned around he could see Claire's reflection in the dresser mirror and realized that she could also see him. "You are downright incorrigible," he said, but smiling.

"Where did you get a word like 'incorrigible'?"

"Hey, I'm an official high school graduate."

"Well, do-bee-do-bee-do."

Carl finished dressing, and Claire put the bags in the Jeep. They decided to eat at the motel restaurant, then take off.

When they were walking to the restaurant, Claire asked where they were going.

"I don't know. South. A long way from Minnesota."

"Can we go to Corpus Christi?" Claire asked.

"Sure, if you want to. I don't care."

After ordering lunch, Carl took out his wallet and passed Claire a piece of paper from it.

"There are some things we need to talk about," he said with his voice lowered conspiratorially. The restaurant was nearly packed. A Muzak speaker in the ceiling above their heads played easy-listening country music.

"What's this?" Claire said, taking the piece of paper.

"Your driver's license."

"I have one. This says Carla Granger. Whose address is this?"

"Give me a chance, will you? My driver's license says Charles Granger. I made up the address. Yours is the same as mine. You're Mrs. Charles Granger."

"Oh, yeah? You married us? I wonder what Dr. Fields would make of that?" Claire said, teasing him.

"Look, Claire, I can only assume they'll come looking for us. It's about the same thing as escaping from prison, isn't it? I just don't know how serious they'll get about it.

"These driver's licenses . . . I guess they'll work. I mean, if we get stopped for speeding or something, it would keep our real names from popping up if there was a warrant or something. But if we get into the kind of trouble that gets us fingerprinted, I mean, that's it."

Claire folded the driver's license and put it in her back pocket. Carl reminded her to tear up the old one.

"I don't know what they'll do," Carl continued. "That bothers me. I guess I want us to assume the worst and act accordingly. We won't be able to use our real names and Social Security numbers to find jobs or anything."

"Your efficiency surprises me. Why did you marry us?"

"I don't know. It seemed like it would raise less questions while we're traveling, checking into motels and like that. They might look for a brother and sister traveling together."

"Do we have any money?"

"A little. Maybe I should have bought a cheaper car, but I liked the Jeep. And see how much the four-wheel drive helped?"

"It did?"

"Oh, yes, you were asleep all that time. Anyway, the house was sold . . . we didn't get very much. Mother's insurance. She had some savings, too.

"She left it all to me, Claire. You weren't mentioned in the will."

"I'm not surprised. How much money?"

"Altogether? About eight thousand dollars left after the car and the money I paid for the fake licenses. And I had to buy some clothes after . . ."

"That's enough money. We'll do fine."

The waitress appeared, bringing their lunch. They waited silently, smiling politely until she put down their plates and refilled their water glasses. When the waitress left, Carl took a bite of his hamburger and chewed greedily. He kept thinking people were listening to them. He felt like a spy or a criminal. The two feelings kept getting mixed up.

"Why do you want to go to Corpus Christi?" Carl asked after the bill had been paid and they were walking out to the Jeep.

"No reason especially. I know some people there I'd like to see. No real reason. It doesn't matter, does it?"

"No, I don't care. We're together."

The phrase "the body of Christ" popped into Claire's mind. It made her tremble with mysterious anticipation.

three

They found the interstate and headed south toward Kansas City. It was after noon. The bright afternoon sun shone directly into their eyes when the highway turned more westerly in Missouri. The stretch of twisting two-lane that appeared when the interstate ended was announced with a sign proclaiming the number of deaths on that road. Carl had to squint even through his dark sunglasses. Carl had Claire check the mileage to Kansas City and realized they would be driving through it at rush hour.

The radio had just started picking up a rock and roll station from Kansas City, and Claire beat time with the music by slapping her hands on the dashboard. The radio was a little loud, but Carl didn't mind putting up with it. He didn't mind anything then. Claire was acting like her old self, the Claire he remembered before she left home: sparkling, bouncy, self-assured, and contented. Even the weather conformed itself to her mood. It was overcast when they left Des Moines. But here they were 125 miles away and there wasn't a cloud in the sky. The solar effect through the Jeep's windows heated the interior so high that Carl turned off the heater and rolled down his window halfway.

Claire talked in staccato bursts. Something would catch her eye, and she would launch excitedly into an animated monologue about whatever she happened to have seen. One time, just over the Iowa border near a town called Bethany, Claire noticed what Carl knew was a dog at the edge of a tree line, although Claire insisted that it was a wolf. For twenty minutes he received a lecture on the habitat, feeding habits, mating rituals, and marking procedures of midwestern timber wolves. She could call up the most esoteric information, some of it stretching back to books she had read ten years before. But she still had trouble recalling the events of two nights ago.

A few miles down the road from the wolf sighting, Claire saw a bumper sticker on the back of a camper that said: "If the camper's rocking, don't bother knocking." Suddenly she began constructing an elaborate story concerning the people in the camper cab, at whom she stared blatantly when Carl passed it. In the most serious tone she told Carl that the couple's names were Joe and Ethel. They had been married for fifteen years and had two children—a boy named Joey and his older sister named Ethely. She said Joe drove a truck for Atlas Van Lines and Ethel checked out groceries at the Piggly Wiggly in Fort Smith, Arkansas. The truck, Carl noticed, had Arkansas plates.

As the story progressed, Claire explained that Joe played around on Ethel and had been for ten years. It's awfully hard to be a good guy on the road so much, she said about him. But Ethel, who had her morals, stayed "true blue to Joe." That's the kind of woman Ethel happened to be, "God-fearing and all that shit."

Claire said, "Too bad about Ethel. You see, one time she got a little tipsy when . . . you see, it was their fifth anniversary and Joe took Ethel to the . . . ah, the Embers Steak House up in Fayetteville, and Ethel, well, Ethel got plastered on zombies. Well, after they got home, with Ethel feeling well pretty warm about everything, she let Joe talk her into posing for a few dirty Polaroids. He got her posing in all these improbable positions on their old bed while Joe marched around, armed with their Polaroid, taking pictures and giving orders: 'Put your legs up a little higher, hon, yeah, that's it.' Click-whirr. 'Yeah, that's right, baby, get on your hands and knees, stick that old thing right up here for Daddy.' Click-whirr. 'Okay, sugar, now get on your back and spread 'em, super, great, yeah, I love it.' Click-whirr. 'Squeeze those boobs, sugar. Oh, yeah.' Click-whirr."

Carl was about to crack up. Claire mimicked a southern

accent and twisted around in the front seat, imitating Ethel's poses. Everytime she said, "click-whirr," she held her hands up like a camera and leered.

"Old Joe promised Ethel those Polaroids would stay locked up in the house so the kids wouldn't stumble across them, and she got his word of honor that he'd *never*, and she meant *never*, show them to a soul. Even Ethel herself couldn't bear to look at them—the flush of full-blown sin just flat turned her red. After she sobered up, of course.

"You know old Joe, that son of a bitch, showed those pictures around at every truck stop from Little Rock to Seattle. He carried them around in a white envelope in his glove compartment, or whatever they call it in a truck. All those truckers would stand around their rigs like pilgrims in a wagon train discussing Indians while Joe passed those photos around like a jug of hard cider.

"Well, it was in September, Joe lent the pictures to this old boy who drove for P-I-E, and that guy made copies of them. Copies got made of the copies until there were maybe ten thousand pictures of old Ethel in assorted sensual poses floating around the truck stops of America. A couple of them even showed up in Japan. There was Ethel with her legs spread and her boobs well in hand stuck beneath the tray in a cash register in Denver, taped to the visor in a Peterbilt working the West Coast run out of Philly, tacked to the notice board in the Dallas ABF freight dispatcher's office. There's Ethel with her buns in the air pinned to the office wall at the Great America Truck Plaza in Big Springs. From New York to L.A., from Miami to Seattle, Ethel became the Betty Grable of the freight haulers.

"First time Ethel came across one of those pictures was in a truck stop outside Omaha. She went into the café for some coffee, and every trucker in the joint stood up and cheered her. A sympathetic waitress took Ethel aside and explained the matter, showed her a yellowed, stained, dog-eared photocopy of Ethel with her hands between her legs. Ethel marched straight out of the place, the men still cheering her, and marched right across the fast lane of Interstate Eighty. Got herself quickly splattered on the radiator of a Kenworth hauling hogs, just like a night bug. After the driver had peeled Ethel off his radiator, there wasn't enough left for him to notice that it was *the* Ethel, the same woman, the very original of the picture he had taped to his sun visor."

Carl no longer felt like laughing. When Claire finally stopped, Carl asked, "Where do you get stuff like that?"

"It's the gospel, I swear." She smiled slyly.

"Then who was that woman in the truck back there, with Joe? Tell me that?" The camper was miles behind.

"Oh, that? That was a store dummy made up to look like Ethel."

"Bullshit."

"Sure. What else could it be? Don't you see? When Ethel got splattered all over the . . . come on, use your imagination a little."

"You're gross."

"Oh, yeah? There's a moral to the story, you know?"

"For sure."

"There's a moral to every human story, even most animal ones. The moral is: The wages of sin is death."

"Trite."

"Oh, *trite?* Another high school graduate notion? Actually, as I recall, that's not the moral of Joe and Ethel's saga."

"What is it?"

"The moral is: Never trust anybody, anytime, for anything."

"Not even your brother?"

"Maybe your brother."

"Maybe?"

"How far do you trust me?" she asked soberly.

"All the way," he said, meaning it.

"Boy, have I got some stories for you." Claire smiled and turned to look out her window at Missouri, which looked like Iowa, which looked like Minnesota—stick trees and brown, bumpy plains.

"Claire, I like seeing you happy. Are you having a good time?"

"I am, Carl. I'm very happy. Thanks to you. And you know I trust you, dear brother."

"I know. Do you think the drugs and stuff from Fairbrook are wearing off?"

"Yeah. I can tell because I'd kill for a drink . . . I didn't say that."

Carl looked at her but did not respond.

"Anyway, I'd like to have memory back. I guess, but maybe not. Maybe I don't want it back."

"It'll come. Dr. Fields said it was a temporary effect."

"He's so full of shit you can smell him a mile away."

"Claire?"

"What?"

"Did you ever have any pictures taken of you . . . like that?"

"Jee-sus. You come up with the strangest questions right out of the blue."

"I just wondered, since you made such a production of the story."

"Well . . . maybe." Then Claire smiled.

She turned back to looking out the window, shutting him out, focusing on nothing.

"We're going to hit Kansas City at rush hour," Carl said, trying to get Claire's attention back.

"It's Saturday," she said.

"Then where are all these cars going?"

They had been in a stream of inbound traffic for ten miles.

"It's the day after Christmas," Claire explained patiently. It pleased her to know the day, even the month. "Santa fucked up again, so they're all returning their presents."

Carl followed a stream of cars and trucks through the downtown freeway, watching attentively when his headlights illuminated road signs. Sunset had lasted a long time in the clear midwestern sky, but it was finally dark. Claire seemed to understand without his saying anything that the radio's volume was becoming a distraction. She turned it down but not off. She did want a drink. Their headlights suddenly caught a stopped car on the shoulder ahead. Carl and Claire realized at the same instant that it was a state patrol car. Carl let up on the accelerator just as Claire cried out, "Cop!" He didn't think he had been speeding. What was the last speed limit sign he saw? Sixty? Fifty? They stared straight ahead and acted melodramatically innocent.

"I wasn't speeding," Carl said to himself as much as to Claire.

"Then why did he pull out right behind us?" Claire said, glancing over her shoulder.

"Don't look back," Carl ordered. But he could already see the red lights reflecting in his mirror.

"Maybe he's after somebody in front of us," Claire suggested hopefully. Carl could hear the tension in her voice.

"Stay calm, for chrissakes."

The patrol car pulled up within a few feet of their rear bumper and flicked its headlights from dim to bright and back. The red lights glowed inside the Jeep. Carl flipped up the turn signal lever and eased off the road.

"What do we do now?" Claire pleaded.

"Find out what he wants," Carl answered calmly. But he had just decided to kill the officer if he tried to arrest them. As he pulled the Jeep over, he bent down and felt for the guard's pistol under the seat. Claire stared straight ahead and did not notice. Better to leave it there and come back for it if something happened. If this was just a simple traffic problem, he didn't want to chance being caught with the gun on him.

Carl stopped and turned off the engine. He checked the traffic, then opened his door to get out, figuring it would be better to keep the cop away from Claire. Before getting out, he said to Claire, "Sit tight and don't worry, and don't look so damn stiff."

The officer approached Carl. He had a pad and a flashlight in his hands.

"Was I speeding, Officer?" Carl asked as the man approached.

"The reason I pulled you over, sir, is that you have no taillights." The officer pointed his flashlight inside the Jeep.

"No taillights? But how could . . . this is a new car!"

"May I see your driver's license, please?" The officer stopped in front of Carl and put his flashlight under his arm, the beam shining on Carl's belt buckle. Carl was glad he had left the pistol in the Jeep.

"I just can't understand how my taillights could be out," Carl said politely as he withdrew his wallet.

"Please remove the license from your wallet, sir."

Carl did as requested and handed the fake license to the officer. He shone the light on it for a long time. Carl hoped he was just a slow reader.

"Is this your current address, Mr. Granger?"

"Yes, sir, it is. My wife and I are on our way to visit some friends in western Kansas." Quit volunteering information, Carl told himself.

"You say this is new?" the officer asked. He reached out and touched the side of the Jeep rather enviously.

"Yes, sir. It was sort of a family Christmas present." Carl smiled as sincerely as he could.

"Would you step back here with me, Mr. Granger? You may replace your license." He handed the license back to Carl, who put it away quickly.

They walked to the rear of the Jeep and stopped between the taillights. "If you'll ask your wife to turn on the lights, I'll show you the problem," the officer said.

Carl nodded and leaned around the side of the Jeep. He knocked on the back window with his knuckles and motioned for Claire to roll down her window. Claire turned around but did not move to turn on the lights. Carl repeated the request in a loud voice. "Turn on the lights, honey." Claire didn't move.

"Excuse me," Carl said to the officer. "I don't think she can hear me." He walked around to Claire's door and tapped on the window. Claire rolled the window down partway.

Whispering, Carl told her it was only the taillights, then: "Turn on the lights, honey." Claire had tears in her eyes. But she reached over and pulled out the knob. Carl went back to join the officer and saw that there were no taillights.

"You can turn them off now, ma'am," the officer yelled up to Claire, and she did as asked. She never turned around.

"But . . . this is a new car."

"My guess is you've got a short somewhere. Could be you threw some mud or slush into the wires somewhere, and they shorted. It happens now and then. What I'm going to ask you to do, Mr. Granger, is follow me to the next exit. There's a Mobil station there with a twenty-four-hour mechanic on duty."

"You want me to follow you then to the next exit?"

"I'm sorry. Did I say follow me? I meant I'll follow you since you have no taillights. Just drive to the next exit. You'll see the station right away. It's a Mobil."

"Yes, sir. I appreciate this."

Carl got back into the Jeep and closed the door. "It's just

some problem with our taillights, Claire. For chrissakes, quit acting like we just robbed a bank." He started the engine and merged with the traffic. The patrol car pulled out right behind. "Scared the piss out of me," Carl commented.

The patrol car's lights stayed in the mirror until Carl pulled into the gas station; then the trooper waved and turned back onto the freeway ramp.

"Thank God," Carl said. "I was afraid he'd hang around talking to us until the lights were fixed."

"Carl," Claire said softly, "I'm scared."

"Look at it this way. We just passed one gigantic test with flying colors. I'm sure he called in for any outstanding warrants on our license plates before pulling us over. He saw my license and nothing happened. We've proved it works; we can be more relaxed now."

"I just wish you could hold me right now. I'm shaking."

He could see that she was. "Why not? After all, we are married."

Carl leaned across the seat and put his arm around Claire's shoulder. She put her head on his shoulder and began to relax. Then Carl said, "Look, what do you say we get this damn thing fixed, get ourselves the hell out of Kansas City, and find a motel with a good restaurant?"

"A contradiction in terms."

"What?"

"A motel with a good restaurant. But I tell you what I would like to do. I'd like to have a drink, maybe dance a little. We've never danced together, Carl. Do you like to?"

"I don't know how."

"Then I'll teach you. There's nothing to it. Can't we just find someplace and let go for a little while? I just need to relax for a while."

"Sure we can. I'm thinking we could drive to, say, Emporia. That's where the toll road begins. We can spend the night there and drive on to Dallas tomorrow. Okay?"

"I've been through Kansas before. I don't think you can get a drink in this state."

"Is that so important?"

"Don't get on my case, kiddo."

"Just asking. We'll find out, all right?"

four

It was almost nine o'clock when they drove into the out-skirts of Emporia and pulled off the interstate into the parking lot of the Prairie Inn—Phones, TV, Pool, Under 18 Discount, Tumbleweed Lounge.

When Carl returned from checking in, he told Claire, "We're really in some kind of wilderness. They don't have bars in this state where you just go in and buy a drink in a glass. But you can get a drink, though."

"You mean, private clubs like in Oklahoma," Claire said.

"I guess, never having been to Oklahoma. I checked us in. What you have to do is buy it from a liquor store; then you can take it to the lounge here in a paper sack and buy setups."

"Sounds like a bogus routine they'd create at Fairbrook."

"Want to stay? There's a liquor store three blocks away."

"What the hell. They have a band here?"

"A jukebox."

"We're stopped now. Maybe this is better. You'd probably get carded in a bar anyway," she said, teasing him.

"I've tried it a few times. I can pass for twenty-one."

"On your best days, maybe."

Carl drove around to their room and parked. They unloaded the suitcases but left everything on the floor while they went for the liquor. Carl gave Claire some money, and she went in to buy it. The clerk checked her ID. Claire told him it was a good thing his sister was "an old lady." She handed him the bottle of bourbon. "Big deal," Carl said. "Anyway, according to *my* driver's license, I'm a few months *older* than you are. So eat that."

Claire decided to change clothes. Carl turned on the TV and watched some variety show. Claire ended up with a pair of black corduroy pants, with the legs tucked into her brown boots, and a puffy white peasant blouse with large poet sleeves. She spun around, modeling for him. "How do I look?" Carl thought she looked as if she didn't have on a bra, and he thought she should. He could see her jiggling when she spun around. But she also looked beautiful, and that's what he told her. Carl elected not to change clothes.

When they found the Tumbleweed, Carl stopped before the door and in a surprised voice told Claire, "This is the first bar I've ever been inside."

"Boy, kiddo, do I have some things to teach you," Claire said, pulling him inside.

The waitress checked both their driver's licenses.

Considering it was nine-thirty on a Saturday night, the Tumbleweed didn't look like Emporia's favorite hangout. It would take a hundred people to fill it; there were perhaps twenty-five there. The dance floor was tiny. It wouldn't hold ten couples at the same time. The dance portion of the floor was made of what looked like stainless steel, and multicolored lights in the ceiling made it appear that paint had dripped on it. A prism ball rotated over the floor, making a kaleidoscope of colors on the walls. There were four couples on the dance floor when Claire pulled Carl out to it.

Carl never had a chance. Claire picked up the beat of the music and spun away from him. Carl stood alone and tried to shake his legs a little. He tried snapping his fingers but couldn't keep the rhythm and felt stupid. Claire came and went like wash on a pulley. Sometimes he could see her, and sometimes she was lost behind the other dancers. He wished he had made a point about the bra. As she twirled, the peasant blouse trapped billows of air under it and blossomed out like a small parachute; a flashing hot yellow strobe occasionally revealed her breasts through the thin material. The flesh of her breasts vibrated as if they had been caught in an out-of-sync film. Everyone watched them or, rather, watched Claire, for Carl did not feel as if he belonged with her. Claire danced as if it were her profession. Carl looked like a drunk trying to act sober. He wondered when she had learned to dance so well. How much of her life was alien to him.

The other dancers watched Claire, and Carl watched them watching. Women glanced furtively, maybe enviously, maybe bitterly—he wasn't sure which. Men stared openly, wantonly. Claire shimmered and shimmied obliviously.

When the fast Rolling Stones song ended, a slow Bee Gees song came on. Claire grabbed Carl and held him closely. "You can do this," she said. "Everybody can do this. Slow dancing is just an excuse for a little simulated fucking."

She could have said anything but that. Carl felt her against him and immediately got an erection. Her breasts were crushed into his chest, and their genitals came together. Claire cleared her throat and laid her head on his shoulder. Carl knew she knew.

"I thought we came here to drink," Carl said, stopping and letting go of her.

"And dance. But if you'd rather . . ."

Carl led her back to their table and ordered Cokes from the bar. Claire watched the dancers until the setups came. She admired one couple who could dance the old swing steps to rock music. She felt flushed and happy. This was freedom. There was a wild, excited feeling in her chest. It no longer mattered that she couldn't remember too much. She only wished Carl would perk up.

"You've changed a bunch," she turned and said to him after the waitress left. "I like you better this way: freer, less . . . uptight."

"Things happen in three years." Carl wondered if she meant she hadn't liked him before.

"Like, look at you sitting in a bar and having a drink of whiskey. Who'da believed it?"

"No big deal." The drink in front of Carl was his first of whiskey. He had consumed maybe a total of ten beers in his life. He poured whiskey into both glasses and filled them with Coke.

The waitress returned with their change. She wore peppermint-stripe short shorts and a horizontally striped red and white halter top. Her breasts, which were massive for such a skinny woman, bulged through the gap above the halter top. Carl thought she looked like a broken barber pole trying to rotate in two directions at once. His eyes followed her away.

"I'll bet she's working her way through the Kansas College of Wheatology," Claire said, gulping her drink.

"Interesting outfit."

"She better not turn around too fast or she'll screw herself into the floor," Claire said, sounding jealous.

"She made me dizzy."

"That's not all she made you," Claire went on, a leering smile crossing her lips.

"Oh, yeah?"

"It looked like you were hypnotized by her *heaving bosom.*" Claire stretched out the description as if she were reading it from a bodice-busting romance novel. "Come on, let's dance." She grabbed Carl's hand and jerked him from the chair. As soon as they were on the stainless steel floor, she danced off into the crowd, leaving Carl to follow as best he could. Carl tried for a while, but soon he gave up trying to keep up with her. He settled down for a glimpse in passing.

They had been in the bar for an hour when someone finally got the courage to ask Claire to dance. Ignoring Carl, Claire accepted and drained her glass before going out to dance. Carl had given up in embarrassment anyway. Her new dancing partner was much better. Carl nursed his third drink and watched them. He started feeling bloated and tight in the kidneys. His cheeks were going numb.

Claire's dancing partner had introduced himself as Tom something-or-other. Maybe he said Norman, or it could have been Corman. He wore black denim jeans, a black satin cowboy shirt with white shiny snaps, and had thick black hair. His black and white cowboy boots shone like patent leather, and the heels clicked on the dance floor. He had the raw, wind-burned face of a Kansas farmer.

Claire and Kansas Tom, as Carl called the man, danced through two fast songs and into a slower one. Carl was having trouble with his eyes; they wouldn't focus clearly on distant objects. Did Kansas Tom have his hands on Claire's ass? Did he just kiss her ear? What was that fancy little dip he just did?

Did he do that just to push his crotch into hers? Carl leaned forward on the table and knocked over his empty glass. You're drunk, he told himself.

He marveled at how Claire held her liquor. She was at least two, maybe three, drinks ahead of him, and still she seemed sober. Not precisely sober, but not drunk. The thought of dancing as wildly as Claire did made his stomach churn. Even watching made him feel dizzy. But there was another feeling mixed up with the dizzy sickness. Carl was proud of being in such a place with the most beautiful woman those people must have ever seen. What did the Tumbleweed crowd think of them? Film people on their way to California, slumming through Kansas on a lark? He closed his eyes to stop the swirling in his head. Then the pictures came. A woman from one of the nearby tables walked over and stood politely waiting for Carl to notice her. Finally Carl, lost in the dream, raised his sunglasses and peered under them.

Excuse me, but isn't that Claire Grant with you?

Yes. Do you want her autograph?

Well, I guess so. But if she's Claire Grant, you must be her brother, Carl Grant, the famous writer and director?

I confess to the crime of brotherhood.

Oh, I'm such a fan of yours, Mr. Grant. I've seen all your films and read all your books. Do you mind if I sit here with you?

If you want.

I can hardly believe this. Here I am in Emporia, Kansas, sitting with the Carl Grant . . .

Carl couldn't believe it either. When he forced his eyes open and destroyed the fantasy, Claire and Kansas Tom were coming back toward the table.

"Don't you pass out on me," Claire said as Carl moved through the void between fantasy and reality.

"Huh?" Carl focused his eyes on Claire. She was holding Kansas Tom's hand.

"You look plowed, kiddo," Claire added.

Carl sat up straight and took his feet out of Claire's chair. There were beads of perspiration on Claire's forehead and a damp patch down the front of her blouse.

"Tommy's got a red Corvette. We're going for a drive, okay?"

But there was no look of questioning or a seeking for approval in her eyes. She was just stating the case.

"I don't know," Carl said, sobering really fast.

"Let's not get into a hassle about this, Carl. I just want to drive a Corvette, like we're going to tour Emporia for a while"—she smiled—"and see the local sights. I won't be gone an hour."

"It's already late, and we need to start out pretty early in the morning." Carl stood up.

"You sleep. You do all the driving anyway. I can sleep in the car." Claire was clearly determined, and Carl started to worry.

"Hey, bud," Kansas Tom interrupted. "I'll have this little kitten back safe and sound." He smiled broadly.

"Look, whatever your name is," Carl said, taking a step closer to him, "I just don't happen to think my wife ought to go out for a ride in your red Corvette. All right?" There was no doubting the anger in Carl's voice.

"Your wife? But you," he said, turning to Claire, "said he was your brother."

"Shit," Claire muttered. "It was just a joke we play." She tugged urgently on Tom's hand. "Tom's okay," she told Carl.

"Hold it a sec, honey," Tom said, but not letting go of Claire's hand and the potentiality expressed through it. "Which is it? You his sister or his wife?"

Carl stared hard at Claire as she said, "He's my brother."

"I don't give a good goddamn what you do," Carl said bitterly. He grabbed the neck of the bourbon bottle and pushed between Claire and Tom. In a few seconds he had disappeared into the darkness by the door.

Claire squeezed Tom's hand and said, "Don't worry about that. He's drunk. He's not used to drinking."

Tom did not want to press his luck. He put his arm around Claire and led her out to the parking lot.

Carl turned on the television set and listened to ten minutes of some movie while he paced the floor, trying to drink from the bottle. But the whiskey was too strong, and he could only swallow small sips without gagging. Sometimes he peeked outside, but there was nothing to see.

He waited for an hour. When Claire didn't return, he got into his pajamas and got into bed with the television on. The movie was *Mighty Joe Young*. He had seen it four times on other late movies. At 1:00 A.M. he was asleep.

Carl slept restlessly and dreamed again—the same dream that had haunted his subconsciousness for more than a month but that disappeared the instant he awakened. It was dark and cold. He couldn't breathe. Smoke curled around his head and entered his lungs. Flames danced around his body. His mother chased Claire around his bed with a flaming torch in her hand. The torch fell on his bed.

Carl jerked upright in bed and swung his arms out to beat away the flames. *"Nooo!"* he screamed, then opened his eyes to find the dream gone. Not a shred of it left in his mind. There was nothing but the sweat and anxiety to tell him he had dreamed again. He concentrated on slowing his breathing and tried to find his bearings in the dark motel room. As his eyes adjusted, he looked over at Claire's bed. He leaned across the space between and put his hand on her bed. It was empty. He looked at his watch. It was a quarter to three.

Carl got out of bed and went to check the bathroom, knowing, though, that she would not be there. He went to the window and looked out at the Jeep, glistening in the moist light from the lamps. "God damn you, Claire," he said.

Now what? He could go out and look for them. How many red Corvettes could there be in Emporia? He could wait. But Claire might never come back. At least not for years. She was always doing that to him—disappearing without a word. He sat on the edge of his bed and tried to think of his options, but he was too angry and too frightened. There was really nothing to do.

Finally he crawled back into bed and pulled the blanket over his head. Sometime after that he fell asleep again. He did not hear Claire come in, undress, and ease herself into bed. The next thing he knew, the phone was ringing with his wake-up call and the hump of Claire's body was visible beneath the covers.

"Why are you so quiet?" Claire asked after Carl had picked up the toll ticket and driven through the gate.

"Hangover."

"That's what you said at breakfast. In fact, that's all you said at breakfast."

"Because it's true. Let me suffer in peace."

"I read someplace that it's not the alcohol itself that gives you a hangover. It's some by-product of the distilling process."

"Does it matter once you've got one where it came from?"

"Shit, don't snap at me. I'm just telling you what I read."

"Is that where you spent last night? In the library?" It was the first time Carl mentioned last night. Claire turned angrily and stared out the side window.

They drove in silence then for a long time. They passed a sign saying: HISTORIC FLINT HILLS. For as far as the eye could see, which was a considerable distance, ranged a sea of undulated brown hills. They had not seen a tree, even some tall stick that could passably pretend to be a tree, for miles. Sometimes, just peeking over a far rise, appeared the top section of an oil derrick. There was very little traffic that Sunday morning. Carl drove seventy-five miles an hour, tempting a speeding ticket, anxious to get the hell out of Kansas. He finally turned off the radio after twisting the dial from one end to the other and able to pick up only church services and one forlorn football game. The Kansas Turnpike stretched ahead like a line of gray paint over a wrinkled brown rug. There were no exits. About every fifty miles there was an island in the median, just a grass patch surrounding a gas station and restaurant. They drove on.

As they skirted Wichita, Claire said, "This is where they build airplanes."

"Aren't you just full of facts? Amazing what you can learn in a library at three in the morning."

It was the first sound between them in two hours. It required them to reacknowledge each other's presence. A minute later Carl said, "Look at the map and see where this damn toll road ends." Claire checked the road atlas, then looked at the back of the toll ticket.

"South Haven, it looks like. About an hour more, I guess. I never could count up all those little red numbers that are supposed to tell you the distance between places."

"I guess we can eat lunch around Oklahoma City then."

"Whatever you say."

"We'll be in Dallas a lot earlier than I thought. Maybe we'll just keep going for a while."

"I'm with you."

"See how far it looks like between Dallas and Austin."

Claire found the right page in the atlas and studied it. "About as far as it is from Oklahoma City to Dallas, it looks like. I've made that drive once, but it was a long time ago."

"You remember that?"

"Yes." Claire sounded surprised. "I do. But only that I did it."

"That's a good sign."

Claire put away the atlas and went back to looking out the window. In a few minutes she said, "It's so empty here."

Carl could hear in her voice that she wanted to apologize, in her way. But he still wasn't in the mood to accept it. The emptiness he thought of was last night's empty bed. And the space between them, which seemed as empty as the brown, bumpy scenery.

"Mind if I try the radio again?" Claire asked.

"I don't care."

While Claire fiddled with the radio knob, Carl opened his window and lit a cigarette. It was very warm. Not far short of hot. He guessed that the temperature was near seventy. Two days after Christmas. They were certainly a long way from Minnesota. Claire had no luck with the radio and turned it off. She took a cigarette from his pack on the dash and lit it off the end of his.

"There's a lighter in there." He pointed to the ashtray.

"I know."

"Nothing on the radio?" Carl asked.

"Guess we'll just have to wait until the churches give up. You ought to know what time churches let out."

"What does that mean?"

"It doesn't mean anything. Jee-sus."

Claire fidgeted around in the seat, opened the glove box and inspected its few contents, tapped on the window with her knuckles, and played with the buttons on her blouse. They left the Kansas Turnpike and passed into Oklahoma.

"Can we stop pretty soon?" Claire asked. "I need to visit a toilet."

Carl nodded and pulled off at the next rest stop, just inside the border. There were a dozen cars and as many trucks parked there. Families were eating picnic lunches at tables surrounding the tourist center building. An elderly couple walked a poodle on the grass in the parking median. Before Carl got the Jeep engine turned off, Claire jumped out and ran to the rest room. Not again, Carl thought, remembering Mason City, Iowa.

Somebody had written "Jesus Saves" on the wall above one of the urinals. Impulsively Carl took out a pen and wrote below it: "Green Stamps."

Claire waited until a woman and her young daughter finished and left; then she went into a stall and sat on the toilet seat. She took the package Tom Corman had given her last night and unwrapped it. She took two whites, popped them in her mouth, and swallowed them without water.

five

"We've got to get something straight, Carl."

"What?"

"You are not my keeper."

"Who says I want to be?"

"And you must stop being jealous of me."

"I'm not."

"Yes, you are. All the time. I am your *sister*. We are not married, no matter what you decided to put on those driver's licenses."

"Some sister."

"I'm not going to argue."

"Why couldn't you just leave me alone?"

"Now we're getting to it, aren't we? It's finally going to come out in the open, isn't it?"

"If it weren't for me, you'd still be in Fairbrook. And they weren't *ever* going to let you out of there."

"I'm not talking about that."

"I know."

"Do you?"

"I don't want to have this conversation."

"Are you tired? Want me to drive?"

"No."

"I'm sorry for the times I hurt you, Carl."

"I'm happy being with you. I'm not hurt."

"I don't know. Sometimes you seem .   "

"Seem what?"

"Hurt."

"I'm not."

"I love you very much, kiddo."

They kept going. Through Dallas, Waco, Austin. They left Interstate 35 south of Austin and took Highway 123 at the Seguin exit. It rained all the way from Seguin to Beeville, and Claire slept. The secondary highway twisted through the flat countryside, and around each curve the Jeep's headlights revealed rows of mesquite trees on both sides. In fifty miles they met only two cars and a pickup truck. Carl thought he could smell the salt-laden Gulf air, but it could have been something in the rain. Claire lay curled up beneath a blanket in the back seat. Instead of the excitement Carl expected to feel as they neared their destination, there was instead only exhaustion and foreboding. He knew where the exhaustion came from, but the anxiety was completely mysterious. Maybe it was the heavy air, the solitude, the strange look of the mesquites, which seemed to take human form and leap onto the highway in front of him. His chest ached from too much smoking. For almost an hour he had been driving dangerously on the last reserves of energy. Twenty cups of coffee sloshed in his stomach and strained his kidneys.

It was Monday morning, dawn, in a light drizzle when Carl and Claire drove into Corpus Christi. He didn't wake Claire until he turned the Jeep onto Shoreline Drive. His tiredness came out in the hoarse rattle of his voice as he reached across the seat and shook Claire. "Wake up, Claire. I can see the ocean."

Shoreline Drive ran east and west with the Gulf to the south and the city of Corpus Christi to the north. Carl drove west, the seawall and ocean's bay to their left and a continual line of motels and restaurants to their right. Streetlamps left fuzzy patches of light on the wet pavement. The clouds hung low like a mist over the bay, from which the masts of moored sailboats appeared ephemerally. "Wake up." Carl shook her again.

There was a little traffic, morning commuters starting for work downtown. Their headlights came out of the fog and mist and rolled past like ghost chariots. Carl drove very slowly, his eyes on the bay and moored boats. Cars passed him.

Claire raised herself up, rubbing her eyes. She leaned against the door and pressed her face to the window glass. "We're here," she said.

"Corpus Christi," Carl confirmed needlessly.

"There's a road up there about a hundred feet. Take it to the left."

Carl saw the road appear and turned on the blinker. It led down to the docks and moorings.

"I'm going to put my feet into the Gulf of Mexico," Claire proclaimed, climbing over into the front seat.

"Won't the water be cold?"

"Who cares?"

Carl made the turn. The road led to a boatyard and row after row of slips. On one side was the open bay; on the other, a beach with concrete spits sticking out 100 yards into the water.

"You can park anywhere along here," Claire told him.

Carl pulled the Jeep over, and Claire jumped out the moment it stopped rolling. She climbed over a low rock wall and landed in the sand. Carl followed her.

The beach was more or less deserted. Far away in the mist they could see two or three people walking at the surf's edge. At the far end from where they stood was a large hotel; a fleet of small Sunfish-class sailboats were pulled onto the sand there. Evenly spaced along the seawall were stately royal palms. It was not a clean beach, Carl noticed: cans, bottles, paper, seaweed, scum, driftwood, dead fish. Carl figured it was Sunday residue not yet cleaned up.

Claire danced through the trash as if it were not there. She was only fifty feet ahead of him, but the mist had already started to close around her. Carl bent over and picked up a long stick and drew lines in the sand with it as he walked along behind Claire. Claire stopped and picked up a small dead fish by the tail, holding it carefully between her thumb and index finger. "Ugh," she said, and tossed it higher on the beach.

"Carl! Come here, look!" Claire stopped at the water's edge and pointed into the mist over the open ocean. "Come here quick!" She waved frantically at him.

Carl jogged up next to her and strained his eyes to see into the soupy atmosphere hanging over the sea.

"Do you see it? Right there. See?"

Like only the specter of a ship, it slid through the fogbank. Carl thought it was an oil tanker, although he could see only its silhouette. It moved imperceptibly to the east. Then it was gone. "Oh, there it is again," he cried, and the ship appeared through a thinness in the mist. In another five seconds it was gone again.

"It's the *Flying Dutchman*," Claire said quietly. "It was here before. It was here to greet me the first time. I have been here before, on this beach, in this very spot, with that very ship. I walked from over there"—she stopped and pointed back toward the seawall—"and put my feet in the water here." She took off her shoes and let small waves tease her feet before dancing back out of its reach. She scurried back and forth at the water's edge like a sand crab. Carl squatted and leaned on the stick for balance, watching Claire play at the water. She spun and danced like a ballerina into the mist, kicking at the water, twirling on her toes in the damp sand, letting the water chase her up and back as she moved farther down the beach. Carl leaned on his stick and watched her move into the mist cloud. Soon she would be out of his sight. He got up and followed her down the beach, keeping well back but not letting her get lost in the thick, wet, salty air. If someone had looked over from the street and seen them, it might have looked as if he were stalking her.

part two

corpus christi

six

Carl and Claire checked into a Quality Court motel directly across Shoreline Drive from the boat harbor and public beach. There had been no rooms available on the sea side of the motel, so they were stuck on an upper floor in back, overlooking the parking lot and the side of a tall bank building. It didn't matter so much. All Carl wanted to do was sleep. Within minutes of checking in, he had fallen asleep, still in his clothes. Claire took off his shoes and covered him with the blanket from her bed.

Not long afterward Claire left the room and walked back to the beach. Although the morning mist had burned away, there was still a thin layer of low clouds. The temperature was almost sixty degrees. Claire left her shoes and socks on the beach and walked along the water's edge from one end of the long beach to the other. She still had most of it to herself. She played with the waves, dug holes in the sand and watched them fill with water, wrote her name in the sand with a stick, inspected the sailboards beached by the hotel.

A bum slept near the seawall, revealed with the lifting of the mist. He lay flat on his back, legs spread in a V, arms crossed over his chest, and a bottle, empty, in his hands. There was sand in his hair, wild and tangled hair. He had not shaved in days. Claire walked over to him and stared. She felt as if she knew him. She squatted there and studied him.

Behind her an old man walked the beach at the water's edge. He carried a metal detector and wore earphones. Suddenly

Claire felt his presence and spun around. RABBIT! His name screamed itself in her mind. She clutched her mouth and scooted across the sand back against the rock wall. A cog had fallen into its slot, a cog that had been spinning aimlessly for months. When it hit the proper niche, a gear turned, then another, and another. Soon Claire's brain was spinning in sync. She remembered. "Rabbit," she whispered through her hand. She could almost see him walking toward her. But when she blinked her eyes, he was gone.

She knew it all then. She knew why she had come to Corpus Christi.

It was four o'clock when she got back to the motel room. Carl still slept soundly. She was tired from the walking—she had walked back out to the house on Lobo Street where she had lived with Rabbit, OP, Susy Creamcheese, Stoney . . . to the park where they used to lie beneath the palms and smoke dope, back to the beach where they had so often made love in the sand.

She looked at Carl, curled up beneath the blanket. His head, shoulders, and one arm were exposed. His hair was messed up from where his arm had lain over his head. He looked so young then. He needed to shave, but that didn't matter. He looked twelve or thirteen, not eighteen. Claire liked watching him sleep. Except he looked so vulnerable, so lost and innocent. He would have to grow up now, she thought. She needed him.

The sand on Claire's feet felt gritty, and she noticed little tracks on the green carpet leading in from the door. She got up and went to the bathtub to wash her feet. Then she undressed completely and got into her bed. She lay on her back, legs spread slightly, and looked down over her body to her feet. She started feeling the effects of the last of the Seconals Tom had given her. She felt the coming of detachment, indifference.

Claire knew she was beautiful, having been told often enough to convince anyone. She was proud of her body, although sometimes, no matter how hard she tried to possess it, the body didn't seem to be a part of who she was inside that shell. Sometimes she could touch her breasts and the hand would feel alien. As if the body were hollow and she could step in and out of it at will. Something to hang in the closet when not being used. It was a borrowed body, and someday she would be forced to return it to the more dominant owner, the one who needed and used that body.

She let her hands move up from her stomach and rest on top of her breasts, each nipple trapped between her index fingers and thumbs. The breasts felt cushioned to her hands. Nobody had ever touched her as well as she could touch herself. No one knew when to be soft and when to be hard, when to squeeze, to rub, to nibble, to kiss.

She could see her reflection in the dresser mirror at the foot of the bed. She felt detached from it, from the image of herself. There was a logical visual correspondence between the body she touched and the body she watched being touched, but which one was real? Claire's sense of reality was as tenuous, as frighteningly undependable as her electrified memory. What could she really depend on? Am I the I that I feel or the I that I see? Or maybe only the I others see? Such thoughts did not come to her humorously or with sarcasm. Too many times in her life had she lost herself, or what she believed was herself, at the root of her being. It always frightened her into a stupor. No matter how much she struggled, she could feel herself slip away as another person filled the body—an evil, hateful, terrible person.

Claire felt hollow. She looked at the mirror image and saw herself as substantially a reflection of some objective vision. She could see the reflection over the plain of her body, feel the hands being moved from some force within the reflecting glass and not from anywhere inside the body it reflected. The hands moved down her stomach, over the flat plate of abdominal muscles, across thighs until the limit of her reach had been met. The hands slowly withdrew and came to rest in the warm, soft flesh between her legs. The hand let its fingers entwine in the light hair and probe willfully on their own at the opening hidden beneath.

Claire closed her eyes, blocking the mirror image, and focused her attention on the fingers only, the way a repeated mantra sharpens the focus of the mind into the power of a single straight line of mental current. Long-period rolling waves radiated from her thighs, surging over her chest and cresting in the back of her head, as if the muscles themselves were guided by the tidal pull of those autonomous fingertips. As the pressure increased, Claire suddenly remembered how Tom Corman had put his fingers inside her, how she turned herself in the bucket seat and leaned over the back of it to give him access. *The* fingers became *his* fingers, and *the* body became *her* body. Things she did not want to remember tried to make themselves present, even dominant, in her mind. She let Tom's fingers plunge deeper and his thumb ride up alongside her clitoris. She rolled her head from side to side to clear away the assault by foreign thoughts; his fingers found their limit. The windshield fogged over. Then his fingers were replaced by something hotter, thicker, more furious an appendage.

Claire did not want him doing that. But someone else did. Someone else always did. As Tom thrust into her, Claire felt herself traveling from someplace deep within the body and stretching out along her arm toward the fogged, opaque rear window she faced. Some other voice urged him.

Claire felt herself compressing and gliding smoothly through an extended index finger, slipping through a pore and out through the glass. She floated around the car, outside, and could see the outline of Tom's ass pressed like a split moon into the front windshield, moisture drops tracking through the glass around it like tears. Claire had seen her doing it before. She tried to find her feelings but could not. Tom humped himself against her, and Claire watched without emotion.

In the bed Claire lost control of herself and rushed toward the demands of her body's orgasm.

She found herself later, she had no idea how much later, sitting in the bathtub with the water running full force over her feet, the drain open so the water would not fully cover her legs. Her face and hair were both wet. She touched a finger to her forehead and caught a drop, tasting it. It was salty on her tongue. Sweat. She lowered her head and watched the water swirl around her feet, then reached out and closed the drain, letting her body slide down until the back of her neck rested on the tub edge. She was putting the pieces together one by one. She had taken herself to Mexico when Carl knocked on the bathroom door.

"Just checking to make sure it was you," Carl said through the closed door.

Claire sat up and noticed that the water was barely an inch from overflowing over the tub. She turned off the water and opened the drain.

"Who were you expecting?" she said teasingly.

"You never know. You're okay?"

"I'm fine, Carl. Fine. I just got started here, and I'm going to wash my hair. Be with you in a while."

"Take your time. But you might keep in mind that I'm in serious need of taking a piss."

"It's not locked."

"That's all right. I can wait."

"Chicken," Claire yelled.

Carl ignored her and went to turn on the television. He sat on the bed and watched Bob Barker yelling at some hysterical women to "Come on down!"

Claire closed the drain again when the water dropped back to a suitable level in the tub. She felt dirty, compelled to clean her body. More hot water was added to the tub until her skin reddened; then she picked up the small bar of soap and briskly scrubbed her arms.

She had to calm herself down. How nice it would be to have a few peyote buttons to chew while she lay in the hot water. Maybe if she turned Carl on, he would be easier to get money from. Tom Corman was happy to pass her a few pills for a little sex. But she was going to need more than a few pills. She slid down in the tub and leisurely soaped her chest and stomach. There were plans to make. She had to have a plan, if for no other reason than to confirm the creeping back of her elusive memory. Remembering some of where she had been made her want to know where she was going.

She hummed "Mr. Tambourine Man" and soaped her legs. She didn't hear Carl go out, heading down to the lobby to use the bathroom there. She laid her head back in the water and soaked her hair. She let her face sink under and blew bubbles with her tongue out, sounding something like a cheap outboard motor. She opened her eyes underwater, and the soap was stinging. She raised up and began soaping her hair.

She remembered the camp between Flores Magón and

Buenaventura—Luz María, Pancho, Emilio, the boy who looked like Rabbit. She knew Rabbit was dead but could not see him that way. Her last image of him was when he climbed out of the truck and told her to stay. She remembered the pain along the road, waking up in a hospital and not knowing, still not knowing, how she had got there. There was a vague memory of walking out of the hospital one evening and standing by a road. Getting a ride, no, two rides, to El Paso. Bleeding again and going into a hospital in El Paso. Then, after walking out of there, moving north on what must have been instinct. She did not know why it took so long to get to Minnesota. She could not account for two weeks. It was cold in Minnesota. She remembered Halloween, kids in costumes roaming the streets.

Claire laid her head back into the water and rinsed her hair. She did not hear Carl return and put his ear next to the bathroom door to check on her.

She remembered the fire. But only seeing the glow of it from two blocks away. And the sirens, she remembered them. Then the sneaking around, discreetly following Carl, taking a bus out to the cemetery, the police finding her there. Then the quick trial, the advice to plead guilty by reason of insanity, the arrival at Fairbrook. Sometimes she thought she might have been inside the house that night, maybe going up to see Carl. Did she see her mother in the hallway?

Corpus Christi. Claire had to find El Lobo and the others. That was her plan. Find Lobo and tell him what happened to Rabbit in the Mexican desert, get him to take her back there.

Carl knocked lightly on the door. "Did you drown?"

"I'm just about finished."

"Just checking."

Like a guard, Claire thought. She opened the drain and stood up to dry herself. What was she going to do with Carl when she went to Mexico? Could he take care of himself? She wrapped the wet towel around herself and went out.

Carl sat on the bed, watching the news on television. He looked up and smiled when Claire came out. She went to her suitcase and got the clothes she wanted, then went back into the bathroom to dress.

Carl could hear her singing "Light My Fire." Her voice was

perfectly pitched, and Carl always thought she could sing professionally. Sometimes she sang in her voice, and other times she sang a verse trying to imitate Jim Morrison. He watched Cobras racing over treetops in Vietnam and listened to Claire.

Claire came out dressed in patched jeans, a flannel shirt with the tails tucked in, a tan web belt, and with a towel wrapped turban-style around her head. She sang to him while standing at the sink in the dressing area.

"Claire?" Carl had been trying to figure out how to get her to talk to him, really talk to him, since he awakened. They were in Corpus Christi, where she wanted to be, they had maybe enough money to last for a year if they were frugal, doubtlessly the police were looking for them in some fashion, and he didn't have the slightest idea what to do next. "Can we talk?"

"Sure we can talk. Boy, what a serious look."

"I want you to talk to me, I mean."

"I do talk to you."

"You know."

"I don't know."

Carl scooted across the bed and turned off the television. Then he stood up and slowly paced around the small space in front of the beds.

"What do you want, Carl?"

Claire pushed herself back on the bed and leaned against the wall. She took one of his cigarettes and lit it. The smoke curled over her upper lip and was sucked up into her nostrils. Carl stopped and sat backward in the desk chair.

"I don't know how to get into this," he said, not looking at her. "Would you throw me a cigarette?" Claire took one from the pack and tossed it to him.

"Just jump right in," she said, pitching the lighter over.

"You remember now, don't you?" he asked. "I mean, I know, I could tell when we were on the beach this morning. I could see it starting to come back. You even said his name."

"Bit by bit. It's coming back."

"You know about Mexico? Where you were before . . . they got you at the funeral?"

She nodded.

"I don't remember how I got from Mexico to Minneapolis or

anything very clearly after that. The funeral, I remember that. The arrest. The trial. Fairbrook. Between, no."

"The fire?"

"No. Nothing."

"Nothing."

"Vaguely I think I was . . . I think I saw the fire."

"Did you start it, like they said?"

"I don't know. No. I don't think I did."

"Could you have?"

"No. At least not with you there. I could have hurt Mother, I think. No, not even that. Such an act means I would have to hate her a lot. I never hated her, really. I didn't care about her much one way or the other. Not a strong enough emotion to start a fire, don't you think?"

"It *was* started. Who?"

"I don't know. It wouldn't surprise me to find out she did it herself."

Carl thought about that. He didn't know. She was coming to warn him, the police said. "Not her," Carl told Claire. "No."

"Did you hate her?" Claire asked, putting out the cigarette.

"No."

"Truth?"

"I don't know."

"Do you hate me?"

The question slipped into his brain unannounced, without preparation. When it registered, Carl's mouth dropped open. "What?"

"I've just wondered sometimes. I think I could understand if you did."

"Of course I don't. I can't believe this."

"If you did hate me, Carl, I would die. You're the only person I've got. How do you like that for a weight to carry around?"

"I can't feel it. I love you."

"I know."

"What a thing to ask me."

"I know."

"I don't understand you, though."

"Well, I don't understand you either."

"I think I'm crazy sometimes," Carl said, looking away from her.

"You do?"

"Sometimes."

"Why?"

"Things. I don't know."

"You know what weight we both have to carry around? Mother. We've got her perched on our shoulders. Mother and God. Sitting up there like a couple of monkeys."

"She's dead."

"You're telling me? I'm her murderer, remember?"

"I don't like sarcasm very much."

"It's just a buffer between me and everything."

"What do we do now?"

"What do you want to do?"

"I don't mean now, like now, I mean from now on."

"Oh."

"I mean tomorrow and the next day and when the money's gone."

"You worry a lot for eighteen."

"You don't?"

"Not about tomorrow."

"Somebody has to."

"Then you can do it for both of us."

"I always have."

"That's something we need to work on."

"I'm looking at you, Claire, and listening to you, but I don't think I know you very well. I mean, I love you, but I don't know you anymore. You're sort of the same, but you're someone I don't know, too."

"You've provided a few surprises yourself. Look, Carl, we hardly see each other for three years . . . I left a kid and came back to a man. How do you think I feel?"

"I always thought of you as a woman, not a kid, I mean."

"Well, I'm older."

"More than that."

"What?"

"I don't know."

"What do you want to know?"

"I don't know that either. Maybe nothing. Maybe I'm afraid to know any more . . . did you sleep with that guy in Kansas? Tom?"

"That's one helluva segue."

"You were gone a long time. Longer than you said."

"I didn't sleep with him. We just drove around. He let me drive his car. That's all. And we talked some, too. I never even kissed the guy.

"Boy, get a load of that smug look on your face," she added.

"That's not a smug look."

"You know, Carl, that's something we really do have to get straightened out. You have to stop being jealous of me. It's not . . . good. I know where you're coming from, and I accept some of the responsibility for it. But, well, you just have to cut it out. There are going to be things in my life . . . men in my life, and that's just the way it is. And you, you ought to have girls. Lots of girls. I'm not going to be around forever. Shit. I'm stumbling over myself. You know what I mean."

"I'm *not* jealous."

"Shit, Carl. You are, too. You always have been. Maybe it was a big mistake . . . it was a big mistake, for me to have . . . shit, shit! Look at me, I can't even say it."

"Fuck your brother."

"God damn. Was it wrong? Was it wrong! Jee-sus, what a conversation this is."

"Was it wrong? I'd like to know."

"Anybody would say it was. But I don't think so. It was something that belonged to that time, to us then. Not now. Not this time. Not us now. I was so lonely, Carl. You were, too."

"Why do you keep teasing me then?"

"I? Tease you?"

"Come on, Claire. You undress in front of me. Walk around with some half towel half-wrapped around you, sneak peeks at me in the mirror, and that stuff."

"I didn't think about it. True. I won't do it anymore. I didn't think about it bothering you this way. We've just always been so close . . ."

"Maybe I do need a girlfriend. But I never . . . I didn't . . . I don't know how you get one. Is that so funny?"

"I wasn't laughing."

"You smiled."

"I'm sorry. What was it like the last three years?"

"What was what like?"

"Your life."

"Like everybody's."

"We really did turn out to be strangers, didn't we?"

"This is giving me a headache."

"Want me to rub your temples?"

"No. I don't want you to touch me. Okay?"

"Sure. But we don't have to . . . Okay."

Carl got up and went into the bathroom. He sat on the edge of the bathtub and buried his face in his hands. He wanted to crawl into bed with Claire and have her rub his head, his chest, below. He wanted to feel her body against his. He wanted to live with her forever. No one should ever try to come between them. He pressed his hands against his eyes and dreamed.

Flames licked at his feet and surrounded him. Was his mother at the door? Did she open it? He heard Claire's voice but couldn't see her through the fire and smoke. The dream wove through his mind over a familiar track.

seven

It was dark when they finally left the room. After the sun went down, the air cooled appreciably. The high had been sixty-five degrees, but at six o'clock it had dropped to forty-nine. When Claire got into the Jeep, she was shaking, but not from the chill. She needed the pills, and there were none. As a weak substitute she had bought a bottle of No-Doz at a nearby drugstore and taken six of them. She thought the caffeine was giving her the shakes.

"Where to?" Carl asked when he started the engine. "Feel like eating?"

"I'm not hungry," Claire answered, trying to get her bearings in the dark.

"Have you eaten all day?"

"Yes," she said, not really remembering. She had not.

"When?"

"While you were asleep. Jesus, Carl. Let's go back to Shoreline and drive east, turn left at the driveway."

"Is it a secret where we're going?"

"I want to see if I can find some people I used to know."

Carl turned left on Shoreline Drive, and they drove beside the bay for a mile. Carl could see mooring lights on the masts of sailboats in the harbor. The sky was crystal-clear; stars were already visible around a quarter moon. Claire's attention was on the street.

"Get on the freeway here," she ordered, and Carl turned onto the entrance ramp, heading north. "It's not far, don't go too fast."

"What am I looking for?"

"I'll know it when I see it."

Carl stayed in the slow lane and drove forty miles an hour.

"There!" Claire called out. "Alameda. Take the Alameda exit and bear right."

Carl turned on the blinker and eased onto the ramp. "What then?"

"Just stay on Alameda until you see Lobo Street. It shouldn't be too far. Don't go under the freeway," she yelled when he started to turn left on Alameda. "Go right, right!"

"Okay already."

"There it is," Claire said more calmly when she saw the Lobo Street sign. "See?"

"I see. Which way?"

"Right. Then go real slow until I see the house. It'll be on the left."

Claire was visibly jumpy. Carl thought she was nervous. He had already guessed they were going to Rabbit's house, to the place where Claire had lived with Rabbit and all those others. One named after the street, Carl figured. "Was El Lobo named for this street?" he asked Claire while she scanned the houses.

"No. I wouldn't doubt that the street was named after him. It means 'wolf' in Spanish."

"Wolf Street?" Carl said to himself.

"There, there!" Claire cried. "Stop." She pointed to a large Victorian-style apartment house across from them. Carl pulled to the curb and stopped. "I was here this morning. I walked over from the beach, and nobody was home. Maybe now . . ." She opened the car door and started across the street. Carl followed at some distance.

Claire knocked on the first apartment door, and when no one answered, she went to the second. Carl followed. No one answered there, and she went across the hall to the third. She expected the first to be empty. It had been Rabbit's. Of course, someone might have already rented it. They had not lived there for more than eight months. El Lobo and Susie Cream-cheese had the second. Stoney, Windy, and Stoney's occasional girlfriend had the third. No one answered there either.

"It's a holiday," Carl said. "Maybe they all went some-where."

"Maybe," Claire answered, feeling panicked. She knocked on the door of the fourth and last apartment. It had been occupied by an old woman they all had called the flower lady because she tended the gardens around the apartment and kept an uneasy truce with the "hippies and dopers" sharing her building.

"There are no lights anywhere," Carl pointed out.

Claire ignored him and knocked again. But no one came.

"We can come back tomorrow," Carl said, tugging on her arm. The dark hallway was spooky.

"Tonight!" Claire said too loudly. "Tonight," said more calmly. "I've *got* to find them."

"Maybe they moved?"

Claire walked back across the hall and rattled the doorknob to apartment one. It was locked. Carl followed her the length of the hall again as she tried each door.

"You're going to end up getting us arrested, Claire. Now just cut it out." He grabbed her arm and tried to pull her away.

Claire jerked her arm back and pushed him. "Leave me alone!" she screamed.

Angrily Carl grabbed her shoulders and pushed her against the wall. He held her there. "Claire! Cut it out! What's wrong with you anyway?" Claire shook her head back and forth and seemed about to cry. "Listen to me," Carl went on. "Listen to me! If the police pick us up, you'll go back. Do you understand me? I'll probably go to jail."

Claire slid from his grasp and slumped onto the floor, burying her face in her arms. Carl could see her back rise and fall with her deep breaths. He knelt beside her and rubbed her back, speaking softly.

"What's the matter? Tell me."

"I'm hurting, that's what's the matter. I'm hurting."

"What hurts?" She didn't answer. "Is it your stomach? What?"

"Oh, Carl."

"Well, I can't guess it. You have to tell me." He put his arm over her back and rubbed her shoulder with his fingers. The only light in the hallway came from the porch light outside. They were deep in the shadows on the floor. "Can't you tell me where it hurts?"

"Carl, you . . . child!"

He removed his arm and leaned back against the wall, dropping to a sitting position with his knees bent in front of him. He and Claire sat side by side, but not touching.

It was a long time to sit in a darkened hallway without speaking and without considering leaving, but they were there that way for five minutes. Carl sat with his arms propped across bent knees and stared at the wallpaper. Claire kept her head down and her face covered by her arms. The first move was Carl's. He took out his cigarettes and lighter. Claire raised her head when he lit the cigarette, his face yellow in the glow. Without asking, he took another from the pack and held it out to Claire by the tip. She reached for it tentatively, like a child reaching for something she expects to be suddenly withdrawn. Carl moved his hand forward to meet hers, and she took it. Carl saw her hand shaking; it was an exaggerated motion when he held the lighter out for her.

"You *are* sick," he said, snapping the lighter closed and plunging them back into the shadows.

"I need something, Carl," she whispered.

"Tell me. We'll go get it."

"Pills."

"Pills?"

"God, Carl. Amphetamines, whites, uppers, Methedrine, Benzedrine!"

"But I thought you were . . ."

"Carl . . . please!"

"Okay." He stood up and took her hand, pulling her to her feet. "Tell me where to go."

She put her arms around him quickly and kissed his hair. Then she pulled him down the hall and out the front door. "Did you bring some money?" she asked as they were crossing the street.

"I've got about a hundred dollars in my wallet. The rest is in the Jeep's door panel on my side."

So that's where it is, Claire said to herself as they got into the Jeep.

Claire could remember only three places they might go to

find a dealer. The first two weren't home, and by the time they got to the third house—a tract-house near the naval air station at the other end of Corpus Christi across Cayo del Oso—Claire was shaking violently and crying. Carl went to the door. "His name's Paul, I think," Claire called out to him when he left the Jeep. "Ask for Paul, and tell him you knew Rabbit."

Carl knocked on the door and heard some commotion inside the house. He couldn't believe he was buying drugs, scoring, as Claire put it. There was a certain thrill in the nervousness he felt.

"Yeah?" a voice called out. The door did not open.

"Paul?"

"Who wants him?"

"I was a friend of Rabbit's."

"Oh, yeah? Rabbit who?"

Carl noticed a Spanish accent in the voice. He half expected to see a gun in his face when, if, the door opened.

"You know who Rabbit is—was. Hey, man, look, do you want me to state my business out here or would you rather just open the door?"

"You a cop? You gotta announce if you a cop, man. Like, you know that."

"I promise. I'm not a cop."

Carl noticed a shaft of light off to one side when someone pulled back a window curtain. Then he heard a chain being released from the door. It opened two inches, and an eye looked him over. "Who's in that car, man?" the voice with the eye said.

"My sister."

"Well, Paul's not here, man."

"You'll do."

"What you want?"

"Is this where you do it? Out on the porch?"

The door opened, and Carl squeezed in. It was a tract-house living room with an open archway leading into a dining room. Only there was no furniture. There were some sleeping bags on the floor, some pillows and cushions, an old dinette chair, bottles and cans everywhere. The windows were covered with army blankets. Two men in navy dungarees leaned against a far wall with a water pipe between them. Another man was lying on one of the sleeping bags, propped on his arm, looking at Carl. The man who had let Carl in was also wearing navy work clothes.

"Are you Paul?" Carl asked.

"What'daya want with him?" the man on the sleeping bag asked. Carl heard a toilet flush.

"You're Paul?" Carl took three steps into the room, followed by the man at the door. "I want to buy some speed."

"Pills or for shooting?"

"Pills."

"How many?"

"How much are they?"

The man raised to a sitting position, crossed his legs lotus-style, and shook out his left arm as if it were asleep.

"I don't know. I hear they go for like two bucks apiece on the streets these days," the man named Paul said.

"All right. Give me ten then."

"Who says I got pills to give you or anybody else? Say you knew Rabbit?"

He wasn't going to take any bullshit, Carl thought. Just tell him the truth and get the hell out. "I met him once. He lived with my sister."

"Oh, yeah? What's your sister's name?"

"Claire . . . Claire Grant."

"Blond chick, long hair, outta sight bod?"

"Sounds like Claire."

"That her in the car outside, man?" the doorman asked, moving sideways back to the window for a peek.

"Yeah. Hey, do you want to sell the stuff or not? 'Cause I got other places to be tonight, and to tell you the truth, I find all this game playing a little boring."

"Joey," Paul said, and waved his arm toward a door on the wall to Carl's right. "Fix this boy up."

"Thanks," Carl said, reaching for his wallet. "Twenty dollars for ten?"

"Forty."

"At two dollars apiece?"

"I said that's what you can get some for on the street. This ain't no sidewalk. I got overhead, expenses."

Carl took two twenties from his wallet and held them out. "Just pitch it down anyplace."

Carl let the money fall straight down from his hand.

"Hey, when you ask your sister something, ask her how come she come out of Mexico and Rabbit don't? Some people wondering how much money she got, you know?"

"I don't know what you're talking about," Carl said.

The doorman came out and handed Carl a vial. The two sailors against the wall puffed contentedly on the pipe. Carl could hear it bubbling and cooling the smoke. Carl couldn't see inside the smoked pill bottle, so he opened the cap and looked in, shaking it around.

"You gon count 'em, or what?" Paul said.

"You look like a trustworthy man," Carl answered sarcastically, replacing the cap and putting the vial in his shirt pocket.

Paul laughed. The sailors looked up, then went back to oblivious puffing. The doorman laughed a few seconds too late for it to sound natural.

Carl backed toward the door, followed by the doorman.

"Y'all come back now, ya heah," Paul said mockingly.

Eat shit, Carl thought as he went out the door.

Claire grabbed the vial from his hand as soon as he got into the Jeep, but she couldn't open the childproof cap. She grabbed at it with her fingernails until Carl jerked it back and opened it. She took three of the white pills and popped them into her mouth dry. Then she curled up against the door and waited, shaking. Carl drove away.

It was ten o'clock when they got back to the motel room. Carl sat on the bed and lit a cigarette. Claire, pacing in front of him, reached into his shirt pocket and took out the pack. She took a cigarette and tossed the pack on the bed. She had not wanted a cigarette; she was looking for the vial. She carried the cigarette between her fingers but did not attempt to light it.

"Feel better?" Carl finally asked. He had not spoken to her in the Jeep as they drove. She had curled up against the door and looked out the window the whole way. But she was smiling when he pulled into the motel parking lot.

"Yes." Claire paced into the dressing area and looked at herself in the mirror. Carl could see her reflection. She saw him watching. She turned around and said, "Thank you."

"It was an experience," he said.

"I don't like getting you involved in stuff like that, people like Paul and that scum." Claire brought her hands repeatedly together in front of her waist, clapping softly.

"I guess I was just surprised that you . . . still needed it so much. I thought . . ."

"It was Fairbrook that did it, Carl." She stopped clapping her hands and came over to stand nearer him. "I was doing okay until they started zapping me on that machine and pumping me full of Elavil and Thorazine, or whatever it was."

"I believe you."

"Don't look at me that way, like I'm a junkie or something. I don't need it all the time. Rabbit, he was a junkie. But he was going to get off the stuff. I've never touched heroin in my life. Not even one single time. This stuff, it just kind of helps get your heart started. Some people have a drink or two, I have some whites. It's all the same difference."

"You don't have to convince me."

"By the way, where are the rest of them?"

"The pills you don't need?"

"Jee-sus, Carl. How many did you get?"

"Ten. You took three."

"Are they in your pocket?" Ten, she thought, maybe two days' worth.

"Why don't I just hang on to them? I won't keep them from you or anything. Just ask and I'll give you one or two."

"Bullshit! What kind of bullshit is that? You are not your sister's keeper, you know?"

"Then what the hell am I doing here?"

Claire sat down beside him and put her hand in his hair. "Carl, Carl, let's not argue. Keep the pills, I don't care. If it makes you feel better." She messed his hair. "Hey, let's go out and do something."

She looked ready to bounce off the walls like a rubber ball. Carl felt as if he should hang on to her to keep her from flying away. He took her hand and held it tightly. He was not tired, but he was not interested in running all over Corpus Christi again.

"Let me show you around. Hey, come on." She tugged on him. "Isn't it pretty close to New Year's Eve anyway?"

Carl looked at the calendar on his wristwatch. "It's Monday, the twenty-eighth." He calculated the days. "New Year's Eve is Thursday."

"Close enough, come on." Claire pulled him up and tried to get him to dance with her to the music she hummed.

She looked so happy and alive, so sensual and emotional. So like a quick trigger. He smiled with her in spite of himself.

"Well, I've got the driver's license; we might as well use it. Know any good bars?"

"Do I! Great." She pulled him toward the door.

It was the first good time Carl had had in longer than he could remember. Claire was flighty, happy, bubbling with energy and happiness. She wanted to walk, to breathe, to sing and dance.

They left the Jeep at the motel and walked into downtown. She put her arm around his waist, and pulled him toward the sidewalk. "Let's walk up to Broadway." She hugged him and took his arm to put it around her shoulders. People they passed on the sidewalk looked at them as if they were honeymooners. There was such an aura.

Claire took him to three bars, and the last one they closed at two o'clock. Carl could barely stand. He had consumed nine glasses of rum and Coke. When he tried to put his hands into his back pockets as they walked back, he couldn't find them. Claire giggled and pulled him closer.

She almost had to carry him up the stairs to their room. When she unlocked the door, Carl fell into the room and just made it to the corner of the bed. He laughed and tried to push himself up.

Claire pulled him onto the bed and turned him over onto his back. "You're plowed, little brother," she said. He flung his arms wide and giggled. "Boy, just wait until tomorrow," she warned. But he looked so good to her, so peaceful, even if silly, and so much a part of her. His hair had fallen into his eyes, and she gently brushed it back.

"Far-out," Carl said, giggling again.

"What's far-out?"

"The bed goes all around."

"Are you going to be sick?"

"Whoopee," he yelled.

He grabbed his mouth and tried to raise himself up.

"Yep, you're going to be sick."

She picked him up and helped him get into the bathroom, just in time to get his head over the toilet. "I'm gonna die," he said between retches.

Claire held his head to keep him from banging it on the toilet edge and rubbed his back with her free hand. "Come on, baby," she whispered, "that's right, get it all out."

Later she got a washcloth and cleaned his face, shirtfront, and the spots on his jeans. She more or less had to carry him back to his bed. His boots were tight, and it took some effort to get them off. She unbuckled his belt, pulled down the zipper, then tugged his jeans down until they were free of his feet. As she started to drop the jeans to the floor, she heard the rattle of the loose pills in the vial. She removed the vial and set it on the nightstand. She looked at him, lying there in white socks, briefs, and his denim shirt. She thought he looked beautifully innocent, too sweet. The shirt went next, then the socks. Carl never stirred; his brain was unreactive. She tried to pull the covers down under him and finally had to roll him over and lift his legs to get the sheet down. She rolled him over again onto his back and started to raise the sheet and blanket. The only light in the room came as a glow through the curtains and the bathroom light. In the shadows Carl's skin looked like glove leather—light, smooth, soft. Claire touched the tip of her right index finger to his chest and drew a line through the fine blond hair across his stomach. She passed her palm over the lump in his briefs but did not touch it. "You are so handsome," she whispered. "You are so good and so kind and so . . . good to me. I love you." She put her fingers beneath the elastic band around the waist of his briefs and pulled steadily downward. Steadily but slowly. She uncovered him quietly, gently. She caught her breath as his briefs passed over his hips and down his thighs. She bent over and removed them from his ankles and feet.

Carl lay flat on his back, legs slightly apart, ankles turned so his toes pointed together, arms at his side, head turned to the left, mouth open, breathing coarsely. His chest moved in a steady, shallow rhythm.

Claire bent to her knees beside the bed and studied his skin, his form, his muscularity and color. She touched his hair, moved it out of his eyes. She leaned over the bed, over him, but kept her weight off it. She could not stop herself from leaning over to touch her lips tenderly to his, smelling the sourness of his breath but inhaling it greedily. She let her eyes trail down his chest to his stomach, where she brushed her hand lightly through the fine hairs there. Her body ached deeply for him.

She moved herself up higher on the bed so she could touch her lips to his navel. She probed it with her tongue, but he did not stir. She could feel his stomach rising to meet her with each breath.

Then she moved down, touching the tip of his young manhood with her fingertip, stroking it as she might touch a kitten. In his unconsciousness Carl gasped slightly, and he grew to fill the hand that grasped him.

With one hand reaching up under her skirt to find the place between her legs and the other cupping him, Claire put a finger into herself and her lips around him. Softly, slowly at first, she stroked him as her mouth sucked and her finger searched. Then she moved him faster, still tenderly, and pushed her tongue against it. Her lips could feel the engorging flood of it before her hand noticed. Carl groaned, moaned, and she tilted her head to look at his eyes, never releasing him from the suction of her mouth. His eyes fluttered beneath the lids but did not open. His mouth stayed open as he made harsh, guttural sounds. His stomach growled beneath her ear. Two fingers framed her clitoris and rubbed.

With the first warm, salty taste of him, she pulled her mouth away and caught his seed in her hand. She lay back on the floor, jerked her dress away, and pushed his seed deeply into her with her fingers. And came then.

She undressed in the bathroom, looking at her face in the mirror. Her skin was flushed pink, and her eyes were wide, dilated. They had told her in the Mexican hospital that she would never conceive again. We'll see, she thought, we'll see.

She covered Carl, then got into her own bed. The sheets were cool against her skin, and she stretched her toes luxuriously. She lay awake for another hour before sleep conquered the diminishing effects of speed.

She dreamed of the bandit camp in Mexico, of Luz María, Emilio, Pancho, the boy . . . of Rabbit lying humped in a puddle of black, fly-covered blood. It was a dream she had never had before; it woke her, and she screamed.

Carl never stirred.

It was dawn.

eight

Carl woke suddenly. He didn't know if he had been dreaming or what. But something jerked him from sleep like a hand slap. He sat up and kicked away the covers. His head throbbed, and he felt like gagging. He couldn't remember taking off his clothes.

Claire's bed was empty. He called her name as he got up to look for his pants. Then he heard it again, the sound that had pulled him from sleep. It was coming from outside the room: a metallic crashing noise, muffled yet clear. Carl hopped over to the window while pulling on his jeans. Through the window he could see the Jeep, its driver's-side door wide open, Claire banging on it with a hammer. The tool kit lay open on the pavement, and several of the tools were scattered around her feet. Claire was crying as she crashed the hammer into the door panel again and again.

"Shit!" Carl muttered, and zipped up his pants as he ran, shirtless, no socks or shoes, out the door. Carl's feet hit the frosty dew on the balcony, and he slid into the railing, banging his shins on the lower rail.

A man and a woman stood on the balcony two doors down. The man asked Carl if the Jeep was his. Carl struggled to his feet and skidded along the balcony, holding the rail for balance. "I already called the police," the man said.

"Mind your own business," Carl told the man as he slid past. He was freezing. The steps were covered in frost, and Carl had to ease himself down carefully. Claire banged away in oblivious anger. Loose pieces of crushed shells peppering the driveway cut his feet as he ran across and jerked the hammer out of Claire's hand.

"What in the hell are you doing?"

Claire tried to break away from him; she clawed at the inside door panel.

Carl heard the siren. When he looked up, there were a dozen motel guests watching from the balcony.

Claire had a wild, incoherent look in her eyes. He could not tell if she even recognized him. Trying to pull her away, he stepped on a screwdriver and sliced his big toe. The combination of pain, cold, and fear made him angry. He jerked Claire back and slapped her hard.

"Hey!" he heard someone yell from the balcony.

Claire did not speak. She made animalistic, crying noises.

The siren sound came closer. Carl realized that if the police saw Claire in such a condition, they would take her away, maybe even fingerprint her. They were lost if the police found her. She would be taken back to Fairbrook and he . . . what? He would be taken to jail? There wasn't time to reason with her. Carl slapped her again, and when she collapsed against him, he pulled her across the driveway and toward the motel. He pulled her into a hallway and sat her on the floor behind an ice machine. The siren seemed very close.

"Don't you dare move," he told Claire, pushing her back against the wall hard. "Do you hear me? You better not move from this spot!"

He backed away from her and pointed his finger firmly toward her face. "You sit right there and don't move, don't make even one sound."

Claire's head was lowered, her chin resting on her chest, but her body shook uncontrollably. Her hands fluttered in her lap like a pair of dying birds. The siren sound seemed right outside.

Carl backed away, then turned and ran as fast as he could on the slick frost back out to the parking lot. He reached the Jeep just as the squad car turned into the motel. The siren faded as Carl saw the black and white. Carl picked up the hammer and began banging on the door panel; only he tried to make it look purposeful. The police car stopped between the Jeep and the motel, blocking Carl from the people watching. Both officers got out and walked toward him. Carl put the hammer on the front seat so they would see his hands empty.

"Gosh, you guys scared me half to death," Carl said, smiling as the cops approached. His skin was covered in goose bumps, and his toe was surrounded by a tiny puddle of blood.

"Leave your hands out where we can see 'em," the first approaching officer said. The second one came around behind Carl, his hand holding the butt of his pistol.

"Hey? What'd I do?" Carl asked, raising his hands.

"Put your hands down," the first officer ordered, "but keep them out where I can see 'em."

"But this is my car," Carl tried to explain.

"Let's see your license," the cop said, "and the registration."

"Sure." Carl patted his back pocket, hoping the wallet was there. It was. Carl could feel the other cop watching him. He removed the wallet and handed his driver's license to the cop. "The registration is in the car," Carl said.

"Get it out, please." The second cop walked around the car with Carl and waited while Carl took the registration out of the glove compartment. He gave it to the officer, who took it around to the cop holding Carl's license.

"Your name is Charles Granger?" the first cop asked.

"Yes, sir. But do you mind telling me what I did?"

The cop studied both the license and the registration; then he handed both to his partner.

"Well, Charles," the first cop said, "we had a call that someone was breaking into a car here. Would you like to tell us why you're standing out in the parking lot here at eight o'clock in the morning, dressed like that, tearing up your car?"

"Oh, is that it?" Carl tried to smile broadly. He was sweating in spite of the thirty-nine-degree air. He laughed nervously. "I'm not trying to break it; I'm trying to fix it."

"I see. What's wrong with it?"

"There were some dents in the door, and I was just trying to knock them out. Not too well, as you can see. I'd about decided to take it to a body shop. Guess I was a little noisy, huh?"

"Aren't you cold, Charles?"

"Oh, you mean . . ." Carl looked down at himself. "Well, sir, I am now. But it was hot banging on the door, so I took off . . . but yes, sir, I'm getting a little cold now."

One cop looked at the other, and both smiled in a bored way. Then one laughed. "I think car repairs in a motel parking lot at eight in the morning isn't a very good idea, Charles."

"Yes, sir, I can see that now." He saw the cop looking at his bloody toe. "I stepped on the screwdriver," Carl explained quickly.

"I guess somebody from Minneapolis wouldn't find it very cold down here," one of the cops said.

"Well, it's getting that way. But, no. A day like this in December in Minneapolis would be like spring."

They gave him back his license and registration. Carl stuck both into his pocket. "I'm sorry about disturbing all those people. I just wasn't thinking, I guess. I'm going to take the car to a body shop soon as I get dressed and let a professional do it."

"That would probably be a good idea, Charles." The two officers returned to their car, and Carl bent down to pick up the spilled tools as the engine started and they drove away. He put the tools back into their bag and shoved it onto the front seat. Then he closed the door and walked back toward the hallway where he had left Claire. When he looked up at the balcony, the audience found other things to look at.

He found Claire where he'd left her, still behind the ice machine. But she had turned over and lay on her arms and knees like a supplicant. Her body shook so violently that Carl could see the muscles in her back rolling like waves. He bent over and lifted her like a lumpy, heavy sack. Holding her close was like trying to contain an exploding ball of rubber bands. He would grab one arm and the other would fly up. Let go of that arm and it would swing out. Her legs wobbled aimlessly. He pulled her up the inside stairwell to avoid the balcony. His anger rose with each lurching, struggling step. All Claire said was: "Money, the money, get the money out, money." They had to walk the last forty feet along the outside balcony. Carl felt as if they were parading through a row of jack-in-the-boxes— faces appeared and quickly disappeared at the windows. He pushed Claire into their room and did not care when she fell on the floor.

"God damn you!" he cried. "God damn you, Claire! You're crazy!" He jerked the blanket from his bed and wrapped it around his shoulders. He stormed around the room while Claire remained on the floor, shaking. "Now we've got to get out of here. You're out of your goddamn mind! What the hell did you think you were doing?"

He walked near her, and Claire flew up like a coiled snake and grabbed his legs. They tumbled backward to the floor, and Claire crawled up Carl's body, pounding on him with both fists as she went. Carl twisted his face away from her fists, but she caught his ear, then his cheek. He grabbed her wrists and twisted her arms away. She tried to butt him with her head. Carl used his weight and strength advantage to buck her off. When he rolled onto her and tried to hold her down, she twisted and shook beneath him like a wrestler. Carl's anger turned to fear. She fought him like a banshee. Then suddenly she stopped. She convulsed, her mouth opened, her eyes wide in terror, her voice struggling to scream. Carl thought she was going to die. In panic, he slapped her and screamed her name. He had once seen a woman slap a convulsive child and stop the shaking that way. She gasped, and the air flew out of her lungs. Carl got up and pulled her to the bed. Her fingers shook spasmodically.

"Oh, God, what do I do?" Carl prayed. "Tell me what to do." He looked for a water glass and noticed the pill vial empty on the nightstand. There had been seven of them when they left the room the night before. Carl wondered if she was dying, overdosed on the pills he had bought for her. How many is too many? he wondered. What could he do? If he called for a doctor, would they discover who she was? Better to be in Fairbrook than dead! She held herself and shook. Sometimes she mumbled about money and speed and hurting. Carl got a glass of water and tried to make her drink some. He cursed himself for not knowing what to do. Everything was coming apart. He blamed himself for getting drunk and not taking care of her, for buying the pills instead of making her get over it, for passing out, for telling her where the money was hidden, for taking her back to Corpus Christi, for being alive and responsible.

Her breaths came out with a hoarse sound, and he gave her more water. She gagged and, turning her head, vomited across the bed and his legs.

"God, I'm sick, I'm so sick," she mumbled. "I'm hurting."

Carl rubbed her forehead and wiped her mouth with a corner of the sheet. "Do you want me to take you to the hospital?" Carl asked.

"No, no, no." Claire shook her head back and forth. "I need . . . I'm sick, so sick."

"What do you want?" Carl cried urgently.

"Can you get me some Seconal? Please, Carl, please. Yes, get some reds or something."

"No more pills, Claire. Jesus, look at you! No more drugs. This is it!"

"Don't, Carl, don't."

"I mean it."

"I'm hurting so bad, Carl. Help me."

"I want to. That's what I want to do."

"Get me something to drink."

Carl touched the water glass to her lips. Claire knocked it away, spilling water across the night table.

"You asshole!" she cried. "You shithead!"

Carl held her arms down to the bed.

"Not water, you idiot! Some bourbon, some vodka, something. Get me a drink."

"No."

The phone rang, and Carl ignored it. The persistent ringing punctuated Claire's crying. She changed the expression on her face from belligerence to complacence.

"It'll help me, Carl, really," she pleaded. "I can get all right with something to drink. Then that's it, I promise. But don't make me feel like this, please, please."

"There's nothing here, Claire, and I'm not going to leave you alone."

"I can get up, I'll go with you," Claire said excitedly.

"Did you hear the phone ringing? I'll bet that was the manager. Did you hear that?"

"Carl, come on, please?"

"Listen to me, Claire. What are you trying to do? I don't understand any of this. Do you want them to take you back to Fairbrook? Is that what you want to happen?"

"No, no."

"What are you doing this for? Why did you take all those pills? I knew I shouldn't have bought those things for you. I knew it. You're scaring me, Claire."

Claire pouted and tried to look sexy. It was pathetic with the vomit on her pillow and in her hair. "Carl, please?"

"You can't manipulate me that way, Claire. It doesn't work."

"Help me," she pleaded softly. When he let go of her arms, she put one hand on his leg.

"This has got to stop here and now. I want to help you . . . that's what I *am* doing."

"You fucking creep!" Claire screamed, and tried to claw his face.

Carl shoved her arms down and started rolling her up inside the blanket, rolling her so tightly that he made a straitjacket for her, only her face visible. Then he sat on her.

"I'm choking!" she cried. "You're killing me!"

Carl didn't answer. He turned her over so her face was toward the mattress, muffling her voice. For one irrational moment he did feel like killing her. It would be so easy, just push her face into the mattress and hold it there. The thought made him wince before he forced it from his mind, replacing it with the problem of what to do with her. He didn't even understand his options.

The phone rang again, startling him. He leaned over without getting off Claire and picked up the receiver. "Yes," he said as calmly as he could. It was the motel manager, saying there had been complaints of noise from his room. Carl apologized, said they were checking out that morning and he would be down soon to settle the bill.

"That was the manager," he told Claire. "We have to leave."

Claire had stopped struggling and was quiet. Carl thought she might have passed out. "Claire," he said, shaking her shoulders.

"What?" she answered brusquely, turning her face to the side.

"If I let you up, will you promise to behave?"

"Yes," she said curtly.

"Really?"

"Yes. I said yes."

Tentatively Carl moved to one side of her but kept his arm across her wrapped body. Claire made no motions. He moved his arm and stood up.

"Do you mind?" she said.

"Remember you promised," he said, unwrapping the blanket from around her. She rolled out of it as he pulled. The tremor remained in her hands; otherwise, she seemed okay. More or less, he thought. She looked sad, almost reflective. Just her hands shook.

"Give me a cigarette?" she asked in a flat, toneless voice.

He got one for her and lit it. She took it from his fingers and puffed greedily on it. She looked tired. Particles of her regurgitation remained in her hair. Her face was pale, puffy.

"I'll pack if you want to clean yourself up," Carl said.

Claire tried to stand, but her legs buckled and she slumped back to the bed, Carl reaching out to catch her. He helped her up and led her to the bathroom.

"I'll stop, Carl. Cut it all out. But not now. I can't now. The sooner you understand and accept that, the better off we'll be. Otherwise, I'll leave." It was her ultimate, final threat. "I'll just leave you."

"Let's get out of here before somebody calls the cops again. Then we'll talk about it." Carl closed the bathroom door behind him as he left.

Why, he wondered, did everything have to always be so messy and so complicated? Why couldn't they ever just live normally the way everybody else did? The thought of Claire's disappearing again terrified him.

He threw their clothes into the suitcases and tried to straighten the room a little. He covered the vomit on the sheets with a bedspread. The shower started. He laid out fresh clothes for Claire, then got himself dressed.

He had to take Claire someplace where they could be

healthy. They had to leave Corpus Christi and all it meant to her, meant to her in a life that no longer mattered, that should never have existed in the first place. He was trying to think of someplace to go when Claire came out of the bathroom and said, "I have to find my friends."

With all their possessions back in the Jeep—a Jeep with a badly dented door and a portion of the panel torn away—they drove onto Shoreline Drive and headed back toward the house on Lobo Street. Claire had won. He would help her find her friends, but then they would leave Corpus Christi, leave Texas, even leave the country. Whatever it took. Carl was unable to see any farther ahead than getting his sister back to the Claire he had known before, the one who loved him, cared for him, protected him, and played with him. He was not much interested in the new one, the one that left him, hurt him, and frightened him. Anyway, he thought, he was curious to meet the people Claire had written to him about.

It looked different in the daylight, seedier, less residential than it had the night before. They had only been in Corpus Christi less than forty-eight hours and Carl had bought drugs, got drunk, and nearly been arrested. He wanted to be somewhere else. A part of him wondered if part of what went wrong with Claire could be attributed to place.

"That's Lobo's truck there," Claire called out excitedly when Carl pulled up in front of the house. A rusting, primer-painted old Ford pickup truck was parked in the driveway beside the house. A sticker in the rear window said: F**K WAR!" Claire sat up straight and brushed her fingers through her hair. "Park behind it," she told Carl, and he turned into the driveway. He couldn't deny feeling a little excited. He had read about these people in Claire's letters for three years.

Claire jumped out of the Jeep and told Carl to hurry up. They went into the hallway and Claire headed directly for apartment two. Carl could hear the music before they got inside the building, the bass so loud it vibrated against his skin.

When the door opened, Carl saw a pretty young woman gasp and back into the room.

"God, Susie," Claire said, going in, "God, it's good to see

you." Carl stood in the open door but did not go in. "It's me," he heard Claire say. The music was so loud that Carl lost the voices once Claire was inside the apartment. Claire seemed to be sucked up by *Sgt. Pepper's Lonely Hearts Club Band.* The girl Claire called Susie looked as if she had seen a ghost. Carl stepped inside the door so he could see but went no farther.

"Lobo!" Susie cried. "Come here!"

Claire had stopped, finally recognizing that Susie was more stunned than pleasantly surprised.

Carl thought the woman named Susie, who must be Susie Creamcheese, was very good-looking, although he had only a glimpse of her when the door opened. Since then Claire had been between them. A movement to Carl's right caught his attention, and he saw a man come through a door there, a tall, rough-looking, black-bearded man wearing a gold earring in his ear, wearing jungle fatigue pants, jump boots, and an olive-drab T-shirt. There was a .45 caliber pistol in his hand pointed at Claire. Carl was about to throw himself between Claire and the gun when the man called her name and lowered it. "Claire?" he repeated, the surprise in his voice as it had been in Susie's gasp.

Claire turned toward him and said, "Lobo, Lobo." Then she ran into his arms, crying. Carl wanted to shrink out of sight.

"God damn! I nearly shot you," Lobo said, holding Claire at arm's length.

Susie joined them, cautiously testing Claire's reality by touching her shoulder. She said, "We thought you were dead."

Claire hugged them both at once. "You should have seen it," she said in a muffled voice. "They just shot him cold. He didn't do anything."

"We didn't know," Lobo said. "All we heard was he got killed in Mexico. There was a thing in the paper . . . you know, 'local man killed in Mexico' kind of thing. Never even mentioned your name, so we figured . . ."

"They *took* you." Susie completed the sentence.

"Oh, God, you feel good," Claire cried, squeezing them. "It was gross, they murdered him and left his body . . ." She started crying again, and Susie started crying with her.

Lobo backed off. "That's really fucked," he said, staring at the pistol in his hand. When he looked up, he saw Carl standing in the doorway. He pulled Claire and Susie apart, then turned Claire around. "Who's your friend?" he asked, nodding toward Carl.

"Oh. My brother. This is my brother, Carl, my brother." Claire held her arm out to Carl and motioned for him to come in.

Carl walked toward them, thinking how odd it felt to be with people who seemed to be closer to Claire than he was.

"Carl," Claire introduced them, "this is Susie and El Lobo. My best friends."

nine

Carl thought it took an awfully long time for Susie Creamcheese and El Lobo to assure themselves of Claire's reality. They were odd people, he thought. For one thing, they never bothered to turn down the stereo yet didn't raise their voices loud enough to be audible over the music unless the hearer happened to be very close to the talker. If you got farther than five feet away, you couldn't hear a word anybody said. The apartment was the sloppiest place Carl had ever seen. Even the posters on the walls weren't hung straight. There was no globe over the ceiling light, which simply hung there bare and flickering. Carl waited for it to burn out. Except for clothing on the floor, there seemed to be very little else of a personal nature. But the clothing lay everywhere. Carl wondered if there were no closets. Boots and shoes—male and female variety—shirts, underwear, a bra over a chair back, a belt coiled on the table, an army fatigue cap, a green beret with a pocketknife stuck through it into the wall. There were some paperbacks and magazines on the floor. When Carl started to sit down at the dining table, he had to move a copy of *Green Mansions*. There were maybe a hundred record albums piled here and there, some records in jackets, some loose. There was a fruit jar on the kitchen counter with a wad of money in it. On the dining table—an ornate round oak one—were tipped-over cans of Lone Star beer, a straw-covered Chianti bottle with cigarette butts in it, two other oversized glass ashtrays filled to overflowing, a plastic bag full of marijuana, a hash pipe, two opened packages of rolling papers, and a box of kitchen matches. The whole apartment smelled like a mixture of sweat, Italian spices, and moldy bread.

The same Beatles album played for the third time. As the others sang along with parts of the songs, Carl was too intimidated to join in, but he felt strangely comfortable with them. He forgot to notice that he had a headache and was starving to death. He tried not to smile his silly 'I'm nervous' smile.

Susie continually reached over and touched Claire's arm. Claire would glance at her and smile. Lobo leaned precariously far back in his chair with his feet propped on the table. Carl looked at his jungle boots. They should have named him Bear, Carl thought, instead of Wolf. He looked more like a bear. He had long, black, curly hair and a full, untrimmed black beard. His face, what could be seen of it, was full and dark, probably Mexican, Carl thought, although he had no accent except the Texas drawl. He was tall, taller than Carl, who was six feet. And he must weigh 225 pounds, Carl figured. His arms, where they protruded from the cutoff T-shirt sleeves, were thick and strong. On his upper left arm was a tattoo of paratrooper jump wings. "AIRBORNE" was printed beneath the wings. Carl wanted to ask about it but was still too uncomfortable. They had more or less ignored him. Lobo smoked a joint without offering it to anyone else. Carl drank the beer Susie had set in front of him.

When he could look at her without feeling obtrusive, Carl let his eyes wander across the table to Susie Creamcheese. She was wearing a man's white T-shirt and no bra. Carl could see the shadow of her nipples. Her face was oval, and her lips were thin. She had large hazel eyes and black, long hair which looked as if it hadn't seen a brush or comb in days. The skin of her forehead was broken out slightly. Yet Carl thought she was as pretty and confident as any woman he had ever seen in person. She had the same Texas twangy speech pattern Lobo did. Maybe, Carl wondered, he was most attracted to her because now and then he caught her looking at him the way he looked at her: secretly, slightly embarrassed, and curiously.

Claire had been telling them about Mexico. She said she now remembered everything that happened but explained that she had been out of touch for so long because of what a doctor called traumatic amnesia. Carl thought he remembered the phrase as "selective recall." He wondered what the difference was. Claire explained why they had to change contacts at the last minute and go with the man Pancho, who drove them into the high desert near Flores Magón, where his bandit friends waited to kill Rabbit and take the money. She told them things Carl had not heard before: about being taken to the bandit camp and abused, about the woman Luz María, who saved her, the miscarriage in the ditch, not knowing where or who she was for weeks, finding herself back in Minneapolis with her memory returning in pieces like a puzzle she couldn't work, then about the fire, the arrest, the trial, the commitment to Fairbrook, and Carl taking her out. When Claire told how Carl had come "to save" her, Carl caught Susie's eyes staring at him. She smiled before looking away. Susie's hand still rested on Claire's forearm as if she were afraid to let go.

Lobo did not say a word for half an hour. He puffed alternately on cigarettes and joints and looked at Claire. He seemed to be working very hard to believe her.

When Claire finished telling her story, she asked Susie to come to the bathroom with her, an insistent tone in her voice. "Be back in a minute," she told Carl, touching his shoulder as they left the room. Carl watched Susie's breasts go by and wanted to touch them just once.

Lobo dropped his chair to the floor and started rolling another joint. He moved in slow motion, deliberate, careful movements. Carl looked at an empty beer can and read the label.

"Huh?" Lobo made a sound like a grunt and held a joint out to Carl.

Carl shrugged his shoulders and said, "I guess so." He had never smoked marijuana before. Lobo lit it and took a deep drag before passing it to Carl. Carl duplicated the motions Lobo made, inhaling deeply, sucking in his breath, holding it, and looking toward the ceiling. The plaster was cracked interestingly in two places. He forgot to hand the joint back to Lobo, who finally reached over and took it. Carl thought the smoke was harsher than a cigarette and had an almost metallic flavor but otherwise wasn't so bad. He didn't feel a thing; he had expected to go insane or something.

Except for the three words just spoken, Carl had not said

anything for half an hour, since just after they had arrived. Being quiet, the silent type, made him feel more a companion to Lobo, who also did not speak, who seemed to be reading thoughts with his eyes and hearing within the depths of his brain. Lobo fascinated him. He could see why Claire had been impressed. These people are so cool, he thought. He took the joint again, inhaled, and wondered what Claire was doing. He forgot to give it back again, and Lobo took it abruptly.

Claire and Susie had not gone into the bathroom. They sat on the end of the bed, side by side, while Susie fished around in her bag for the pills Claire needed.

"Look at all this shit," Susie said. Most of the pills were loose, and she took out handfuls and dropped them onto the bed. "Where are those little things?" She pulled out yellow jackets, reds, some synthetic mescaline.

"Maybe you don't have any speed?" Claire said with a slight trace of annoyance.

"Sure I do. Just a minute." She turned the leather bag over and spilled everything out onto the bed: cigarettes, matches, a tampon, a hairbrush, a tin of aspirin, two loose cigarettes, a yellowed old roach, a prescription bottle of Valium, a comb, a beer can opener, four paper clips, a roach clip, more loose pills, and no little white ones.

"Where did you leave them?" Claire asked.

"Hey, I'll just ask Lobo where they are."

"No." Claire stopped her. "Carl's got this idea I ought to get off the uppers."

"Your brother is pretty goddamn good-looking, you know?"

"Susie! Where are the fucking whites?"

"All right, all right. Man, just a minute, let me think. Your brother's kind of a prude, huh?"

"Susie!"

"I think Lobo put them somewhere. I don't do that shit; bad for my nerves."

"Well, shit, then go ask Lobo to come in here. And keep Carl in there."

"My pleasure," Susie said, shoving everything back into her bag and dropping it on the dresser on her way out.

*   *   *

Carl heard the door open and turned around to see Susie coming back. She looked so good the way she moved that he wanted to cry from the joy of just watching her.

"Baby," Susie said to Lobo, "Claire wants to see you in there for a minute." Carl started to stand, but Susie touched his shoulder, gently but persistently pushing him back. "Why don't you and I get to know each other?" she said.

Without a word Lobo dropped his chair to the floor and got up, handing what remained of the joint to Carl. "Fucking games," he muttered, then went into the bedroom.

Susie Creamcheese took the chair abandoned by Lobo next to Carl and sat with her body turned toward him. Carl's head felt lighter. His vision was clear, and he stared blatantly. It was only vaguely like being drunk. There was no feeling of bloatedness and no sweet taste in his mouth. He took some extended delight in watching his right forefinger move up and down, tapping its own mysterious rhythm. Susie smiled at him, and he looked back at his finger, smiling secretly back.

"I guess you like that record," he said finally. It was starting to play through for the fourth time.

"Oh," Susie said as if she had not noticed. She got up and went to the stereo, her blue jeans coming alive. She moved in slow motion, and Carl thought he would die from desire.

"What do you like?" she asked, lifting the tone arm and plunging the room into the first silence since Carl's arrival.

Carl almost shouted but stopped himself after the first word. "I didn't mind that. I mean, you didn't have to change it if that's what you wanted, I don't care."

Susie laughed and turned her attention to the records on the floor. Carl drained his beer and stuck his finger in the hole in the can. He could hear quiet conversation coming from the other room. He wanted to take a nap.

Susie put on an Iron Butterfly album, and it was louder than before. Carl looked at the Baggie of grass on the table and wondered if he could roll a joint by himself. He liked the feeling.

Susie took the same chair and helped Carl get his finger out of the can.

"Claire wrote to me about you guys," Carl said, needing to say something, anything.

"Oh, yeah? Like what'd she say?" Susie asked, moving the can out of Carl's reach.

"I don't remember," Carl said, laughing.

"Far-out," Susie said.

He wanted to put his hands on her breasts.

When Claire and Lobo finally came out of the bedroom, Susie was teaching Carl how to roll a joint. "Lick it this way," she said, seductively rolling her tongue around it.

"Lick what?" Claire asked, walking up next to Carl and putting her hand on his shoulder.

Carl tilted his head back to look at her and smiled.

"Jee-sus K-rist," she said. "You're blasted."

Susie shrugged, innocently denying her participation.

"Have you been fucking with my baby brother?" Claire teased Susie. Susie shrugged again in the same way.

Lobo fished around in the refrigerator and pulled out a can of beer. He handed it to Claire, then got another for himself.

Carl watched everything in his perfect world. He had to look away from Susie to keep from touching her.

"Well, where is everybody?" Claire asked, sitting down at the table. Lobo took his beer, turned down the stereo a little, then sprawled on the overstuffed couch next to it.

"OP had her kid," Susie said.

"She did? What kind?" Claire wanted to know.

"Boy kind. Last month."

"Month before last," Lobo inserted.

"Well, one of those months. Hey, I remember. It was the day before Thanksgiving, I remember."

"No, it wasn't," Lobo corrected disinterestedly. "It was sometime in the middle of October."

"What happened the day before Thanksgiving then?"

Carl looked back and forth between Lobo and Susie as if he were watching a Ping-Pong match.

"Forget it," Lobo said.

"Aww, tell me. Something happened with OP the day before Thanksgiving." Susie sounded convinced and wasn't about to be deterred.

"A boy," Claire said to herself.

Carl looked at Claire's sound, then back to Susie, to wait for the next comment. He puffed on the joint alone. Nobody asked for it.

"It died," Lobo said matter-of-factly.

"It died?" Susie questioned, raising her eyebrows.

"OP's kid died the day before Thanksgiving," Lobo explained, then laid his head back on the arm of the couch.

"Oh . . . I remember," Susie whispered so that only Carl, who was closest, could hear her.

"OP's baby died?" Claire straightened up, and her body stiffened.

"I remember. He was a little baby, very tiny, and he died the day before Thanksgiving," Susie said.

"What do you mean, 'he died'?" Claire's voice raised a pitch. "Died of what? How?"

"He was very tiny, and he never even got out of the hospital," Susie said reflectively. "OP was so big, too. Just like the last time, you know?"

"Premature?" Claire asked.

"Drugged, like the other one she almost had," Lobo said from the couch, not opening his eyes.

"Acid? You mean the baby . . . and the acid?"

"Who knows?" Lobo said. They could barely hear his voice over the music from Iron Butterfly. "That's her second one, though."

Claire's stomach turned and twisted as she suddenly remembered the feeling when she aborted on the side of the highway in Mexico: the pain, the blood, the fetus in the dust. "Shit," she said with an exhaling of hot breath. "What the fuck did she do to herself?"

"OP went home to Missouri or Mississippi or one of those places," Susie said.

"I didn't mean where she went. I meant . . . oh, forget it."

"I hate that fucking record," Lobo said, reaching over to change it.

"How about some CCR?" Susie suggested, going over to find the album.

Carl wanted to lay his head on the table and sleep. He was getting smashed.

While Susie looked for the record, she talked. "We got a card from her at Christmas, and I could find it later if you want to see it. I don't know where Lobo put it. But it had a neat dove on the front. Lobo, do you know where OP's Christmas card is? I put it on the dresser or on the table, someplace like that. Anyway, Windy went to Frisco again. She says she met the drummer for the Grateful Dead. Fuck her way into the music business, you know? Stoney ought to be here pretty soon because he got back from wherever he went two days ago." Susie found the record and put it on the stereo. Lobo let it play for about ten seconds, then took it off and put on a Moody Blues album. When the music started, full blast, Susie raised her voice to compensate. "I think Leadhead went to Baja or somewhere like that, but he'll be back before New Year's Day, he said. But now you're here and we're here and when Stoney gets here and if Windy finally shows up, when Leadhead gets back too, then we'll all be together again . . . except for OP."

"And Rabbit," Claire added, pulling the Baggie and papers to her. "Shit, OP's kid. That's fucked."

Carl felt very sad. Claire lit the joint and handed it across to Susie. Carl followed it with his eyes. Susie finished and offered it to Carl, but before he could take it, Claire reached out and pushed his hand away. "Take it easy, kiddo," she said, taking the joint back.

"Hey!" he said, but didn't feel like making an issue of it.

Lobo turned over with his face against the back of the couch and seemed to have fallen asleep.

Carl thought he would starve to death before anyone else thought about food. His throat started to burn from the thick smoke in the air. He laid his head on the table under his folded arms.

"Maybe I'd better go put your brother in the bed," Susie suggested.

"You keep your hands off him," Claire said, although her voice was not menacing. "I'll do it."

She stood and stopped next to Carl. "Look at him." She smiled. "Isn't he so fucking good-looking it makes you want to cream?"

"No shit," Susie confirmed. "I like 'em young and innocent."

"Come on, you big doper," Claire said, lifting Carl from under his arms. "Jee-sus," she groaned, unable to pick him up.

Susie came around, and between the two of them they were able to get him on his feet and moving toward the bedroom door. Claire reached out and pushed the door open; then they took him in. Carl felt them moving him but didn't care enough to protest. Lying down seemed like a pretty good idea. He was dizzy, but he liked the feeling.

They put him on the bed, and Susie picked up a blanket from the floor to place over him. Both women stood and stared at him for a long minute. "He looks like he's about ten," Susie said. "Now I see why Rabbit always felt so competitive with him."

"Did he tell you that?" Claire asked sharply.

"More than once, lady, more than once."

"Bullshit."

"Have it your way."

They went back into the living room, and Susie said, "Would you check this out? Here we are ready to go and the guys are both zonked. So who's the weaker sex?"

Wordlessly Lobo raised his arm into the air and stuck his middle finger up. Statement made, he withdrew it and snuggled closer to the couch back.

"Did Rabbit really say that about Carl?" Claire asked when she and Susie sat back down at the table.

"Did he have to say it, Claire? Shee-it."

ten

In the middle of the afternoon Susie went to the store to get something for them to eat. Carl was still asleep. Lobo was bitching because he had to go back to work in three days. Sometimes he looked at Claire with those jungle-fed eyes and frightened her. But he always had. Ever since he showed up at Rabbit's door more than three years ago, still in uniform, three days out of the jungle, he scared everybody but Rabbit. Rabbit would say, "Just don't try to wake him up, and don't argue with him when he's drunk; he's otherwise harmless." Even Susie, who said she loved him, could get awfully frightened sometimes. She told Claire that once Lobo woke up in the middle of the night and started choking her. Only Rabbit, hearing the commotion and pulling Lobo off, saved her, Susie believed. Lobo told Susie that he didn't care if she made it with other guys, but then, when she did and he found out about it, he nearly beat the man to death. Yet he never hit Susie, or any of the women who lived there, even the ones who just came and went. Which is not to say he never wanted to. On more than one occasion he put his fist through the plaster wall to keep from putting it through Susie. It was that knowledge that tempered Claire's fear of him. But now there was something else at work, her need for him.

Lobo was the only one of them who worked. Some of the women had turned tricks—never Claire, but Windy had, Susie before Lobo—and Rabbit mooched, dealt drugs, and borrowed from his brother; the others sold drugs, sometimes played in bands. Lobo had a job, the same job he had held for three years. He was a mechanic in a small garage on South Staples. He said, "I won't live off no bunch of women and fucking hippies." But he contentedly lived with them. He was, in a way, their protector. They were never once ripped off in Corpus Christi. Everybody in the drug culture knew where El Lobo lived and who his friends were.

When Susie left for the store, Lobo reached over and turned off the stereo. "Fucking all the time music," he said in general. "Fucking hippie shit." He pushed some albums around the floor with his foot until he uncovered the one he wanted. He put the Merle Haggard record on and turned the volume down to a more acceptable level.

Claire opened a beer for him and took it to the couch. He nodded a thanks and took a long drink. Feeling her way, cautious not to intrude on whatever mood Lobo had decided to put himself in, she sat on the arm of the couch farthest from him. She waited for a moment, to see if he minded, then said, "I think maybe you blame me . . . about Rabbit."

Without looking at her, Lobo said, "Nah. What could you do anyway? The dude been trying to die for a long time. He didn't care."

"I think he did care, Lobo. Really. He didn't just die. They murdered him—for nothing."

"All killing is for nothing," he said reflectively.

"But I mean really for nothing."

"Huh," Lobo grunted, and drank more beer.

"I'm sorry. I know he was your best friend."

Lobo nodded.

"I feel responsible because I wasn't fucked-up and he was and I felt something was wrong right from the beginning. Rabbit didn't know which way was up by the time we got there." She sounded as if she might cry at any moment.

"Fate shits on you sometimes. Nobody's responsible."

"I feel it anyway, and I want to do something about it."

"Yeah. I knew it was sour from the first. Yeah, I feel it."

Claire had never heard Lobo admit to any sense of responsibility before, and she had never heard him say he felt *anything*. She wished he would look at her. Maybe it wasn't going to be as difficult as she thought. Claire moved off the couch arm and sat on the floor near Lobo's feet. If you need to beg, she thought, you ought to be in the position of a beggar. She was tempted to touch his leg but thought better of it. She and Lobo had slept together twice, but that was more than two years ago and they'd both been smashed and it hadn't meant anything more than the feeling. Besides, when Lobo wanted to be touched, he picked up the hand and placed it where he wanted it.

"I see them in my dreams, my nightmares, sometimes," Claire said, trying to catch Lobo's eyes with hers. "The killers, those bloody goddamn bandits who killed Rabbit just for the"— Luz María's voice appeared suddenly in her mind, a rough voice saying *"emoción"*—"for the thrill of it. They could have had the money, kept the drugs, let us go; but no, they killed just for the thrill of it. Left Rabbit with his blood soaking in the dirt . . . maybe still alive, suffering, and just drove away." She felt the tears come. Through the mist she saw Lobo's eyes find hers. His hand, like a bear's paw, moved toward her face, and she closed her eyes to wait for the electrical touch of it. But he did not touch her face. His fingers went to her hair, and she felt him moving locks of it off her forehead, a tender, sensual touch. She opened her eyes, and two rolling tears were released, falling down both cheeks. She moved her hand along the cushion, let her fingers crawl slowly, like a spider, toward his leg. When her hand came within a few inches of his knee, she stopped and waited. Then Lobo picked up her hand and put it on his leg. His fingers brushed through the front of her hair.

"Shit," he said almost as a release of air, "let's just go down there and waste the motherfuckers."

Claire sniffed deeply and squeezed his leg slightly. With her free hand she wiped her eyes.

"We owe Rabbit that much," Lobo said.

"Would you do that?" Claire asked. "Would you find them and kill them?"

"That's what all this is about, isn't it? That's why you showed up here again, why you're sitting down there crying, why you're acting like fucking me is number one on your list?"

"I . . . no."

"Don't mean nothing. You're right anyway. I thought about it already. I just wanted to see where your head's at. It would give me a fine pleasure to blow those motherfuckers away. And you know who they are and where they are."

"I do, Lobo. I know their faces, where their camp is, I know. You really will? You're not just . . . No, I know you wouldn't tease about it."

"How much money you got?"

"Money? I don't know. Carl has it. A few thousand dollars; maybe as much as seven or eight."

"I'll need five."

"Five thousand dollars?"

"To start. Then we'll need money for the road . . . say, another two or three. Susie's got a wad stashed in here somewhere. We gonna do this, we do it right."

"Whatever you say. I'll talk to Carl."

"What are you going to do with that kid?"

"I don't know."

"He's kind of weird. He fucking retarded or something?"

"Retarded? No. He's young, Lobo, really young. And naïve as a day-old kitten."

"Well, he stays. I don't want his death on my conscience. It's not his problem anyway. Susie'll go, you, Stoney if he wants to, Leadhead won't be back probably soon enough, that's it. We don't need no army anyway. Charlie taught us that lesson well enough. Two or three sappers could take out a fucking platoon and never be seen."

"Carl's got a pretty strong will. He might not want to stay."

"I don't fucking care what he wants. Deal with him."

Claire could see the excitement building in Lobo. There was a spark in his eyes that seemed to monitor the memories flashing through his mind. It made him exciting to her. It no longer frightened her.

Claire's hand slipped up Lobo's thigh, but he stared at the wall behind her, lost in the jungles of Vietnam, planning, calculating, filling his soul.

"I can make pretty fair grunts out of you guys in a couple of days," he was saying. "You don't need to know that much. Just how to keep your asses quiet and how to shoot. You'll just be diversions."

The door opened, and Susie returned with a bag of groceries. Claire did not move her hand fast enough, but just far enough so Susie couldn't be sure how far up Lobo's leg it had been.

"Want me to go out and come in again?" Susie said, taking the grocery sack to the table.

"Djew get some Twinkies?" Lobo asked. Claire moved away from him and went to turn the record over.

"Did I get Twinkies?" She pulled two boxes of them from the sack and held them out like prizes. "Here"—she tossed one of the boxes to Lobo—"stuff your face." She turned her back to Lobo and Claire while she jerked things out of the sack. "God-damn cowboy music," she muttered too low for anyone to hear.

Claire walked over to the table and began helping Susie put the groceries away. She got Susie's attention, then mouthed the words, "Nothing happened."

"He's a big boy," Susie whispered. Lobo tore into the Twinkie box.

Taking two cans of beans from the table to the kitchen shelf, Susie dropped them with a loud bang. A minute later Carl came out of the bedroom. Claire welcomed the distraction from Susie's jealous mood.

"Look who's alive?" she said when Carl staggered into the living room.

"What happened?" Carl asked. He went to the tap and ran a glass of water to drink.

Susie and Claire laughed knowingly. Lobo was in another world: heat, wet, fire, jungle, death.

Stoney came that night. A tall, lanky red-haired man with a scruffy beard, wispy mustache, and bulging eyes. He opened the door without knocking and said, "Far-fuckin'-out," when he saw Claire sitting on the floor by the stereo. He tossed a blanket roll on a chair and pulled Claire up to hug her. He smelled as if he had bathed in a vat of beer. He pulled Claire against him and squeezed her like a child would a teddy bear. Carl stood at the sink, where he had been washing the dishes— unable to stand the filth any longer—and marveled at the world Claire had lived in during those years away. He had never had a friend, he realized, and Claire with hers made him miss it. Claire was his only friend, but apparently he was only one of hers, if that.

"There any beer here?" Stoney asked, breaking away from Claire and heading for the refrigerator. "Sorry about Rabbit," he added. He nodded at Carl and said hello as he opened the refrigerator and found a can of Lone Star.

Carl wondered if he ought to offer to shake hands. Apparently nobody was going to introduce them.

Finally he said, "My name's Carl. Claire's brother."

"Hey, man, nice to meetcha. I thought you were younger."

Before Carl could say anything else, Lobo said, "We're going to Mexico."

"Far-out," Stoney replied, looking for the can opener.

Carl pulled it out of the sink and handed it to him.

"Hey, thanks, man." He opened the beer in a spray of foam. Going back over and sitting cross-legged on the floor in front of Claire, he said, "So where you been? *They*"—he cocked his thumb in the direction of Lobo and Susie, who were on the couch—"thought you were dead. Not me, no, sir. I figured you'd split."

Carl felt odd man out and went back to the dishes. There was mold on some of the plates.

Claire told her story again, appropriately punctuated with comments from Stoney, who concentrated on making cocaine lines on a piece of construction paper. "This is some really far-out shit, man," he said to Lobo. Then he told Claire to go on. When Claire finished her story, Stoney solemnly shook his head, patted Claire's leg, then held out the construction paper and said, "Shall we have a go at this fine shit?" He moved over to the coffee table in front of the couch and put the paper on it. Lobo was quietly rolling a dollar bill. "Hey," Stoney called out to Carl, "get on over here and dig the shit." Then, whispering to Claire: "What the fuck's he doing anyway?"

"Take it easy," Claire whispered back. "He's not into this."

"He's *your* brother? She-it."

Carl didn't have any idea what cocaine was. He'd never seen it. He walked over, wanting very badly to be a part of them but at the same time thinking they were crazy. He sat beside Claire, and she put her arm around his shoulders. Leaning over, she whispered into his ear, "Don't do anything you don't feel like doing, okay?"

"I can take care of myself," he told her.

Claire squeezed his shoulders and made a kissing motion at him. Carl watched Lobo lean over and sniff an entire line of the white powder through the rolled bill and into his nostril. Then he quickly moved over and inhaled a second line into the other nostril. His head drifted backward, and he held the bill out for Susie. "God *damn!*" he cried out. "Far-fucking-out." The bill passed from Susie to Stoney, who handed it to Claire. There were four lines left, but Stoney began cutting new ones on the table. Claire slid it across and in front of Carl, questioning him with her eyes. Carl took the bill from her and imitated the others. He had to inhale twice on each line to get it all. It stung his nose, then filled his head with helium. It floated backward, and he lay back on his arms for support. It was terrifyingly wonderful. Lobo put a pill in his mouth, then reached across the table and slipped a second one into Carl's hand. Carl looked at the pill for a moment, then swallowed it dry. If Lobo could do it, so could he. Carl thought his head was going to fly away by itself and circle the room, bouncing off the walls and ceiling like a balloon. The Doors sang from the stereo. They sang directly into his brain as if the circuit were open only between his ears and the speakers. He had an erection that started in his toes and stretched up through his groin and into his face. He had to catch himself to keep from falling over backward when he leaned back to look at the ceiling. The drums and bass pounded in his chest. He thought he was about to come and everything inside him would explode all over the room. His skin went into shock, electrified and exposed. His mouth fell open.

"What did you give him?" Claire asked Lobo.

"Just a little acid," Lobo said. "Just a couple hundred mikes."

Claire frowned at Lobo, then leaned over and put her hand on Carl's cheek. "Is it okay?" she asked him.

All Carl could hear was the music.

Later Carl raised his head out of Claire's lap, where it had been for an hour, and watched Lobo and Susie. Lobo's feet were propped on the coffee table and spread. Looking between the worn soles of his boots, Carl could see Susie's head going up and down over Lobo's lap like a pump. It was the most beautiful motion he had ever seen. They were circled in an orange aura. Lobo's head lay back against the wall, his arms behind his head, his eyes closed. Susie's hair had fallen over to cover her face and the object inside her mouth. All Carl could see was the motion of her head, up and down, up and down, up and down. It was hypnotic.

Stoney lay flat on his back, studying the ceiling. Claire's head lay on Stoney's stomach, and his steady breathing was rocking her to sleep. Her hand rubbed absentmindedly up and down Carl's backbone. Each stroke sent shivers through Carl's skin. The world focused down through Carl's eyes onto the sight of Susie's hair moving up and down. It was as though she were moving over him, not Lobo. Claire's hand on his back became Susie's. Carl became Lobo. The dimensionless configurations of reality became so blurred that Carl thought he could feel his body merging with Lobo's. He caught the rhythm of Lobo's breathing, the posture of his head, the spread of his legs, the gap in his mouth. Susie's hair moved autosexually. He had not found friends: Carl had found a brother in Lobo, a sister in Susie, and both of them were then inextricably bound up with himself. He found the experience spiritual, if not religious.

It seemed to have gone on forever, but it didn't last long. Carl eased back into reality, the usual one, a couple of hours after taking the last four cocaine hits. At some point he must have slept, he figured, because he couldn't account for the time. He had moved or been moved. Claire slept beside him, curled into a fetal position against his back. When he moved to sit up, she made an unintelligible sound. Stoney and Lobo sat on the couch, talking intently but in whispers. Susie was not in the room. When Carl eased himself away from Claire and sat up, Stoney looked over and said, "Far-out shit, huh?"

Carl got up slowly and agreed, "Yeah, far-out." He had to use the bathroom. He had not urinated since early in the afternoon, when he got up from his nap. It was now ten o'clock. He went through the bedroom and into the bathroom. The door was open, and the light on.

Susie leaned over the sink, washing her face. From the side Carl could only see her hair hanging down, and he flashed back to the sight of that hair pumping over Lobo's lap, not sure if he had actually seen it or imagined it. He stopped in the door and stared at her. Susie rasied herself up and saw Carl's reflection in the mirror.

"Hi," she said, wiping her face with a towel.

"Excuse me," Carl said, backing out.

"Oh, that's all right. I'm finished." She tossed the towel on the counter and faced him. "That was some shit, huh?"

"Far-out," Carl said, the words sounding strange and unfamiliar.

It was like a standoff. Susie stood by the sink, and Carl in the doorway, waiting silently, each waiting for the other to do something or at least move one way or the other. Carl put his hands in his pockets, unconsciously keeping them from reaching out to touch her breasts.

"Your sister doesn't know you very well," Susie said.

"Oh, yeah?"

"Nobody ever really understands someone they think of as a kid brother."

"I guess not."

"I bet there's a lot Claire doesn't know about you."

"Probably."

Someone turned on the stereo in the other room. "Pinball Wizard" filled the apartment. Susie moved inside her clothes, and Carl's eyes spontaneously fell to her chest.

Mysteriously compelled, urged, Carl moved toward her. When he looked up, Susie was closing her eyes and leaning her head toward him. They did not quite kiss. Their lips came so close that a static charge could have connected them. He could feel his chest heaving against hers, although only their shirts brushed. He still had his hands in his pockets. As he backed his head away slowly, Susie opened her eyes, and they were bright. "Whew," she breathed. Carl thought he would faint. "Jesus Christ," she whispered. Without taking her eyes away from his, Susie moved slowly around him and into the darkness of the bedroom. Carl turned on his axis until she faded into the dark. Then he closed the door and sat down on the edge of the counter, staring blankly at the wall. He was totally, eternally, desperately, ecstatically in love.

Susie had not been unaffected.

They sat around on the floor, smoking dope, until 2:00 A.M. A wine bottle passed around and around until it was gone; then another appeared. They didn't talk much. The stereo played loudly. Carl had already begun associating the music with that apartment and thought he could never hear those songs again without returning to that night. Sometimes he saw Susie looking at him, but he was too afraid and too embarrassed to do more than glance at her occasionally. He wanted to puff himself up and be great for her, be heroic, steal the show. But he sat quietly and listened when the others talked. He smoked when it passed and drank when the bottle came around. He was floating away again, but it was nothing compared to the cocaine and pills. He was a little surprised at how little Claire's presence meant to him then. If she'd wanted to get up and walk out, he wouldn't have noticed or cared. All his thoughts were on Susie. He fantasized a life for them in minute detail. His brain made connections in new places, with new feelings, in new ways. He felt fresh, alive, vital. And his heart fluttered dangerously. He sat between Stoney and Claire, across from Lobo and Susie. Susie's hand rested possessively on Lobo's leg. Lobo's hands lay in his lap, when they weren't dealing with the bottle or the joint.

Their stories and jokes didn't mean anything to Carl. But he wasn't listening anyway. He made up elaborate pictures for himself and Susie.

Lobo talked about love and sex. Carl heard him say, "There are times when I believe that sex is not only separable from love but superior to it." His voice was low and hoarse. "But I also recognize the tacit presupposition that I know what love is. I don't. But I do know what sex is. I've been in sex lots of times, but I've never been in love."

"No shit," Susie said, and Carl wanted to yell to her, "I love you."

Everybody but Carl laughed. And Carl was afraid his thought had come out verbally. But they were laughing at Susie's comment.

Lobo said he was going to write a book and call it *A History
of the Flesh*.

Carl felt sick. It came on him like a blow in the face. He was
barely able to run into the bathroom before throwing up into
the toilet. Down on his knees, retching into the bowl, he felt a
cool cloth on the back of his neck and a warm hand rubbing his
back. He couldn't turn to look but wanted it to be Susie's hand.
Then he heard Claire's voice, soothing and low, saying, "It's all
right, darling, it's all right." He was embarrassed enough to
think of suicide. "Come on," Claire said when he was finished,
"let me take you to bed." A dead man couldn't object, so Carl let
her lead him to the bed and put him beneath the sheet. She
took off his shoes and told him to sleep well. "You'll be fine
tomorrow," she said, leaving him alone.

Later that morning, it was still dark, Carl felt someone getting into bed beside him. Hesitantly he turned his head to see,
hoping against hope that it was Susie, only to see Claire pulling the sheet up to her neck. He scrunched down into his pillow
again and tried to deal with a headache the size of Minnesota.

eleven

Carl was the first to awaken Wednesday morning. The bedroom smelled stale, and he could hear the forced-air heater kick on. It was hot in the room. He got out of bed carefully, trying not to disturb Claire, who breathed steadily on the other side. He noticed he was still in the clothes from yesterday. The apartment was quiet except for the heater's sound and some muffled noises when cars passed on the street outside. Carl remembered that they had left all their luggage inside the Jeep yesterday.

He tiptoed into the bathroom to relieve the pressure from who-knows-how-many cans of beer and remembered standing there the night before with his lips brushing against Susie's. It weakened him, and he had to prop himself up on the counter with both hands. He didn't have a toothbrush, so he rinsed his mouth with water from the tap and brushed his hair with his fingers. He closed the door when he urinated so the noise wouldn't awaken Claire. In spite of being famished, he felt happier than he could ever remember being. Susie had wanted to kiss him. He had affected her. She liked him. Maybe—he was willing to cut off his arm to insure it—she even loved him.

There was no way to get outside to the Jeep where his clothes were without going through the living room, where he presumed the others were sleeping. He didn't want to make them angry waking them, but particularly he didn't want to chance seeing Susie in Lobo's arms. What choice did he have? He couldn't sit in the bathroom until everyone else decided to get

up. He looked at his watch and saw that it was ten after nine.
Maybe if he was very quiet.

The door between the bedroom and living room wasn't closed
all the way, and Carl had to move it only a few inches to pass
through. It was darker in the living room, where the curtains
were still drawn. But he could see Stoney first, inside a sleeping bag in the middle of the floor. The night's residue was still
scattered around the floor. The smoky staleness was thicker in
the air. When his eyes adjusted to the dimness, he could see
that the couch made into a bed and Lobo slept there with Susie.
It was almost hot in the room. Carl figured the thermostat
must be on eighty. He tiptoed across one side of the room,
trying to avoid kicking one of the cans on the floor, glancing at
Lobo and Susie after each step.

Lobo slept on his stomach, only his head visible above the
sheet. Separated by at least two feet from him, Susie lay on her
side, facing away from Lobo, her right arm over her head. One
leg stuck out from the sheet, and it reflected the small amount
of light in the room as if it were phosphorescent. He saw her
jeans and T-shirt lying across the back of the couch. If he stood
there long enough, he wondered, would the sheet eventually
fall away?

Carl made it to the door without stumbling over any of the
debris and went into the hallway. There must have been a
thirty-degree contrast between the apartment and the hall.
When he went outside, there was another fifteen-degree drop.
It was thirty-five degrees outside and sparkling clear. The frost
had not yet begun melting in the bright sun. Carl did not have
to try it to know that his socks would give his feet the security
of ice skates on the frosted porch, so he pulled off his socks and
jogged unsteadily out to the Jeep.

Sitting in the Jeep was a reminder of the radical contrast
between the world he really lived in and the one where he had
spent the night. Here were all his familiar things: his luggage,
sunglasses, extra packs of cigarettes, road map, empty Coke
can, ashtray holding cigarette butts stretching all the way
back to Minnesota, his smell, Claire's smell. He sat behind the
wheel and stared at the back of Lobo's primer pickup truck.
The urge came and went in one instant, but during that moment he wanted to start the engine and drive away, alone,

heading for something he knew, something he understood, something he could deal with. How odd it felt, but somehow he knew then that he would stay, not so much because of Claire but because of Susie. He told himself he was a jerk, then got out a bag for himself and one for Claire.

It took them a long time to move themselves in the morning. Carl had brought in the bags, changed clothes in the bathroom, then sat on the toilet and smoked a cigarette. He thought he would starve to death before anybody else got up. After waiting half an hour, he took off his shoes and crept back through the living room and out to the Jeep. He drove down Alameda until he found a pancake house and gorged himself. By the time he got back it was eleven o'clock. Claire was in the shower, Stoney was gone, Lobo was at the dining table, writing something, and Susie was still asleep.

Lobo looked up when Carl came in, then went back to his notes. Carl asked if Claire had gotten up. "Shower," Lobo said without looking up again.

"I got some breakfast," Carl said to make conversation. He sat at the table across from Lobo with his back to the sleeping Susie. Otherwise, he would have been tempted to stare at her in front of Lobo. He kept his voice low.

"Uh-huh," Lobo said, writing slowly but continually.

Carl heard the shower water stop. He looked at the refrigerator, the stick tree outside the window, the rings on the table, the stack of clean dishes on the counter, a cigarette butt stuck on top of a Lone Star can, the fruit jar bank, the ceiling, the wall.

Finally Claire came into the living room. She was wearing jeans, a bulky white sweater, and boots. She was brushing her damp hair.

"You brought the bags in. Good," she said. "Where'd you go?"

"Breakfast," he said, adopting Lobo's grunting type of response.

"Okay," Lobo said, looking up at Claire. "Sit down. I've got this worked out." He tapped the paper with his pencil.

Claire sat down between Carl and Lobo and kept brushing out her hair.

"I'll need four thousand up front to cover this," Lobo said.

"I haven't talked to Carl yet," Claire said, glancing between them.

"Talked to me about what? Four thousand dollars!"

"It's *his* money, or what?" Lobo asked, staring at Claire.

"Well, sort of . . . more or less."

"Fuck!" Lobo threw the pencil on the table and stood up. He went to the refrigerator and got a beer.

"Hey!" Carl heard Susie's voice from behind him. When he turned around, she was sitting up in the bed, the sheet clutched to her chest. Her hair had fallen into her face, hiding her eyes and most of her cheeks.

"It's about time," Claire said.

"Is it day already?" Susie asked huskily. In one motion she swung her legs off the sofa bed, dropped the sheet, and reached for her T-shirt.

Carl choked soundlessly. She wore only panty briefs. Oblivious to his stares, Susie pulled the T-shirt over her head and sat down to pull on her jeans. Carl had already forgotten the mention of money.

Lobo sat down again and swigged the beer. "Well, what is it?" he said. "You can forget it without the money. This stuff doesn't grow on the trees down here. And I for damn sure ain't going down there without it."

Susie walked into the bedroom, rubbing her eyes. When she was gone, Carl turned around and looked at Claire. "Roll in your tongue, kiddo," she said, winking at him.

To change the subject, Carl asked Claire what she wanted some money for.

"I was going to talk to you about it last night, but well, I don't know."

"Talk to me about what?"

"Fuck," Lobo muttered, and went into the bedroom.

"I need some of the money you've got in the Jeep."

"Yeah, four thousand dollars. I heard."

"More than that."

"We've only got about eight."

"We might need it all."

"I'm not giving you all that money just to buy drugs with. You can forget it."

"We're not going to buy drugs."

"Well?"

"Guns, I think. Whatever Lobo needs it for."

"Guns? You mean, *guns?*" Carl mimicked firing a pistol.

"Stuff like that."

"Have you gone crazy! I can't even imagine what you **want** with . . . Jesus, Claire. That's all the money we've got. I mean, there's no more. We don't even have jobs. That money might last us a year if we're careful. Then I can get a job somewhere, we'll get a house or something . . . guns? What in the hell are you . . . or Lobo . . . going to do with four thousand dollars' worth of guns, for chrissakes?"

"If you'll simmer down and be quiet, I'll tell you."

"Well, I can hardly wait to hear this one."

"Don't be an asshole."

"Me? Me? You want to take all the money we've got and buy some goddamn guns!"

"Are you going to shut up, or what?"

Carl raised his arms as if to say "Who me?" He fumbled around in his shirt pocket for a cigarette.

"Give me one of those."

Carl took out two cigarettes and lit both. He liked the style of it.

"We're taking the money"—Claire emphasized the "tak- ing"—"because Lobo, Susie, Stoney, me, Leadhead, if we can find him, are going into Mexico to get the motherfuckers that killed Rabbit. Lobo's going to get—"

"You're what?"

"You heard me. Look, Carl, this isn't up for debate. I'm just telling you what we're going to do; then you're going out there and get the money out of the Jeep. If you don't, then I . . ."

"Then you will? Huh? The fuck you will! You're all crazy! Loonies! Nut cases! I should have left you in Fairbrook; you belong there."

"Don't be a problem."

"A problem! Me? A problem?" He laughed a little too hysterically. *"You* guys are going to Mexico to . . . what? Kill some people? Get killed? Tell me."

"I don't care if you understand or not."

"I guess you're right. It doesn't matter. Because you're not touching one . . . peso of that money."

"You can't stop it, Carl, so don't try. I know where it is. If I tell Lobo to go out there and get it, he will, and you won't be able to stop him. It would be very stupid to try."

"This is a joke, isn't it? You aren't even a little bit serious."

"Totally serious. We're going. Lobo, Susie . . ."

"Susie knows about this? She's going?"

"Of course. Look, Carl, I want you to understand why we're doing this. But whether you do or not, we're going."

"You're not going anywhere I don't go."

"Let go, Carl. Just let it go, let me go. It can't be like this forever."

"So you're going off to Mexico to kill some people? Okay, then so am I. Who do we kill, huh? I hope there's some kids. I've never killed any children. Women? Can I kill a couple of women? What kind of gun do I get? I want a machine gun. Then I can kill a bunch of people."

"Get serious!"

"Oh, you want serious?"

"Carl."

"I'll give you serious. We're getting the hell out of here right now. Leave the bags, I don't care. I mean, right now. And we're getting in the Jeep and driving the hell out of this fucked-up place. That's serious." He stood up. "I think that stuff has fried your brain."

"Sit down," Claire ordered.

"No. We're leaving."

"Sit down, Carl. I want to tell you about a night I spent in Mexico last July. I want to tell you about a man that got killed in the Mexican desert by some capitalistic hopheads . . . about your sister's rape, about a miscarriage on the side of a dirt road. I want to tell you about the death of the father of my dead baby." There were tears in her eyes. Carl sat down, and she held his hand. "I want to tell you why we're going to Mexico and you can't do one single thing to stop it."

Then she told him everything, including a few expert lies.

Lobo helped Carl remove the Jeep's door panel. The money was wrapped in a taped garbage bag. Carl tore off the wrapping and counted out $4,000 in fifties and twenties.

"What does this buy?" Carl asked when he handed the money to Lobo.

"I know a guy that took an AK-47 out of Nam; he'll sell it if the price is right. I've got a forty-five and a CAR-15; personal prizes. The forty-five won't be much use because I ain't getting that close."

Lobo sat down beside the Jeep and leaned back against the side panel. He put the money in his toolbox and opened a beer. "Want one?" he asked Carl. Although it was up to fifty degrees at midday, Carl was chilled. Lobo sat in his jungle fatigues, a nylon jacket, his boots, and a baseball cap with a set of jump wings embroidered on the front. Carl squatted just off the damp grass and took a beer. Lobo seemed to like his audience.

"I know a guy over in Refugio who has a contact for the other stuff: some M-16's, some KA-Bars, might even be able to get some Claymores and clackers."

Carl nodded, but he didn't have any idea what Lobo was talking about.

"Tell ya what, though. We can't just go humpin' in there like a bunch of grunts." He laughed to himself. "One fucking Cobra and we could just sit back and watch it on TV. Hell, we could just walk in if we wanted and count the KBHs."

"The K-B-Hs?"

"Killed by helicopter."

Lobo drained his beer and stood up. Carl tried to guzzle the remainder of his but couldn't get it all down in one swallow.

"Let's fix up your Jeep here, man, then get inside," Lobo said, picking up the door panel.

Carl had not been sure he couldn't either talk Claire out of the scheme or just take her, even if by force, and leave. But first he got mad. Claire embellished the story, adding a multiple rape and graphic depictions of Rabbit's murder. And Carl felt the anger rising in him as she spoke. He told himself that it was sensible, it was just, to revenge such actions. Yet it wasn't anger that changed his mind, not justice or revenge. Not at root. He didn't want to be alone; he didn't want to leave Lobo and Susie. He would help because he wanted them to be his friends.

He presented Claire with certain unalterable conditions. First, he would go. Second, he would also go with Lobo to buy the guns. Third, they would leave $1,000 in Corpus Christi so they wouldn't come back with no money at all.

Reluctantly, after some argument, Claire agreed to all three. In a way she was very proud of him. Her baby brother was no kid. When Carl and Lobo started outside to get the money, Claire kissed her brother spontaneously, whispering into his ear, "I love you." But there was another feeling; below the love and the fresh respect, Claire was afraid.

After Claire had told Lobo they all were going, a clear change came over him. As if some primordial instinct had gripped him. The navy blue baseball cap with the jump wings on the front appeared. He took to squatting on his haunches instead of sitting in a chair. His eyes roamed the room furtively. When a traffic helicopter flew near the apartment, Lobo looked up in the direction of its sound with an almost wistful look in his eyes. His choppy speech became peppered with boonie rat slang, even to once calling Carl a "cherry boonie rat." The others tried to pick up his mood, his rhythm, all but Susie, who seemed a little frightened by Lobo's changes. She had lived with him off and on for a long time. She made it a point to touch him as much as possible—a hand placed gently on a shoulder, fingers run through hair, arm around his waist.

"If I can get a pound of Charlie-Four and some caps . . ." Lobo would say, and Susie would always make him stop and translate. "C-Four plastic explosive and blasting caps," Lobo would tell her. She made him explain that a clacker was a firing device for a Claymore mine and that a Claymore was charged with C-4 and exploded out hundreds of steel ball bearings. She wanted everybody to hear what those cute little military words really meant. She would go anywhere Lobo wanted to take her, into hell and out if he wanted, but she wanted there to be no doubts about the destination. If Lobo wanted to do this crazy thing out of some sense of loyalty to Rabbit, then so be it. She would go with him. Rabbit wasn't that important, she believed, but Lobo was. And he was Lobo's best friend. What she didn't like was the feeling that Claire had started it all, that Lobo would have let it go if Claire hadn't talked him into it with an obviously fantasized sob story. Maybe it had been bad in Mexico, but if it had been so bad, how had she walked out of it? But you didn't argue with Lobo. Her last hope, that Carl would refuse the money or somehow be able to talk them out of it, died that morning when Carl joined in, apparently with a willing excitement. She should have tried to talk to him first.

Now, in two hours, Carl and Lobo were leaving for Refugio. It was the day before New Year's Eve. Some celebration. On New Year's Day, they all would be on the road to Mexico.

She looked over at Carl, who sat alone on the couch, drinking beer. He had been in the apartment just over twenty-four hours, coming in like a kid fresh out of high school with maybe enough experience to know the difference between tobacco and marijuana, maybe. Now there he sat with a red bandanna tied around his head, his cowboy boots propped on the coffee table, drinking beer with one hand and sucking on a joint in the other. He was wearing Lobo's old field jacket—at least three sizes too big, with the sergeant stripes, the airborne and ranger patches, the cloth jump wings and combat infantryman's badge all ripped off, only their shadows remaining. He was much too good-looking to look so silly, Susie thought.

When Lobo was ready to go, he walked over to Carl and slapped his boots. "Let's fuckin' dee-dee mau, man."

Carl stood up and took another toke on the joint; then he handed it to Claire. Susie put her arms around Lobo and kissed him. Claire hugged Carl.

"You goddamn well better take care of my brother," Claire told Lobo.

With a smile Lobo said, "Hell, the kid's going to take care of me!"

With a six-pack of beer under his arm, Lobo blew a kiss to Claire and Susie, then followed Carl out the door.

Claire turned to Susie and shrugged. Susie said, "I feel like a war bride or something."

"Boys will be boys," Claire said, finishing the joint Carl had left with her.

twelve

Lobo drove the Jeep. He said he was more familiar with the roads. Because they both had been drinking beer and there was a dime bag of grass in the glove compartment, plus a half dozen rolled joints in Lobo's shirt pocket, they kept to the back roads and obeyed the traffic laws. They crossed Corpus Christi Bay, through Portland, turned in Gregory up to Taft, then onto 136 toward Copano Bay without saying much of anything to each other.

Lobo passed a joint, and Carl took it, although he took shallow puffs, wanting to keep his head clear. He was nervous, but it was clouded by an anticipatory feeling. He waited for Lobo to say something, to get a conversation started, but for the first half hour he had said nothing at all. He played the radio loud, tuned to a cowboy station.

Carl looked at the nothing around them. The land was unbearably flat; an anthill would be a prominent rise. And not many trees. Mesquites and some scrub. Everything was brown and lifeless. A lot of old billboards. Some oil pumps, bobbing like Erector set monsters, sucked up and down in black, oozing puddles. A long-legged white bird—a crane, egret, something—perched on the arm of one of the oil wells and rode it like a teeter-totter.

Carl wanted to ask Lobo what being in Vietnam was like, but he didn't know how Lobo would take it. He wanted to ask him if he had ever knowingly killed anybody. If he had been wounded. He wanted to ask how they were supposed to drive into Mexico with a bunch of guns in the car and then find these bandits or whatever they were and kill them—he could hardly fathom such a possibility—then drive back into Texas and live as if nothing ever happened. And what would they do in the likelihood that one or more of them got hurt or killed?

Lobo drove with his hands at the top of the steering wheel, tapping his fingers in time with the music.

Carl saw a sign saying: "REFUGIO 15 miles." Lobo had not spoken. Once in a while they passed a house. Every one of them had at least one abandoned car in the yard. Carl decided that people took better care of their property in Minnesota. Even houses with an oil well in the yard were still little more than shanties. Carl thought that anyone with an oil well in his yard would have to be rich.

Finally Lobo said something, so obliquely that the sound of his voice startled Carl.

"You probably ought to stay in the car."

"Are we there?"

"Couple of miles. Don't worry, I ain't gonna run out with the money."

"I never thought you were."

"Uh-huh," Lobo said sarcastically. "We'll pick up Jack; then he'll probably be taking us somewhere else. Maybe you ought not do a lot of talking when he gets in the car."

"Sure, no problem."

"Good boy. You'll do all right, kid."

Carl wished Lobo wouldn't call him boy and kid. He decided to tell him. After all, he thought, I'm in this, too, and it's my money. "Why don't you try using my name?"

"Heeey! Just a habit, hell. Didn't mean to offend you."

"That's all right. It just gets on my nerves after a while."

"Like being a cherry in the Nam. Everybody gets it at first, but it feels real good to get rid of. Hey, Carl, you're gonna be okay. I got a feeling."

"Thanks." Carl almost asked him what Vietnam was like, but then Lobo turned down a narrow gravel lane and headed for a house barely visible behind a stand of mesquites.

Claire was blasted on speed. She had been in a cleaning frenzy for the better part of an hour. She had spent ten minutes scrubbing stains off the kitchen table with a sponge and brush.

Susie tried to stay out of the way. Once when she didn't move her feet fast enough, Claire mopped right over them. Finally, seeking sanctuary, Susie jumped up on the kitchen counter, which had already been scrubbed thoroughly, and sat there with her legs dangling off.

"And I go running for the shelter of mother's little helpers," Susie sang. Just watching Claire was making her tired and irritable.

"Is there some point to all this, or what?" Susie asked. "I mean, shit, you'd think the place was up for sale or something."

"I can't stand all this filth!" Claire replied in a burst of words. "How do you guys live this way?" She attacked the coffee table with her sponge and brush. "You could help, you know?"

"Yes, ma'am, at your command, ma'am." Susie jumped down from the counter and saluted, but Claire didn't see her. "What would you have me do?"

"You might try picking up the records before they get walked all over."

Susie saluted again and made some production of scurrying about picking up the record albums off the floor. They were quickly finding the rhythms of life before Rabbit's death in Mexico: Claire going up as Susie was coming down.

"This place is gross," Claire proclaimed.

"Well, I think your old apartment next door is still vacant," Susie replied, tiring of the game of pick up the records.

"Oh, don't be a bitch, Susie."

"Bitch? That's it! You do it, for whatever good it'll do. We're all supposed to hotfoot it down to Mexico because you got some freaked notion of revenging Rabbit." Susie tossed a record on the couch. "Rabbit was a junkie, and he was asking for it. *You* were supposed to stop him, take care of him."

"I tried," Claire said, turning to look at Susie, suddenly regretful and complacent. "I knew it was wrong."

"But you went. And Rabbit got his ass blown off." Susie regretted the statement the moment it flew from her lips.

Claire fell to her knees and bawled. Susie came to her immediately and sat beside her, her arm around Claire's shoulders, stroking her hair with her other hand.

"Hey, shit, I'm sorry. Everybody knows how you felt about

Rabbit. Me and my big mouth, huh? Come on, Claire. Don't cry, Jesus. I'm sorry." Susie tried to raise Claire's face. "Come on, look at me." She put her head on Claire's shoulder. "I'm fucked-up, hey, don't pay any attention to me."

"A big part . . . of me . . . died . . . when they . . . murdered him," Claire said in gasps. "I loved him, Susie."

"Hey, I know you did. We all loved him. You the most, though. We'll fix it, though, won't we?"

"Yeah, we're going to fix it."

"Lobo needed to do this. It's a good idea, Claire. He's been really down since Rabbit . . ."

Claire turned her face and kissed Susie. They hugged each other there on the floor, rocking back and forth like old people wasting away in rocking chairs.

Carl watched Lobo walk up to the house. He was just as contented to wait in the Jeep. A vicious-looking German shepherd flew up and snarled at Carl through the closed window when they stopped. But Lobo got out and said, "Shut the fuck up, Peyote!" The dog bounced around the Jeep and followed Lobo to the porch. Carl didn't believe he would have such control. When Lobo went inside the house, Peyote charged back to the Jeep and barked at Carl's door until a voice from inside the house yelled, "Shut up, Peyote!" The dog yelped once more for effect, then trotted off to the porch to guard the front door. *What the hell am I doing here?* Carl thought. *If I died out here, nobody would ever know.*

Lobo was in the house less than ten minutes. When he came out, a second man followed. He looked a lot like Lobo—tall and muscular, thickly bearded, dressed in cast-off army fatigues. He got into the back seat.

"Jack, Carl." Lobo made his introductions.

Carl turned around and stuck out his hand. Jack shook it quickly, then turned his attention back to Lobo. "Turn left on the road," Jack said, "and I'll direct you from there."

They went to Highway 77 and headed toward Victoria, some forty miles away. It was getting dark. Carl noticed it was getting close to five o'clock. They had been on the road for a few silent minutes when Jack said, "Okay to talk?"

"His money," Lobo answered.

"Okay," Jack went on. "Animal's got only one AK that I know of; you can get all the M-16's and ammo you want and can pay for. I'm sure he's got some Charlie-Four, but I don't know how much. Clackers, of course. I tell ya, the dude's got a fucking arsenal up there. He's got him a couple of M-60's. I seen 'em myself up there. Ammo for it, too. Probably got some M-79's if you want 'em."

"Sounds good," Lobo said, nodding.

"What kinda ball game you guys gonna play?"

"Don't make no difference, does it?" Lobo said.

"Fuck, man, I don't care nohow. But you could leave some real fucked-up people with shit like that."

"Maybe we going back in the boonies . . . get our friends out."

"Shee-it."

"Don't matter."

"Get to Victoria, take the one-seventy-five cutoff, and head echo. Hey, you dudes got any dew?"

Lobo reached into his shirt pocket and handed back a joint. "Far-fuckin'-out, bro."

Jack lit the joint and sucked the smoke deep into his lungs. Grunting, he passed it up to Carl, who waved it off, as did Lobo when offered to him. "Suit yersefs," Jack said with an exhale. "Like old times, huh, man?" Jack sucked in more smoke.

"We didn't have us no Jeeps like this, man," Lobo said. "Goddamn airborne, got us humping rucks through the boonies."

"Yeah, man, I heah ya talking."

Jack sat back in the seat and finished the joint alone. Lobo concentrated on the driving, drinking occasionally from the beer he kept stuck between his legs. They drove in silence for ten minutes.

"Hey, echo off on the one-seven-five," Jack called out when they got near the highway exit.

Carl didn't have any idea what they were talking about, but Lobo turned east on Highway 175.

They followed Jack's directions until they pulled up in front of a large tin building on a side road south of the city of Victoria. A sign over the door said: "SMITH'S AUTO PARTS."

"Animal did his motherfucker over there in the rear, but he

pulled out some good connections, man, I tell ya." Jack opened the door and got out.

"Sit tight," Lobo told Carl, and followed Jack.

It was nearly six o'clock and fully dark. Carl sat in the Jeep, smoking cigarettes and sipping a warm beer, for more than an hour. When Lobo came out, followed by Jack and two other men, they were carrying three large crates and a burlap bag of some weight. Carl sat quietly and tried to be unobtrusive while the crates and sack were loaded into the rear of the Jeep. Then all four men went back inside and came out with another crate and two more gunnysacks. When those were loaded, all four men went back inside. Nobody had said a word.

Twenty more minutes passed before Lobo and Jack came out, alone.

"Got any more of that dew? Fine, fine shit, man." Jack accepted the joint Lobo pulled from his pocket. This time Lobo took hits when Jack passed it up. Carl opened another beer and waved the joint off. He figured they were driving down the highway in his Jeep with who knows how many illegal weapons in the back end; somebody had to keep a straight eye on things.

"What time is it?" Claire asked Susie.

"I don't have a watch."

"About eight, do you think?"

"Probably."

"I wish Lobo said where they were . . . or at least how long it would take, you know?"

"Lobo takes care of business."

"Yeah, but Carl . . ."

"You know, Claire? That brother of yours is no kid. I'll bet he could take care of himself anytime. If he's got a problem, maybe it's the way you mother him . . . or wife him."

"You don't know what you're talking about."

"Hey, don't jump my case."

Claire looked down at her hands on the table. The fingers had just started to tremble. Earlier she had promised herself to cut down on the speed, but it seemed less and less a good idea. She felt chilled.

Susie sat across the table from Claire. She was wearing panties and one of Lobo's oversize olive T-shirts. One leg was bent up with her foot in the chair seat so she could paint her toenails psychedelic orange.

Claire stood up and went into the bedroom.

"Don't go away mad," Susie said without looking up.

"Be right back."

Claire went to Lobo's pill cache and sorted through it until she found the white ones. She took two of them with a drink from the bathroom tap. That's it, she told herself as the water washed them down her throat, no more . . . well, only one a day from now on, just to get right with things, but no more than one. Then she went back and sat across the table from Susie.

After bending over to blow-dry her toes, Susie looked up and said, "That brother of yours gave me a kiss in the bathroom last night and about knocked my drawers off."

"Carl? Carl kissed you?"

"You better believe he kissed me. I tell you, I tingled from one end to the other. It would have been a little inconvenient, but the thought of raping him in the bathtub did cross my mind."

"I can't believe it."

"You see what I mean? You better open your eyes about that guy; he's not some baby brother you can diddle with and forget it."

"You kissed him or he kissed you."

"He kissed me . . . then I kissed him right back. Good stuff."

An image of Carl kissing Susie came into Claire's mind, but it did not even closely correspond with the reality of it. She saw Carl shove Susie against the bathroom wall and stick his tongue into her mouth, his hands pushing under her T-shirt, his crotch bumping furiously against hers.

"I think," Susie went on, "that if you loosened up on him a little, he'd be all right."

"I'm not holding him back," Claire answered without much conviction.

"Then I'm free to have a go at him?"

"No, you're not."

"Aha!"

"Don't 'aha' me. If Carl wants to fuck you, that's his business. But I don't want him getting into it with Lobo. I've seen some of Lobo's leftovers, after you . . . I remember the guy Lobo left in the critical ward. You put Carl between you and Lobo and I'll tear your eyes out—slowly."

"Wow. I think all that speed has cooked your brain."

"Believe me."

"Oh, I believe you." Susie put up her other foot and calmly began painting the toenails. "But I tell you what. If Lobo could have you, he wouldn't give a flying damn what Carl and I do."

"That's a crock."

"Oh, yeah?"

"Is that all? Just 'oh, yeah'?"

"Hey, the only thing that kept Lobo off your bones this whole time has been, was, Rabbit. You were Rabbit's. Lobo respected that. Jesus, are you blind as well as stoned?"

"I don't believe you."

"Okay. Nobody's making you."

"He's never even made half a pass at me. Never."

"Lobo's got his standards. There was always Rabbit there. Besides, you're lying."

"What?"

"You're lying, Claire. Lobo told me."

"He told you?"

"He sure as hell did. I know you two got it on two or three times back when you first showed up here." Susie blew on her toes, then looked up at Claire. Claire tried to look back but couldn't.

"I didn't know you knew."

"Shit. I don't care. I don't own Lobo. Besides, in those days me and him hardly even knew each other. He also told me he never put a hand on you after Rabbit told him he was in love with you."

"I wasn't lying on purpose. I just didn't know Lobo told you."

"Well, he did. Hey, no big thing, you know? I made it with Rabbit a few times myself."

"Yeah, I know."

"So? I made it with Rabbit, you made it with Lobo. Kinda makes us sisters, huh?"

"Lobo still . . ."

"Yeah, he still."

"How do you feel about that?"

"What's this? Psychology one-oh-one? Like I said, I don't own the man. *Nobody* owns Lobo."

"But he thinks he owns you."

"Only because I let him."

Claire's imagination took control. Her head filled with incoherent images and pictures. The speed grabbed her body and stiffened it. She could no longer understand what was being said. Susie was still talking, but Claire was sinking inside herself.

". . . but if Carl wants to, I'm going to let him, or help him, whatever. Lobo can fend for himself, with you if he wants to. Me, I don't care a lot, know what I mean? I mean, Lobo never loved me. It was you, Claire, always you. And now Rabbit's gone, and now you got him talked into this freaking Mexican revenge trip. You wouldn't care if we all got killed, just to satisfy your sense of . . . I don't know what. What are we doing this for anyway? Hey! Claire? . . ."

Claire stared past Susie at the door.

"Well, fuck it anyway," Susie said, and blew on her toes some more.

By eight o'clock Lobo and Carl had left Jack off in Refugio and were on their way back to Corpus. Carl had been waiting until Jack got out to ask Lobo how much he had spent. About $3,000, Lobo told him. "Don't worry, it wasn't a rip-off."

"I don't think anybody would ever try to rip you off," Carl said.

Lobo laughed. "Yeah, you're all right."

Carl looked out the window so Lobo wouldn't see the grin on his face. He felt pretty good about the way things were working out. He felt Lobo really liked him. He wished his friends in Minneapolis could see him now.

"Yeah," Lobo said, verbalizing his thoughts, "we did all right, Carl. We got us three M-16's with a thousand rounds, an AK-47 with five hundred rounds, four Claymores, a pound of Charlie-Four, half a dozen caps, ten pounds of dynamite, and get this . . . this is the real kicker. We got us one brand-new still-in-the-box genu-wine Thumper. And ten grenades."

Carl pulled out two warm beers and handed one to Lobo. "You know," he said, "I know what an M-16 is . . . otherwise?"

"Well, I'll tell you. An AK-47 is a Russian job, a Kalishnikov, one fine motherfucking assault rifle, seven-point-six-two-millimeter semi or full automatic. What else? Claymores? Antipersonnel mines fired with a one-pound charge of Charlie-Four."

"Charlie-Four?"

"C-Four plastic explosive. Versatile shit, man. You can cook with it, clear a jungle with it, or kill with it."

"And what's this genu-wine Thumper?"

"M-79, forty millimeter grenade launcher. You know? Whish, THUMP, BOOOOOM!"

"This is really serious, isn't it?" Carl's imagination could handle the possibilities of a few rifles, maybe even a stick or two of dynamite, but he drew a blank when it came to mines, grenade launchers, and plastic explosives.

"You bet your sweet ass."

Carl felt a tremor run through his muscles. The can shook in his hand, so he moved it to his side out of Lobo's vision. "Far-out," he said with very little conviction.

"There's this guy in the Nam used to juice up and read poems to us right in the boonies, man."

Carl looked over at Lobo, who was looking at the highway and talking, it seemed, just to hear the sound of his voice.

"Guys picking leeches off their balls, trying not to cry, and Swede—'cause he was from Minnesota, like where you're from; his name was Andersen with an *E,* instead of an *O*—pulling on this rotgut in a can he humped everywhere and reading us poetry. Sometimes you could hear him whispering that shit at night. He was the squad's RTO, and sometimes he'd even read that shit right through the PRC-25. One time the colonel's flying around in this Huey, telling us to go kill this, go kill that . . . you know? So Swede he's on the radio, saying 'roger' and that kind of shit; then he starts saying this poem to the colonel. Swede had this low, really deep voice, sounded like what's that guy in that movie *Liberty Valance?*"

"John Wayne?" Carl guessed.

"Nah, that other guy. Tall guy, gray hair, face like the meanest vulture in the valley?"

"Oh, yeah. Lee Marvin."

"Yeah, right. That dude. Swede's got a voice like Lee Marvin. Only kind of an accent, like you guys from Minnesota talk. Say 'out' like it's got two *o*'s.

"Reason I remembered Swede is 'cause you look a lot like him. He had that kind of blond hair like you and was young-looking, even though he must have been the oldest guy in the squad or just about. He was twenty-two, twenty-three, I think. Graduated from college in Minnesota, some small little-ass college in the backwoods."

They drove down the highway at fifty miles an hour in a light mist, just enough moisture to require the windshield wipers. A night bug crashing into the glass left a two-inch-wide two-foot-long yellow streak until the wipers could cut through it. They were in a void except for the short distance penetrated by the headlights.

"That voice would scare the shit out of you, it coming out of this kid's body, this kid's face. Like a ventriloquist. If you didn't know Swede or never heard him say anything, you'd never believe it was him on the radio. He'd keep his mouth shut and save his ass from a lot of bad trouble sometimes.

"Anyway, the colonel's flying around in this slick, telling us to count the bodies, and Swede's saying 'roger.' Then the colonel says to tell the L-T that we're doing a fine job down there in the boonies and mother country is proud of her boys.

"I'm sitting there five feet from Swede, pulling leeches off my ass, and I start laughing at this mother country fucking bullshit, and I say to Swede to tell the colonel that we done been fucked in the ass royal by mother country.

"Swede takes a pull on his can and keys the radio; then right out of nowhere he says this poem—for the colonel, the gooks, and God and everybody to hear. He says: 'If in some smothering dreams, you too could pace/ Behind the wagon that we flung him in,/ And watch the white eyes writhing in his face,/ His hanging face, like a devil's sick of sin,/ If you could hear, at every jolt, the blood/ Come gargling from the froth-corrupted lungs/ Bitter as the cud/ Of vile, incurable sores on innocent tongues,—/ My friend, you would not tell with such high zest/ To children ardent for some desperate glory,/ The old Lie: *Dulce et decorum est/ Pro patria mori.*'

"That last part's in Latin. It means, 'Sweet and proper it is to die for the fatherland.' Later I asked Swede what that poem was and he told me it was by this World War One grunt named Wilfred Owen. I looked it up and memorized the motherfucker.

"Can you dig it? I mean, I figured—you had to hear that voice low like that over the radio—that any minute we'd have a company of Charlies come out of the jungle throwing down their AKs and giving up. Hell, I was ready to give it up.

"But Jee-sus X. The colonel's voice comes back through the speaker; he's yelling, 'What's your name and rank, soldier.' That shit goes on, and Swede just grins and turns up the squelch. No more colonel.

"That got to be the most famous poem in I Corps. You had black-ass jarheads never got through the tenth grade running around trying to get 'that gotdamn Willie Owen pome.' Guys blasted on dew and pills saying *'Dulce et decorum est'* and laughing their heads off. Rumor got out that Willie Owen was a Spec-4 in the one-oh-one. Seems there was this boonie rat named William Owen in the Hundred and First Airborne, and guys started thinking he wrote it. Guys buying him all kinds of drinks and sharing their dew with him. Owen got to where he even tried his hand at writing some poetry, which is when they got onto his case. He couldn't write for shit.

"Goddamn Swede. He ate it up. A man needs to be famous for something, especially when you're about to get your ass blown off."

When Lobo dropped his empty beer can to the floor, Carl opened another for him. It was the last beer. He wanted to say something but couldn't think of anything. Lobo took a deep swig of Lone Star.

"You want to know what happened to Swede?" Lobo asked, glancing over at Carl, then quickly back to the road.

"Yeah," Carl said with interest.

"All that poetry stuff went to his head. He just wouldn't drop it, no matter what. One night he's on an LP—a listening post—with two other guys, and he's saying poems into the PRC-25; just whispering 'em, you know, but loud enough. Charlie dropped a B-40 rocket right in their hole: BAM!" Lobo threw up his hands, then dropped them back to the wheel. "Fucked up all three of those guys so bad we couldn't find nothing to put in bags but parts."

"I knew that was going to happen," Carl said. "I just knew it."

"But he sure died famous."

thirteen

Stoney never showed up again. Nobody but Carl seemed surprised. Carl had thought Stoney was going to Mexico with them. Now there were four.

Lobo took the grenade launcher out of its box and spent some hours cleaning the grease from it. After that he took apart each of the M-16's and the AK-47 to inspect them. When he added his own CAR-15 and forty-five pistol to the other weapons lined up on the living room floor, it looked quite impressive to the others. Maybe even sobering. Lobo added a Buck hunting knife, two Ka-Bar combat knives, and a pair of binoculars to the arsenal.

He spent all of New Year's Eve day working on the weapons. Carl, Claire, and Susie ran various errands under his direction. Carl washed the Jeep and changed the oil and filter. Claire and Susie went into Corpus to a sporting goods store and bought nearly $1,000 worth of camping equipment. Then they shopped for food.

Lobo did not intend to use the camping gear for that purpose; they would, he planned, be in and out of Mexico within twenty-four hours. The tents would be used to disguise the weapons, the backpacks would carry the ammunition, and the C-4 explosive would be hidden inside a gutted camp stove.

They would take none of it out of Mexico with them. When it was finished, Lobo planned to take all the weapons and gear and burn it.

Carl, Lobo said, looked all right, but Susie would have to do something about her stringy hair. They all would dress like college kids on holiday. Even Lobo planned to get his hair cut and trim his beard.

"If we try to cross looking like a bunch of hippie dopers," he explained, "they'll tear through everything in the Jeep. We're going to be four of the nicest fucking college kids you've ever seen, just going down to Mexico for a Christmas holiday campout." He looked at Claire and added, "Nobody, but nobody, crosses the border blasted on anything."

They packed the Jeep that night. Claire thought that Lobo looked incredibly handsome dressed in his best pair of blue jeans, a powder blue oxford button-down-collar shirt, and with his hair neatly cut and combed. Although he didn't look like Joe Fraternity. He was too old, and he looked it. Lobo was four years older than both Claire and Susie, who were twenty-one and twenty-two respectively. At least four years, because sometimes he said he was twenty-five and sometimes twenty-six. If Claire had stopped to figure it out, she would have realized he was probably older than that by a year or two. He was in Vietnam from early 1966 to March 1967, and she knew he was a senior in college the year he went into the army. If he was in the army at least three years, and since he was discharged in March 1967, that meant he would have been around twenty-one in 1964. Claire watched him loading the camping gear into the back of the Jeep and thought that whatever age he wanted to be, he was too old to be a college student. Maybe if he shaved off the beard, she wondered.

Susie had once peeked at Lobo's driver's license. Only she, and Rabbit, had known that Lobo's name was James Earl Marlar and that he was born on January 10, 1942. In fact, only Lobo and Rabbit had known, among that group of communal transients, that Susie was two years younger than she claimed, and that her name was Susan Lear Kraft—Rabbit had named her Creamcheese.

Susie was banished to the shower to wash her hair. Then Claire was supposed to "do something with it," Lobo ordered. Carl packed the ammunition on the bed.

When Susie came out of the shower, her hair hanging wet and limp over her forehead and down to her shoulders—shoulders bare above the towel wrapped around her—she crept up behind Carl and threw her hands over his eyes. "Guess who?" she said playfully. Carl, holding a carton of 5.56 mm shells in his hands, could feel her body pressed into his back. "Che Guevara," he said.

"Che Guevara feels like this?" Susie asked in a husky voice, pushing herself closer to him.

"Well, I suppose not," Carl said teasingly. He dropped the shells on the bed and felt her fingers with his. "How many guesses do I get?"

"Take all the time you need," Susie said, pushing closer still.

"It may take hours." He could feel her hips moving very slowly, tentatively, against his.

"You can have the rest of 1970," she said. "That's about two hours."

Carl could feel the dampness of the towel against his shirt. He wanted to turn around and make love to her right there on the floor. He had a terrible erection. He wanted her to move her hands down there.

Suddenly she moved her hands away from his eyes and leaned over his shoulder to peck his cheek quickly with her lips. Then she turned around and sat on the edge of the bed, her legs stretching out in front of her forever. Desperately needing to occupy his hands, Carl picked up the shell carton and started packing it on top of others in one of the backpacks. "I knew it was you all the time," he said, feeling immediately like an idiot.

"What was it that gave me away?"

"Truthfully, or you want a good story?"

"Both."

"The truth, the smell of your fingers. I've got this thing about the way different women smell, their skin, I mean."

"Oh? You've sampled widely, I suppose."

Carl blushed.

"You may have Claire fooled, but not me."

"What do you mean?"

"You know what I mean."

Carl couldn't look at her and still breathe, so he focused his attention on the packing.

"That I've had a lot of experience with women?" he said. "I haven't . . . not very much." Carl wondered what she would say if he told her the only woman he had actually gone all the way with was his sister. How could somebody say a thing like that?

Susie fiddled around with her towel, tucking in the corner and tugging at the lower edge of it. It was not a well-disguised attempt to get Carl to look at her.

"Helluva way to spend New Year's Eve, don't you think?" she said, distractedly opening a carton of shells.

Carl took the shell box and closed the lid, then tried to stuff it into the pack.

"It's all the same to me. I've never been to a New Year's Eve party in my life. Usually I just watched the stuff on TV."

"You're kidding."

"No, I'm not. It just never worked out, I guess."

"Well, we're going to fix that tonight. Tonight you're going to have a New Year's Eve party."

"I think Lobo wants to leave pretty early in the morning. I heard him say we'd go to bed early."

"Who cares what Lobo says? Besides, I didn't say we *wouldn't* go to bed early, did I?" Susie stood up next to Carl and put her hand on his shoulder. "I've even got a present for you."

"Oh, yeah?" Carl turned his head to look at her.

"This," Susie said, smiling; then she opened the towel.

Carl got only a glimpse of her, for she quickly closed the towel and with a light giggle ran back into the bathroom and closed the door. Carl didn't move; not a muscle, not even his eyelids blinked, as if he had been turned into a pillar of salt.

Outside, Lobo and Claire finished packing the Jeep with everything but the ammunition Carl had on the bed. Lobo had climbed up inside the rear and meticulously stacked the items Claire handed him. When the last piece was properly placed, Lobo crawled over into the back seat, where Claire had gone to make sure there was nothing left there. When he came over the seat, they were sitting side by side, Claire on her knees and Lobo sitting.

"I think that's it, except for the stuff Carl's finishing," Claire said. It was dark inside the Jeep, only the glow from a lamp across the street illuminating their faces.

"They go in the very back. I'll put them in from the rear door."

When he reached for the door handle to get out, Claire put her hand on his and stopped him.

"Lobo," she said softly. "Thank you."

"What for?" he asked, looking back at her.

"For this. For all this." She had not taken her hand away. "For Rabbit."

"Forget it. I loved him like a brother. This isn't just for you, you know." He paused for a minute and looked into her eyes. "This feels good," he said finally.

"I feel good, too."

Lobo seemed to be waiting for her to move her hand away from his. But neither her hand nor her eyes moved.

"I want you tonight," Claire said in a whisper, a deep, throaty, breathless whisper.

"Shit," Lobo said, but with the tone a man might use when he'd just been shot in the chest, like a final exclamation of resignation to his fate.

Claire leaned forward and kissed him. Lobo moved his hand out from under hers and put it behind her head, forcing her mouth hard against his. Claire dug her fingers into his shoulder.

They were like that when Carl came out bringing the four loaded backpacks. He couldn't see them until he was at the rear door. His stomach lurched up into his throat, and his chest felt cut to the bone. He barely stifled a scream. They did not see him. Carl put the packs down behind the Jeep and walked back toward the house. He was hyperventilating by the time he got on the porch.

He walked straight through the living room, through the bedroom, and into the bathroom without knocking. Susie sat on the toilet seat, fighting with the immense tangles in her hair. She looked up surprised just as Carl lifted her and kissed her. When she was able to pull her mouth away, she said, "Hey, slow down, okay? This is great, but let's just do it a little slower, all right?" Carl wasn't much interested in slow. He led her by the hand into the bedroom and pulled the towel away as he laid her down.

"Boy," Susie said as she helped him pull down his pants, "something sure lit your fire."

When Lobo got out of the Jeep and went around to close the rear door, he saw the packs lying on the ground. "Come here," he told Claire. Claire walked around the other side and nearly stumbled over one of them. "Carl?" she said, knowing the answer.

"Well?" Lobo questioned, waiting for Claire to say something.

"I don't know. I guess he saw us."

"Well, I mean, was he just being polite, or is he pissed?"

"He might be pissed. He's got a pretty wide jealous streak."

"We don't need this now," Lobo said angrily, picking up the packs one at a time and loading them. "What's the deal with you two?"

"No deal," Claire's lie apparent. "I'd better go talk to him."

"You do that. I'll finish this."

Claire's nerves sparked as she walked toward the house. She reached into her pocket and took a pill from a vial and swallowed it dry.

Lobo finished loading the Jeep, then leaned against the front fender waiting for something, anything to happen. In less than five minutes Claire returned. She was smiling. She walked directly up to Lobo, threw her arms around his neck, and kissed him.

"Problem solved, all around," she said, smiling again.

"Oh, yeah?"

"He and Susie are in there fucking their heads off." Claire almost laughed.

"Oh, yeah?"

"Does that bother you?"

"I don't tell her what to do."

"And I don't tell Carl. Problem solved." She pushed herself against him, and they kissed again.

"Don't count on it," Lobo said when she let go of him.

But the switch had been made. That night Carl and Susie slept in the bed; Claire and Lobo slept in the living room on the sofa bed. Only once, when Claire tiptoed through the bedroom on her way to the bathroom and saw Carl lying on his back with Susie's arm draped possessively over his chest, her hair spread out over his shoulder, did she feel a little sick, the nausea of jealousy. She shook it from her mind, took some Seconal to help her sleep, and didn't look at them on her way back to the living room.

The morning of the first day of 1971 they awakened one at a time, starting with Lobo at six-thirty. His movements awakened Claire, and her trip to the bathroom awakened Carl. When he moved out from under Susie's shoulder, she awakened. By six forty-five they all were up and dressing.

There seemed very little urgency to Carl. Did none of them realize where they were going, what they were going to do? They might as well have been leaving for an afternoon picnic. Carl thought they ought to do things like check the stove, turn off all the electrical appliances, at least unplug the stereo. Who would pick up their mail? Oh, well, it was none of his business. But when he asked Lobo if he wanted the thermostat turned off, Lobo answered, "Why? We'll be back in three or four days. Can't let the plants freeze."

It was obvious Lobo would drive. He didn't wait to ask but got behind the driver's seat. He still had the keys from the night before. The other seating arrangements were quickly determined when Claire got into the front seat next to Lobo.

Susie had been clinging to Carl all morning. When they got into the back seat, Susie leaned the back of her head against Carl's shoulder and propped her feet on the opposite window ledge. Lobo looked past them when he turned around to back out. When they were on the street and under way, Claire put her arm across the seat back and let her hand rest possessively on Lobo's shoulder. So Carl kissed Susie's hair, producing a soft, pleasant moan from her.

Lobo did not bother to explain their route, but he had decided to stay in Texas for as long as possible before crossing the border. He would cut straight across to Laredo, then north through Eagle Pass, through Del Rio, then the long haul through the middle of nowhere to El Paso. They would cross the border there, cutting straight south on Mexico 45 to the Buenaventura cutoff. They would be on the road for 700 miles before crossing the border. Lobo was going to drive it in one shot before sleeping in El Paso.

They had been on the road only half an hour when Claire took two Seconals to balance out the speed she took that morning, and soon her head fell over into Lobo's lap, where she slept. Lobo refused all offers of beer, marijuana, or cocaine. He did take two Dexedrines.

In spite of his sharing a couple of joints with Susie, Carl's mind was revved up as fast as the whine of the Jeep's knobby tires. Susie sang along with the radio.

College kids going camping, my ass, Carl thought. We're all going straight to hell! He looked straight ahead out the windshield, the weight of Susie's head on his arm becoming a burden, and in his mind he could see what he had never seen before: a desert in Mexico, a landscape filled with cacti and bandits behind every rock, adobe huts with naked children playing in front. At the end of the highway he could see himself like a wild man running loose in the dirt with his rifle roaring, John Wayne storming Iwo Jima, only Mexican babies fell dead.

When finally he closed his eyes, the body appearing was his own. Claire knelt by him, crying hysterically and saying how sorry she was. The dead man had a smile on his face.

part three

mexico

fourteen

They reached El Paso sometime after midnight on Saturday, the second day of January. Carl and Susie were asleep, curled up around each other on the back seat. Claire was awake, talking with Lobo to keep him from falling asleep. Lobo didn't think it would be too smart to cross the border at one o'clock in the morning, so he drove them to a motel near Fort Bliss. He sent Claire to register, and she got one room.

"We'll cross at noon," Lobo told them when they settled into the room. "It's Saturday, it'll be crowded at the bridge, and they won't feel much like fucking around with us. Hell, nobody cares what you take in, just what you bring back—and we ain't bringing nothing back."

There were two double beds in a nondescript room. There was a speaker on the wall with knobs beneath it. Susie fiddled around with the controls, trying to find a radio station playing something besides Tex-Mex music and screaming Del Rio radio preachers.

"Let's sleep," Lobo said, pushing her hand out of the way and turning off the radio. "This will probably be it until we come back tomorrow."

"Yes, sir, general," Susie replied sarcastically.

Lobo glared at her, then went into the bathroom.

"Do you believe this military trip he's on?" Susie whispered to the others. "Put a gun in a little boy's hand and watch out."

Carl had never fully awakened after they got out of the Jeep. All he wanted to do was get into one of the beds, but he wondered if he should wait to see how they were divided up.

Claire opened a pill bottle and took two Seconals to help her get to sleep. She was so wound up, so anticipatory that she wasn't sure even the downers would knock her out.

Susie decided for everyone. She took Carl's hand and led him to the nearest bed. "We'll take this one," she told Claire. Then she unsnapped her jeans and started pushing them down.

Carl and Claire found themselves standing a few feet apart with Susie undressing between them. Claire looked at him and without speaking tried to get him to understand that no matter what it might feel like, everything was working out the way it had to. She shrugged her shoulders, then turned around and started unbuttoning her blouse. Carl walked over and turned out the light. The toilet flushed. When Carl's eyes adjusted to the darkness, he made his way to the bed. Susie had already crawled under the covers. Claire finished undressing and got into the other bed. Carl watched until she was covered, then took off his clothes. Susie did not wait for him to settle down before rolling over and putting her hand on his crotch. Lobo came out of the bathroom, surveyed the situation, then sat on the end of the bed Claire was in and started unlacing his black boots. Before Lobo finished undressing, Claire rolled out of the bed and went into the bathroom. Susie was climbing on top of Carl then, and Carl could see Claire go past. He tried to lose himself in Susie's hair.

Susie began to moan and make puffing, animalistic noises as she worked Carl inside her and moved her hips in tight circles. Carl was completely embarrassed and self-conscious. The bedsprings squeaked. He turned his head to the side and could see the outline of Lobo's back. Lobo sat on the side of the bed, facing the wall. Claire had not come back. "Come on, baby," Susie whispered into his ear. Carl closed his eyes and tried to concentrate on the feeling. "Oh, baby, come on . . . come on," Susie said louder. She hovered over him in a push-up position, her breasts bouncing off his chest as she twisted herself on him. The blanket fell back, exposing them from the hips upward.

Carl looked over at Lobo again. Lobo was standing, putting on his jeans, then slipping his shirt over his head.

This is crazy, Carl said to himself. Crazy!

"God *damn*," Lobo muttered in a low voice; then he walked around the ends of the beds and toward the door.

Carl saw Susie turn her head to watch him go. In the loudest voice yet, she cried out, "Ohhh, ohhh . . . that's sooo goooood!"

Lobo slammed the door when he went out. Susie slowed down. Carl felt himself wilting out of her. Susie let herself down until she lay on his chest, her head buried in the pillow next to his head. Carl saw light from the bathroom door as Claire came out. He could see her looking for Lobo, but not looking directly at them. Susie breathed heavily into his ear, and her chest heaved against his. He could feel the beating of her heart.

Claire picked up her clothes off the floor and went back into the bathroom.

Susie rolled off Carl and lay on her back next to him, one arm lying over her face. Her breasts sparkled with sweat.

In a minute Claire came out of the bathroom and walked across the room and out the door, closing it quietly behind her. Carl felt like crying: a combination of anger, frustration, hatred, fear, and embarrassment—acute, desperate embarrassment.

"Too tired?" he heard Susie ask.

"Guess so," he said, pulling up the blanket to cover them.

"Hey, I can dig it. Boy, though, it was great for me."

Why? Carl wanted to ask. Because Lobo was watching you?

"Good," he said, turning over with his back to her. At that moment he didn't like her very much at all.

Claire could see Lobo sitting in the Jeep, the ember from a cigarette rising and falling reflected in the windshield. She went around to the other side and got in.

"I apologize for my brother," she said.

Lobo sucked deeply on the cigarette and let the ash fall into his lap. "Wasn't him."

Claire took the pack off the dash and lit one for herself. Her face reflected back orange from the windshield when the match flared. "I think she's good for Carl, though. At least, right now. Maybe not later, but now it's okay for him, takes his mind off things, and he needs that now."

Lobo didn't answer.

"You want to tell me what's wrong?" Claire asked.

"Tell you what, if I ever do find out what's wrong with me, it'll probably be the thing gone wrong with you as well, with all of us in this fucked-up place; and I'm pretty sure that whatever it is gone wrong, it'll be sad, and it'll leave us totally fucked-up and hopeless in the face of it."

"I was talking about what's wrong with you right now, right here; not your cosmic version of the fate of man."

"Same difference."

She decided not to ask him to start the engine so they could run the heater. It was only chilly, not really cold. But she didn't have any shoes on, and her toes felt frozen. She noticed that Lobo was also barefooted. He probably didn't have the key anyway.

"Are we going to be all right tomorrow . . . or is it tonight?"

"Do you mean are we going to die?"

"Not that exactly. I wasn't thinking about that."

"What were you thinking about?" Lobo asked; he had not looked at her once. He opened the wing vent and flicked the cigarette out, then reached up and took another from the pack. Claire waited until he lit it before answering.

"I guess I was wondering if we're crazy, if I'm crazy . . . I guess I want you to tell me this is the right thing to do."

"Which 'this'? Me and you? Susie and your brother in there making it? Going after Rabbit's killers? Sitting in a cold Jeep in a motel parking lot in El Paso at one-thirty in the fucking morning on New Year's Day—pardon me, it is now the day after."

"Going into Mexico," Claire answered quietly.

"Oh, that. Scared?"

"Oddly, no."

"Then you're crazy."

"Aren't you?"

"Crazy or scared?"

"Either."

"Both. Always."

It was the most personal revelation Lobo had ever made to her. Claire wanted to kiss him but decided not to. He didn't seem receptive.

He went on after a moment. "Before I ever went into action the first time, I thought I'd like it, glory in it, love it, relish it, even need it. I thought I could be the best killer the army had. I thought I was fearless. They called me Lobo because I was quiet and cunning and vicious, deadly, like a wolf. After a couple of fire fights they started calling me El Lobo. *The* Wolf. Because I was the best. I thought war was created for me, and I was right about everything. Almost everything. I was still scared all the time. You know what scares me?"

Claire shook her head, but Lobo didn't see her or need to. His face glowed when he puffed on the cigarette.

"That I was right about everything else. That scared me, because I loved it. I loved it so much I couldn't even stand being back in base camps. They made me wiggy. Only time I felt like I belonged was in the boonies. The original boonie rat. I even loved the smell of my own fear, the getting-it-out-in-the-open smell of my own goddamned fear. Although I never knew then what I was afraid of. It wasn't dying. It wasn't getting hurt.

"You know, I never got hurt. Not a bullet touched this body. Not a piece of shrapnel, nothing. Just leeches and rot. The enemy couldn't touch me. But I sure fucked up a mess of them.

"You know, guys used to glue themselves to my ass, trying to stay alive out there. They said I was charmed. They said I had the mojo working for me. During mortars guys'd be clawing to crawl into the same hole with me. 'Hey,' they'd say, 'El Lobo got the mojo on his side.' Crazy motherfuckers would follow me anywhere. 'Ain't nothin' gon happen to my ass in that dude's shadow, no, sir.' They'd say that.

"Guy over in Bravo who could draw anything made up these cards, like business cards, that size, made out of red paper with a wolf's head drawn very neatly in black ink. He gave them to me. Each card had fancy block letters under the wolf's head; said 'EL LOBO.' I still got a few."

Lobo fished into his back pocket and pulled out a wallet. He took a rectangular red card out of it and handed it to Claire. She held it up to the window so the streetlamp would shine over it.

"He was very good," she said, handing the card back.

Lobo replaced it and put the wallet away. "I left one on each body. If there wasn't a body, I put it on whatever part was left laying around. Sometimes I just stuck one on a tree or left one in some hooch in some ville. Even old Charlie knew better than to fuck with El Lobo. Like those guys in the one-oh-one who used to leave an ace of spades on dead gooks. But that was for a whole fucking division. El Lobo was just El Lobo. One man."

Lobo flicked the cigarette out the wing vent and lit another. Claire sat on her feet to keep them warm.

"Jesus, I loved it," he said.

"Maybe that's why I'm not scared," Claire said after his silence. "Because when we go into Mexico today, I'll be walking in El Lobo's shadow."

"You don't understand diddly, do you?" His voice was angry. "You really don't get it, do you?"

"I guess I don't."

"Damn straight."

"Why don't you tell me what I don't understand?"

"Those guys, those dudes stuck on my shadow to cover their asses . . . most of them are dead. There ain't no barrier in a shadow. Mojo don't spread very thin. It's how you think about it. It's what's in your mind.

"You think you're using me, don't you? Never mind, you don't have to answer that. I know. You think you suckered me into doing this little ball game in the Mexican desert for who knows what fucked-up reason. Maybe you're just still pissed-off. It don't matter. But you're way wrong, lady. It's me using you. Holy Mother of God, I need this! I had to feel this way again. I had to get hold of the stink of my own goddamned fear and strangle it one more time.

"But you, you with this stupid fucking vendetta thing . . . you get people killed. Nam was full of that shit. Dudes out there *believing* in the justice of their cause. Shit, lady, Rabbit don't care nohow. You got this idea it's the right thing to do, it's justice. An eye for an eye. I don't know what all you think.

"But I tell you, there ain't no point in killing a-tall, not one bloody goddamned purpose in it whatsoever, except to conquer your own fear of dying.

"You think this government gave a piss in the wind about any dumb grunt's individual death over there? Shit. Only way they could serve their notion of justice, not to mention cover their financial asses, was to sucker a bunch of dumb kids into *believing* in the cause. The believers are all fucked-up, buried in some garbage bag somewhere. The survivors, the killers, we all came home with no way to go but back. It was the backfire of all time. You see, the believers had to think to maintain that belief, and it's thinking that gets you killed. The killers didn't do any thinking. They just killed everything that moved or might have moved in order to keep from dying from their own fear. You let that kind of emotion go free and you'll never get it locked up again. That's the mojo; terror is the mojo."

Claire didn't know what to say when he stopped suddenly. She didn't even understand most of it. Anything she said might come out wrong and make him angry. His eyes, seen reflected in the furiously glowing ember of his cigarette, were seductively indifferent. While Claire tried to organize her thoughts, Lobo continued; only his voice lowered, and he spoke more slowly.

"If these people are professional bandits, as it appears they are, then it's not inconceivable that one of us gets wasted. I don't think you believe that, Claire. That's why you're not afraid. The good guys always win; the bad guys always die. Your cause is just. God is on your side. Well, let me set your train back on the track: Bad guys are the only winners. The guys who are so afraid of their own death that they are single-mindedly devoted to covering their own ass—they win, they live. The rest? I don't know. Maybe they get some kind of deal in heaven."

He flipped the fourth cigarette out the window and said, "Well, do you reckon they've finished humping themselves so a guy can get a little sleep?" Without waiting for an answer, he opened the door and got out.

Claire sat in stunned, futile silence and watched him go back into the room. She tucked her feet tighter beneath her and hugged her sides. She felt as if she had been pushed over a cliff and could see herself tumbling inexorably toward the black crevice below.

She decided that she didn't believe anything he said. Lobo was magic; that was all she knew and all she needed to know.

She wanted him to touch her, to make love to her, to save her.

But when she crawled into bed next to him, Lobo was on his side, facing the wall and breathing steadily. She reached out cautiously and touched a fingertip to a stranded lock of his black hair, careful not to wake him. At that moment she was agonizingly in love with him.

Carl was sent to the motel café for coffee and sweet rolls. Susie decided to go with him, to help him carry the stuff back. Lobo and Claire sat on the bed with a Mexican road map laid out between them. A light drizzle fell, and the sky was the color of mushroom soup.

"Okay," Lobo was saying, "it looks like about a hundred ten miles to El Sueco."

"That sounds right. Two and a half hours on those roads, which aren't all that bad until we turn west. Then it's a rocky roller coaster."

"Then thirty-five or forty miles west to Flores Magón?"

"Uh-huh. It took over an hour in the truck. But it was an old truck and didn't run that well."

Claire looked up at Lobo now and then. He ignored their conversation in the Jeep. She just wished he would kiss her once or at least smile nicely at her.

"Point to the camp."

"Well, like I said, I can only get it approximate." She pointed to a spot just north of the road between Flores Magón and Buenaventura. "But there. Yes, right there. I don't think there were many roads off the highway, certainly not to the north. There's nothing up there. See"—she pushed her finger over the empty space north of the road—"there's nothing in there clear back to the border except the mountains. Not even a single village."

"Uh-huh," Lobo said, studying the map. "You saw only one road in or out?"

"Yes. That I'm sure of. There's only one road. And it's not even really a road. It's like a trail through some scrub brush and trees running through a kind of valley between two rounded hills."

"How far up the road, or the trail, to the camp?"

"Not far. Less than a mile, I'm sure."

"How far from the camp can a car be seen on the road? Did anyone look out?"

"Not until you're right on the camp. The road bends around a lot, and it's hidden by the hills on both sides. I didn't notice if there was a guard. I don't think so."

"Tell me again precisely how many people you saw total, how many separate structures, how many vehicles?"

Carl and Susie returned while Claire went over everything again. They passed around the coffee and rolls; then Claire picked up where she had left off. Carl stood behind Lobo and looked over his shoulder. Susie plopped down on the other bed and ate a roll.

They spent another twenty minutes with the map; then Lobo told them to "saddle up." He sent Carl to check out while he double-checked the room to ensure they had left nothing but trash behind. Claire and Susie waited outside, protected from the drizzle by the awning over the walkway. Claire was getting shaky. Lobo allowed her only one pill until after they had safely crossed the border. It was eleven-thirty, and he intended to be in Mexican territory by twelve-fifteen. That would put them near the camp by sunset, which would be early if the cloudy weather held.

Susie turned to Claire, looked her directly in the eyes, and said, "Okay, joke's over."

"What joke?"

"We are *not* going to do this."

"Oh, yes, we are."

"Come on." Susie looked a little frightened.

"We're going. You can come or not, as you choose."

"I thought this was just a lark, some big ego trip for Lobo. I mean, when he bought all those guns and bombs, or whatever, I started to wonder. God, Claire. Come on, you're not that crazy!"

"Wanna bet?"

"This is *not* funny."

"You're right about that."

Carl drove up and parked in front of them, leaving the engine running. Lobo came out and locked the door behind him.

"Let's go," he ordered.

"Susie doesn't want to go," Claire said.

When Lobo turned and glared at her, Susie quickly said, "I didn't say that. I just didn't think this was really . . ."

"Nobody has to go," Lobo said sympathetically. "Nobody ever gets shoved out the door."

"Have any of you considered what will happen to us if we get caught?"

Nobody answered.

"They have firing squads in Mexico, for chrissakes!"

"We won't get caught," Claire said.

"Who died and appointed you God?" Susie cried.

Carl watched the strange scene through the smears of the windshield wipers. He couldn't hear a word.

"I don't have time to debate this, nor the inclination. Get in the Jeep," Lobo ordered Claire.

She threw up her arms in disgust, then went to the Jeep. She got into the front seat.

"Okay," Lobo said to Susie, "what's really bugging you?"

"I didn't really believe . . ."

"Fuck that shit." Lobo bluntly stopped her. "You knew."

Susie lowered her head. Lobo reached out and tilted it back with his fingers under her chin.

"Lobo . . . I'm scared to death."

"Good girl. You should be. Don't worry, nothing's going to happen to you. I guarantee it." He smiled at her.

"I thought maybe now, after . . . what happened with Carl and all, I thought you didn't, you wouldn't care about me anymore. Then you wouldn't . . . protect me."

"Hey"—Lobo put his hand on her cheek—"you just stay in my shadow." He laughed.

Susie smiled and threw her arms around him, burying her face in his chest.

"What's going on?" Carl asked Claire.

"It's just me and you, kiddo, just like it's always been," Claire said. Her lips tightened, and she looked out the side window, away from Carl and away from Lobo and Susie, who were walking to the Jeep.

Lobo opened the driver's door and told Carl to move over. Carl didn't know whether to slide across the seat or get out and go to the back with Susie. Claire answered that question by getting out and going to the back seat. Carl slid across and waited for Lobo to get in.

"This looks like two married couples," Carl said with a smile, but no one laughed or smiled with him. "You know? Men in the front seat, women in the back," he tried to explain.

"Yeah, we got it the first time," Susie said.

"What did I do?" Carl said quietly, mostly to himself.

"Everything's cool, brother," Lobo said, then drove out to the highway.

fifteen

Deciding to make the border crossing at noon was based on Lobo's experiences smuggling, in the days when it was Rabbit and him, before Claire started going. Traffic across the short bridge was continual and hectic on a Saturday anyway, and noon seemed to be one of the two peaks; the other came around midnight. The border patrol guards seemed more interested in moving the traffic than harassing a carload of college kids. Hippies they would have stopped anyway. Lobo made one quick stop on their way to the border: to buy a University of Texas—El Paso sticker for the Jeep's rear window.

Lobo told the American guard that their destination was a camping overnighter at Lake de Palos just south of the village of Los Papalotes. The guard looked in the back seat at Claire and Susie, both of whom smiled at him, then patted Lobo on the shoulder, winked, and waved him on. On the Mexican side the guard simply flagged him through.

"Nothing to it," Carl said.

"It's always easy going in," Lobo corrected.

Lobo parked near the Juárez open market and bought two quarts of tequila. Then they left the city and headed south on Highway 45. The first bottle was opened and passed around, each taking a single swallow from the bottle.

Carl was edgy and wanted to talk, but the others seemed content, even determined to be silent while they worked on the tequila. In the rearview mirror Carl could see part of Claire's face and noticed her popping two pills into her mouth the next time the bottle passed. Susie sat directly behind him, and he couldn't see her without turning his head.

The tequila burned his throat and hit his stomach like a ball of fire. After the third pass he could feel it in his head. He wondered if they ought to be getting drunk, although he seemed to be the only one feeling it. He wondered what the others were thinking.

Half an hour out of Juárez they passed through the village of Samalayuca. Carl saw an antique Coke sign hanging in front of an adobe store and gas station. He wondered if they could stop on the way back so he could steal the sign.

He wondered, Is this how it is? Nobody talks? Everybody thinks of whatever they need to think about? Can I stop this? He felt as if the entire North American continent had been ripped from the globe and tilted to the north so he was tumbling head over heels southward into the alien land of Mexico whether he wanted to or not. He couldn't see anything worth looking at, the gray desert and the gray, misty sky blended together a few hundred yards in the distance. He wondered if, or how much really, Lobo was thinking for him. A side glance at Lobo told him nothing. Lobo drove. But Carl felt a reckless power coming from him, coming across the seat almost as a heat wave. In Minnesota such a sky would bring snow. In Mexico it brought mist. The temperature was seventy-five degrees, but cooling as their elevation increased.

He felt passionately aware of everything, except the consequences, which were still only malformed thoughts. The smell of tequila in his nose, the sky and splotchy mist for his eyes, the sweat staining the back of his shirt were as real as anything he had ever known. And all the while he could feel himself falling irresistibly southward down the plane of the continent.

He took the tequila bottle each time it passed.

It had been dark the last time Claire passed along that road. And she had been lying in the back of a pickup truck, with Rabbit's hand sometimes with a will of its own reaching over to touch her, a kind of movement of assurance. Claire did not see outside herself the way Carl did. Her eye turned inside and drifted backward through the ephemeral cloth of time. Even her stomach rolled in cramps. The only smell coming to her brain for translation and explanation was of manure and chickens, the pickup's usual cargo.

The Jeep began emerging from the mist. The low clouds rolled and broke up at the near horizon. It would be a clear night in the mountains. They were past the lake of their stated destination, passing through the town of Villa Ahumada. Released rays of the afternoon sun shot through the clouds and spotlighted sections of the desert.

Claire put her hand on the seat, then surprised herself when Rabbit did not take it. For an instant she was in the Jeep again, but her eyes closed and darkness returned. The pickup jolted her back.

Somewhere along that highway Rabbit had touched her face and looked over at her with his perpetually sad brown eyes. Eyes Claire believed had the ability to see beyond her skin and bones, into the darkest, most inaccessible reaches of her . . . she could not bring herself even to think the word "soul," so she unconsciously translated it to "mind." She could see those eyes. With his mouth closed, Rabbit's face showed only the hump of his nose and his wide eyes. Maybe, she wondered, that's why he seemed to be all eyes. Eyes she had fallen in love with; even when she didn't like him, she loved his eyes.

She revised their fateful stop in the high desert. Rabbit killed all the bandits, and when he and Claire drove away, their bodies littered the sand like so much garbage in a roadside dump.

Carl and Susie had been talking nervously for half an hour, feeling very young and free, and Claire didn't hear a word of it.

It was early twilight when they reached El Sueco. Lobo stopped to fill the gas tank. After that he parked the Jeep at the side of the station and went into the rest room, carrying his duffel bag. When he returned, he had changed clothes; changed into jungle camouflage fatigues, the navy blue baseball cap with the jump wings on the peak, and his black boots. He looked as if he had just walked out of a war zone hidden somewhere behind the gas station.

He tossed the duffel bag onto the back seat between Claire and Susie, then drove out to the highway.

"There are black sweaters and caps in the top there," he said. "You two put them on. Under that there's a shirt and cap for Carl."

Carl looked around to see what his uniform would be. After Susie had taken out the sweaters, she handed the bag to Carl. He took out a top like the one Lobo wore and a black watch cap.

"It's not that cold," Carl said, putting the cap on the dash.

"It's not for the cold," Lobo said patiently. "It's to keep your goddamned blond hair from shining like a beacon."

"Oh," Carl said, taking it off the dash and trying it on.

"What about us?" Claire asked.

"You won't be that close."

He turned west on the road to Flores Magón and Buenaventura. The sun, humped up yellow and shimmering at the horizon, looked as if it were melting into the highway ahead.

"It should be dark by the time we get there," Lobo said to himself.

Claire and Susie pulled the sweaters over their heads without removing their blouses. The evening air was crisp. Venus was out, flickering low on the skyline.

"The glow up there should be the village of Flores Magón," Claire said, flashing back to that other night momentarily, then back to the present. "About five or six miles beyond is where we . . . where they killed Rabbit." She wanted to see it again, if for no other reason than to fuel her anger. "I'll show you the turn."

"How far beyond that to the camp?" Lobo asked.

"I'm not sure. It can't be far, maybe five miles at most. It took us less than ten minutes, maybe fifteen, to get there afterward. I wasn't in much shape to notice."

"We don't have time to tour any memorials."

"I want to stop."

"No."

"Yes," Claire insisted.

Carl and Susie looked back and forth at them.

"And I say no."

"What difference does it make? Five minutes more or less. We *are* going to stop!"

"Don't get fucking hysterical."

"I'm not hysterical. Look, I want to stop. Unless you would like to stop on our way out. I want to tell Rabbit what we're going to do."

"Shit," Lobo muttered, but in such a voice that Claire knew he would stop.

"Thank you," she said.

Lobo shrugged his shoulders, Susie slumped down in the seat, and Carl smiled at Claire. He thought it was a nice gesture.

They drove through Flores Magón and into the nothingness beyond it. The constellations were appearing as the last glow of the sun faded into the desert. The mountains loomed on both sides of the road as shadows.

"Slow down," Claire ordered, sitting up to peer into the darkness between Lobo and Carl. "I think it's right up here. The next road you see to the right has to be it. There's a broken-down wire fence running alongside a shallow ditch. Then the road turns off right where . . . there! Stop!"

Lobo pulled off onto the trail and drove slowly between the mounds on both sides. The trail was deeply carved and rutted; the Jeep bounced over them even at five miles an hour.

"I can't believe you let some asshole drive you up a road like this," Lobo said, twisting the wheel sharply back and forth to avoid the worst of the holes.

"Slow down," Claire said.

"If I go any slower, I'll be stopped."

"There!"

There was nothing ahead at all, not even a wide place in the road. The road continued in a slight curve around a sloping hill.

"Stop right here!"

Lobo stopped and turned off the engine. The confining silence, the cessation of motion struck each of them mute. When Lobo turned off the headlights, it felt as if they had fallen into a deep hole. When Claire slowly opened the door, the dome light did not go on. Lobo had removed the bulb before they left.

Their eyes were adjusting to the dark by the time Claire walked around to the front of the Jeep. There was only a sliver of moon, but the night still had the faint leftover light of day in it. Claire walked to a spot about ten feet in front of the Jeep and stopped. Carl had the urge to get out and be with his sister, but when he put his hand on the door handle, Lobo reached over and touched his shoulder. When Carl looked at him, Lobo shook his head. Carl sat back and watched with the others.

Claire didn't think his blood would be there, having given itself up to the earth and the air. She knelt down and touched the still-warm sand. She couldn't really tell if it had been that precise spot or a place five inches away, or five feet away, or fifteen feet. She would will it to be the spot she touched with her right hand, palm flat on the road.

All they could see from within the Jeep was Claire's shining hair. The slope of her back, covered in the black sweater, did not exist except as a presumption from the location of her hair.

Claire couldn't cry. But she wasn't trying. She tried to reach Rabbit, to have him fuel her anger with justice. She clawed up some dirt and believed she was holding a piece of Rabbit in her hand. Then she whispered to him: "Lobo, Susie, my brother, Carl, and I are here with you, Rabbit. We've come here to find the men who killed you, to kill them. To pay them for leaving you here to die and for taking me away from you, for me to die. But I didn't die. If there is any of your spirit still in this place, watch over us. Guide us. Rabbit . . . I loved you. I lost our baby. That's not true. They ripped our baby out of my belly and left it lying in the dirt on the side of a road. I think he was a boy. I never told you. I'm sorry. What would we have named him? Would you have wanted to call him Jess, after you? Rabbit junior would sound kind of funny, don't you think? If it was a girl, we could have called her Bunny." She giggled to herself.

Lobo touched Carl's shoulder again, and when Carl looked, Lobo said, "Go get her." Carl opened the door and got out.

"Oh, where are you, Rabbit?" she pleaded. "Did they come back and bury you?"

Carl put his hand on her shoulder, and Claire jumped. "Lobo says time to go."

"Carl, come down here." She pulled his hand until he was squatting beside her. "Touch the earth here." She placed his hand where hers had been. "Feel it?"

Carl felt the warm, gritty sand.

"Feel his presence? This is where he fell, where the life flooded out of his body and puddled in the sand. His blood is in this sand."

Carl thought it sounded as if she were mourning the death of Jesus Christ. He wanted to take his hand away. It felt somehow immoral to be rubbing the sand there. He could almost see her as Mary Magdalene weeping at the foot of the cross, touching the blood from Jesus' side as it fell into the dirt.

"Let's go." He pulled her up.

Claire turned around and walked with him back to the Jeep. When Claire got in, she put her dirt-covered hand on Lobo's shoulder and said, "Let's go start a war."

"I don't believe any of this," Susie exclaimed. "We're crazy! I mean, desperately, fucked-up, over-the-line crazy."

"Shut up!" Carl spun his head around and yelled at her.

"Well, pardon my shit," Susie said under her breath.

Carl was suddenly terrified. He thought he was going to vomit all over himself. His mind had fixed on the image of Jesus hanging from the cross, His blood dripping steadily into the sand. Oh, my God, he thought, what am I about to do?

Lobo got the Jeep turned around, and they headed back to the highway. Carl picked the bottle of tequila out of the seat and drank as much of it as he could between the bumps.

Claire had shifted gears. She was ready to go; she was flying. Two more whites slipped down her throat, and her eyes sparked as she leaned on the back of the front seat and watched the road. She was full of directions: slow down, speed up, turn here, go that way, slow down, it's not far now. They drove for ten minutes before Claire spotted the road up to the camp. "Here, here!" she cried happily. "This is it!"

Lobo pulled the Jeep off the highway and stopped, leaving the engine running.

"Okay, people, this is it," he said. Then he asked Claire to tell him again how far they could drive up the road before their lights would become visible.

"Five hundred yards easy," she told him.

Lobo turned up the road and drove slowly until he came to the first sharp curve in the road. Then he stopped, turned off the lights, turned off the engine, and told everybody to be quiet. They waited in the silence for him to say something or do something. He listened. After a minute of that, Susie said in a low, unsure voice, "I'm not going to do this."

Lobo turned and looked at her. "You're in my shadow," he said softly. Then he reached out and touched her cheek.

"No," she whispered, shaking her head, starting to cry. "I can't."

"Not now," Lobo said.

"I can't," she repeated insistently.

"Fuck it," Claire said, pushing Lobo's arm away. "Leave her. We can do it." She took Lobo's arm and moved his hand to her chest, placing his hand over her right breast. She squeezed his hand with her own. "We can do it," she said again.

Carl was in a kind of shock. He looked straight out the windshield and choked down his bile.

"Stay in the Jeep and shut up," Lobo told Susie as he jerked his hand away from Claire's breast. "Come on"—he motioned to Carl—"let's load up."

Carl was in such a condition that doing what he was told was the only thing he could do. He felt completely unable to make any move, even think, on his own volition. He got out and followed Lobo around back. Claire joined them there. Lobo and Carl unwrapped the weapons from the tents, and Claire took the ammunition out of the packs.

"You take the Thumper," Lobo told Claire, handing it to her. Then he handed her the bandolier holding six grenades like big fat bullets.

The M-79 grenade launcher looked something like a stubby sawed-off shotgun with an extra-wide barrel. Claire held it to her shoulder.

"No, not that way," Lobo said. He took it back and showed her how to hold it at her side with her arm gripping the short stock. "You don't have to aim or anything," he said. "Just elevate it about this far, point it in the general direction of the center of the camp, or anywhere you see a group of people together, and pull the trigger. That's all you have to do."

"Okay," Claire said, practicing holding it the way Lobo had.

Lobo tossed an M-16 to Carl, then took out one for himself.

Carl inserted the clip the way Lobo had shown him before. When Lobo gave him ten extra clips, Carl dropped them into the medical bag he carried over his shoulder.

"Carl and I are going up on the ridge to see what this place looks like," Lobo said to Claire. "You stay put and don't make any noise. If any kind of vehicle tries to come down this road, either way, just point that thing straight at it and pull the trigger."

"I will," she said excitedly.

"And settle down. Don't start getting spooky. Calm, okay?"

"Yeah, sure. Just don't stay up there all night."

"We'll be back within an hour. If you want something to do, how about talking to Susie; get her head on straight?"

"Forget Susie, we don't need her."

"We need everybody."

"Okay, okay."

Carl watched a lizard sitting on a rock just a few feet in front of him. He felt envious. In an hour the lizard could just run under a rock and hide. Could he? Could he do this?

"Come on, Ace," Lobo said, pushing Carl ahead of him.

Carl duplicated Lobo like a cow and a calf. When Lobo stopped, Carl put his feet in the same track. When Lobo crouched, he did as well. They moved around the base of the first hill in unison. Then came the climb. Carl carried his M-16 the way Lobo did, by the handle, and used his left hand for balance as they began climbing the ridge. "Don't make a sound," Lobo whispered. Carl nodded. He couldn't have spoken if he had wanted to.

It took them twenty minutes to work their way up to the top of the hill and over to the slope running into the camp. From that vantage point Lobo could see down to the road and more than 300 yards to the camp. The word "camp" had conjured an image of tents to him, and the sight of nearly a half dozen adobe and corrugated tin shacks came as a surprise. It did not have the look of a permanent village, but evidently a lot of time was spent there. Lantern light shone through the windows of half the shacks. In the glow Carl could see two men sitting on the back of a pickup truck, smoking. Lobo had crawled about ten feet ahead of Carl so he could see better. Carl kept his body flat to the ground and raised his head to see. He did not let go of his weapon.

There were five vehicles in the center of the camp. Three of them were parked together, two others separated at either end of the others by at least fifty feet. A man sat out front of one shack, and he seemed to be asleep. He had not moved in five minutes. They were the only people in sight. There were no animals, not even a dog.

Lobo crawled back to Carl and whispered, "I think we were lucky to even find these people here. This looks like just a way station or something. I don't think they live here on a permanent basis. Probably just when they do business out here."

Lucky, Carl thought. Yes, how lucky.

"Come on, let's get back. I can't tell if they're all there. Others might come in at any time."

It took less time to get back because Lobo knew the way. They were at the Jeep fifteen minutes after leaving the top of the ridge.

"Piece of cake," he told Claire, who waited for them by the Jeep. She had not said a word to Susie. "But let's just do it and haul ass."

"Susie says fuck off."

"Don't matter. You keep an eye on that road where we came in. Ace and I are going to put two Claymores in the middle of the road up that way."

Ace, that's me, Carl realized. Ace. He liked it. Now he had a name, too. This is a war, he thought. I'm in a war.

"Come on." Lobo pulled on his shirt sleeve. "We got to hustle."

Carl slung his M-16 and took one of the Claymore mines. Claire sat on the Jeep's rear bumper with the Thumper aimed down the road.

Lobo and Carl walked 100 yards up the road to the place where the hills closed in so tightly that there was no way to keep from heading a vehicle directly down the center.

Carl watched Lobo dig in the mines and arm them. Maybe, he thought, this is all we have to do. If we just mine the road, we're bound to get them driving out sooner or later. We can just go out on the highway and wait for the bang.

"Come on, Ace, get your hands dirty."

Carl got down on his knees and helped Lobo cover the mines.

"This is one fine fucking operation, Ace, let me tell you," Lobo said, turning and smiling at Carl so that his teeth caught the little light and stood out as if they were painted. Carl thought of his hair and pulled the cap down tighter.

"You scared?" Lobo asked when they were walking back.

"Can't you smell it?" Carl said, the first words he had spoken since they left for the ridge.

"You're gonna make it, Ace."

Carl laughed faintly.

sixteen

Lobo told Claire to keep the Thumper, and he gave her one of the pistols. She managed to jam the pistol barrel into her back pocket. He gave her two extra clips, which she put into her front pockets.

Their eyes had adjusted well enough to the darkness that they could see the area around them fairly clearly. Except there was nothing to see. Just sand and dirt, hills, some scrub brush and rocks.

Carl took one of the forty-fives and stuck it inside his belt, then put two extra clips into his pocket. He didn't want to chance mixing them up with the M-16 clips in his medical bag, regardless of the fact they were not similar in size.

Lobo told them he was going to leave the Jeep keys in the ignition on the off chance whoever might be carrying them got hit.

Claire pulled her hair back and stuffed it beneath a black watch cap. Carl squatted near the front of the Jeep, his eyes on the road ahead, the M-16 held in front of him for support: the pose of the universal soldier. He heard some commotion at the Jeep and looked back to see Lobo pulling Susie out. He didn't want to watch and turned his gaze back down the dark road where the two Claymores lay embedded in the sand.

Carl didn't know how he felt about Susie then. He preferred not to think about her at all. Or think about anyone. He spent his efforts trying to imagine himself a soldier, a warrior, and that the desert he saw was a war zone. It was the only way it made sense to him, the only way he could do what they were about to do. Susie's fears revealed his own, and he didn't want to see them. But he hated himself for ignoring her. He gripped the M-16 so tightly that his knuckles turned white. Was he in love with Susie? He didn't know, he didn't want to know.

Lobo had pulled Susie to the back of the Jeep and was showing her how to load and fire the Thumper. Claire gladly relinquished the grenade launcher in favor of the third M-16. She didn't want to be in the background, lobbing grenades into the camp. She needed to be up front, with Carl and Lobo, seeing the effects of her firing.

"I can't *do* this," Susie pleaded when Lobo shoved the Thumper into her chest so she had to hold it.

"It's not a point we're going to debate," Lobo told her. He took the bandolier from Claire and draped it over Susie's head and shoulder. "Just choose your targets well because there's only six grenades."

"Don't make me do this," she begged.

"I need you, Susie. Somebody has to be up there on the ridge, scaring the piss out of them. That's all you have to do, just scare them to death."

"But *I'm* scared to death!"

"You're fine, baby. Just follow my shadow."

"Would you shut up with that goddamn shadow business!"

Lobo leaned his face into Susie's and spit out the words: "Fuck this up, and I'll shoot your ass myself. Okay?"

Carl stood slowly and walked back to the Jeep, holding the M-16 at rest. He stopped behind Lobo and touched his shoulder. Lobo turned around. "Just leave her."

"Who asked you?"

"Nobody had to ask me. Look, what the hell. Just leave her here."

"What's this? Some goddamn mini-rebellion?"

Susie walked around Lobo and stood next to Carl, as if pulled to his protection. She put her hand on his arm, and Carl felt his chest swelling.

Lobo took two steps closer, until he and Carl were only a breath apart. Carl's grip tightened on the M-16, but he didn't know what he'd do if Lobo tried something. "What's the point?"

Carl asked, unwilling to let his eyes move away from Lobo's eyes.

"The point is, I say she goes."

As if a wind had blown between them, Claire pushed her way into the center of the three of them and jerked Susie away from Carl. "God damn it, Lobo, let it lay. Tell her to walk home or something. But just let's get this done." Claire turned around and jerked the Thumper out of Susie's hands, then ripped the bandolier from her shoulder. "I'll take the goddamn thing!" Claire threw the bandolier over her head and slung the M-16 so she could carry the M-79.

Susie ran to the Jeep and got into the back seat.

Shoving past Carl, Lobo started climbing the hill without a word. Carl waited for Claire to start; then he followed her. As he passed the Jeep, Carl was the only one to look back at Susie. He blew her a kiss. It made him feel extremely brave, even though he was on the verge of throwing up the tequila that still sloshed around in his belly. He was glad Susie had been looking when he blew the kiss.

Carl and Lobo crouched together at the top of the final ridge before the camp. Claire sat in the dirt a few feet behind them, the Thumper lying across her lap. The scene below was basically unchanged. The two men were no longer sitting on the truck; they had moved twenty feet away and were now sitting on two barrels. A dog had appeared, and it was sniffing around the men's feet. One of them kicked it away. The dog's yelp could be heard faintly by the three people on the hill, but they were not able to hear the men.

Lobo crawled back to Claire, and Carl followed. Lobo brought their heads close together and whispered his final directions.

"Ace," he said to Carl, "follow that arroyo to the base of those two boulders. The first two buildings from the left are yours. I'll take the two on the right."

Turning his face to Claire, he continued. "I'm going to work my way down the ditch until I get to that clump of bushes over there. It'll probably take me five minutes to get into position. You won't be able to see me there, so watch Carl. I'll signal to

Carl, and he in turn will signal back to you. At that sign, fire the first grenade at that pickup truck. Reload immediately, and wait to see where the people come from. Carl and I will hold our fire until we see what they're going to do. Fire the other grenades at any target you think appropriate.

"Hopefully we'll get them all the first few bursts. But we aren't going to hang around for a body count. Understood?" Carl and Claire nodded. "You watch Carl, and Carl, you watch me. When I split, you two split. Back up this ridge and over to the Jeep. If there's anybody inclined to follow us, the Claymores will stop them in the road. Questions?"

"There's a woman in there . . . Luz María," Claire whispered.

"Fine time to tell me that."

"I'm just saying that if you see a woman, don't shoot her."

"Jesus Christ," Lobo muttered. Then he tapped Carl's shoulder and motioned for him to start working his way down the hill.

Carl slid feet first into the arroyo and moved quietly down through the twists and turns toward the twin rocks Lobo had directed him to. A thin fog hung in the arroyo at waist height. He felt disembodied. The walls of the deep ditch hid everything except the starlit sky from Carl's view. He moved slowly, unable to see his feet clearly in the low-lying haze. He wondered if he would be able to see Lobo's hand signal. There was 100 yards to go.

Every movie hero he had ever seen guided his feet. He didn't know who he was, nor did he care. His heart jumped against his chest wall and he felt extraordinarily hot. Adrenaline fired his muscles hyperkinetically. There was nothing to do but keep slipping down the arroyo toward the twin rocks.

Lobo had an easier time of it, his feet used to moving through rough terrain without the benefit of guidance from his eyes. He also felt the adrenaline flush. His steps were quick but sure. Supporting his weight with his right arm, he moved down the steep incline without stirring a single loose rock or moving a cloud of dust. Lobo had the feeling of coming home. It only bothered him that it all looked too easy.

Claire could hardly stand the waiting. She had lost sight of both Carl and Lobo within a minute of when they left the top.

She could see the twin rocks and stared at them so intently that her eyes burned. It seemed as if an hour had gone by, and still, there was no sign of Carl. She wished she had a watch. How long had it really been? Two minutes? Three? Ten? She broke the M-79 and checked the round, then reclosed it carefully to avoid any sound. She wondered if it kicked and how bad? Lobo had never said. Should she hold it very tight? What would happen if it kicked out of her hands? Would she be able to recognize the man who killed Rabbit? Emilio, Luz María's son. Could she hit a man running? What would a grenade do to Emilio if she could hit him with it? She hoped it would blow him into a hundred bloody pieces—in slow motion. Lobo had told her some men in his team took ears off Vietcong. Maybe she would take some part of Emilio. His balls, she thought, and smiled. Feed them to some chickens, she decided. How long can it take to move two hundred yards, downhill all the way?

At one point Susie thought she saw a light flash instantaneously across the Jeep. She twisted around to look back, but there was nothing in the dark road as far as she could see. Maybe a car had passed on the highway? She moved around the Jeep's interior, checking the door locks. They were still locked. She wondered how loud it would be. Would there be explosions? She was about to urinate on herself but was too scared to get out of the Jeep. Then she heard a muffled, dim THUMP.

When Claire saw Carl wave his hand, she directed the stubby, fat barrel to the elevation Lobo had prescribed and squeezed the trigger. Her eyes were closed when the grenade thumped out of the barrel. It kicked as if someone had grabbed the barrel and lifted it. She expected a flash but maybe missed it because her eyes were closed. Suddenly, just as she opened her eyes, a pickup truck jerked spasmodically into the air and lit up like a strobe. She saw the ball of fire an instant before the roaring blast rumbled by her. The quiet, still night erupted with the crackling pop of the truck burning and the staccato rattling of automatic-weapon fire. Claire thought it sounded like hail hitting a tin roof and rolling off it. She could see the muzzle flashes from Carl's weapon—like a stuttering tiny flame from where Claire watched in fascination. She could see the line of tracers arcing across the camp from below and to her right, from where Lobo was.

How long had she stood there dumbly watching? She pulled another of the fat, bullet-shaped grenades from the bandolier and inserted it into the breech of the M-79. *Target. Appropriate targets.* She strained her eyes, trying to find the target she wanted in the chaos of the camp.

A black cloud rose above the flames of the truck, stretching hundreds of feet into the crisp desert sky and mushrooming. The dog lay still on its side. Both the men who had been sitting on the barrels were still. Claire realized that their fire was being returned; she could see flashes from two of the shacks. One of them must have an automatic weapon, she realized, for one window showed a continuous series of flashes. No one moved outside. Hail rattled on the tin roof.

Claire elevated the Thumper and squeezed. The second round hit fifty feet behind and to the left side of the shack from where she could see the muzzle flashes. The blast rattled back to her, and the fireball disappeared nearly as quickly as it appeared. She tried to calculate the range and distance, loaded again, and fired. THUMP! The third grenade exploded in front of the shack, but much nearer. A thin stream of fire licked up the wall by the door.

Nothing about it felt real to Claire. It was like watching a film at a drive-in movie with speakers turned up too loud. Except she was starting to smell it: powder, sulfur.

Three men ran from the burning shack, and Claire saw the first one tumble over like an acrobat, then lie still. The other two split up and ran in opposite directions. She could see the puffs of dust around them. She raised the M-79 and fired. THUMP! The grenade fell far short of the first shack and did nothing more than throw dirt into air. She had two rounds left. Two men came out of the first shack and ran behind an old Chevy. The second shack in the row, the one Claire had nearly hit, was engulfed in flames—two columns of black smoke rose into the night sky.

With the M-79 in one hand and the M-16 in the other, Claire

pushed off the ridgeline and started down the arroyo in the
direction Carl had gone. How the hell, she thought, can I hit
anything from way the hell up here?

Muzzle flashes came from six different windows in the four
remaining shacks. The air was filled with a mixture of sounds:
hail rolling off a tin roof, rocks being rattled inside a wooden
box, boards being slapped together at five-second intervals, the
truck's gas tank finally exploding, wood from the shack popping in the fire.

Once in the arroyo, there was nothing left for Claire but the
noises.

For Susie, it was like the Fourth of July. She could see the
dancing glow of fire from over the nearest hill, but not the
flames. The black smoke billowed upward in widening towers.
The noises were incoherent. She held her sides and rocked back
and forth, crying. The bright lights came up behind her so
quickly that by the time it registered on her, there were four
men pulling on the Jeep doors, trying to force them open.

They screamed in Spanish at her, and she screamed in terror
back. They didn't struggle with the doors for long. As Susie
tried to crouch on the floor, one of the men drew back and
smashed the rear window with the butt of a rifle. He reached in
through the hole and unlocked the door. Susie felt the hands
ripping at her shoulders as she was dragged out into the dirt.
They all screamed at her at once, all in Spanish, and she curled
up in the dirt, crying. Two of them jerked her up, and they
pulled her to the car parked behind the Jeep. Someone opened
a back door, and she was shoved headfirst onto the seat. Someone threw her legs over and jumped in beside her. Someone sat
on top of her. She felt the car moving, but she couldn't see.
Someone slapped her in the face. "Help me!" she screamed
three times before she was slapped again. She felt the car speed
up and the man on top of her sliding sideways as the car
rounded the curve. She felt a hand ripping out her hair, then a
sudden pressure that compressed her entire body. It was the
last sensation she would ever have. When the front tires hit
the Claymores, the old white Ford raised into the air and
flipped onto its back, burning like a blast furnace.

*   *   *

Lobo felt the thud in his feet as it passed through the ground from nearly 400 yards behind him. He turned and put his back to the scrub brush that had been his barrier and saw the white, then yellow flash come over the rise. No vehicles had left the camp. That meant someone must have been trying to come into the camp from outside. And it meant they would have found Susie in the Jeep, unless she had already run. He rolled back over to his stomach and searched for a target. He could hear the popping of Carl's M-16, firing in short bursts with longer and longer pauses between. The oppportune targets were gone. Where was Claire?

Lobo was ecstatic, high as he had ever been in the jungle, not knowing or caring where he was then. He sighted down the barrel and followed a man running in a manic zigzag between the hulks of two trucks. Lobo followed him for five seconds before squeezing the trigger. The man flipped over and folded up like a broken puppet. Lobo jerked out the clip and inserted a fresh one, having only one left. There was firing coming from one shack and pistol fire from the only other one left unburn-ing. Carl must have hit the Chevy's gas tank; the concussion when it exploded hit Lobo's face like the prop wash from a small plane. Sand whipped up and stung his eyes. He rolled over twice and fired short bursts into the only shack from which returning fire still came. He hoped the two men hiding behind the Chevy went up with it. He rolled over again and got behind a large rock. The shooters in the shack had zeroed in on his bush, and bullets tore through it, snapping limbs off and sending them sailing through the air. Then he saw Claire. "God damn you!" he screamed.

When Claire went by Carl, he thought he was seeing things. Nothing was real anyway, so why should the sight of Claire running by be any different? He pointed the M-16 at objects, squeezed the trigger, and out there somewhere the objects fell down or ran away. Bullets tinged and chipped off pieces of the rocks around him, but he felt detached from it. As if he were immune. Even the people who fell when he fired his weapon at them were only playing out their roles. In a few minutes somebody would call out, "time out," and they all would get up and go about their usual business. But then Claire ran screaming by him, yelling like some hellish banshee. She ran straight for the center of the camp and stopped. Carl could see dirt exploding near her feet. She leveled the Thumper and fired directly through the door of the third shack. The THUMP and BLAMMM came so close together that they seemed one sound in different pitches. The blast threw Claire backward nearly five feet and dumped her over two hay bales. As Carl stood, he saw Lobo running from the right, charging toward Claire like a crazy thing.

Lobo ran quick, like a determined buck weaving through a forest, firing in a sixty-degree horizontal arc from the waist. The exploded shack collapsed on itself in a shower of sparks and fire. Only one of the five shacks remained standing, and continual firing came from its windows. Lobo whirled toward the last shack and emptied a clip into its walls to cover himself. At the same time he bent over and kept running toward Claire.

Carl jumped forward into the open and also ran toward Claire, who lay motionless between the hay bales. He had moved a few feet when he tripped and fell on his face, digging the barrel of his M-16 into the sand. He rolled over when the earth around him began erupting in small puffs. By the time he had scrambled to his knees and looked up, Lobo was almost to Claire. Carl's knee was bleeding, but he didn't feel it; blood spurted through a torn hole in his jeans. His hand blistered when he grabbed the hot barrel of the M-16, but he didn't feel that either. All he could see was Claire and Lobo running toward her. Lobo!

Lobo suddenly stopping as if he had run into an invisible wall. He just stopped and stood there forever. Then, as if some hand had grabbed his left arm and jerked, Lobo spun a 180 and faced Carl, not fifteen feet between them. A dark stain covered the entire front of Lobo's shirt. Carl saw muzzle flashes from the shack, and Lobo sailed into the air toward Carl, landing facedown not ten feet away.

"No!" Carl heard himself screaming. Lobo raised his head from the neck and stretched out his hand, palm up, as if asking Carl to take it. Carl crawled closer until he could touch Lobo's empty hand, but as he did, it fell to the earth and Lobo's eyes closed. Rounds puffed the dirt near Carl, and he rolled to his side, holding the M-16 out in one hand, firing wildly into the sky.

Carl felt the fury in him like hot coals in his stomach, then the awesome feeling that he was alone out there. Continuing to fire erratically toward the shack, he crawled to Claire and put his face on top of hers. The face was blackened, the front of her hair and her eyebrows singed, but he could feel her steady breathing against his ear. He pushed himself up and behind a hay bale, pulling the dropped M-79 grenade launcher to his side. He took the bandolier from Claire and took out the last round, loading it. Bullets puffed the dirt around the hay bale.

Carl held the Thumper against his shoulder like a shotgun and fired. The grenade blasted through the window of the last shack and exploded.

There was no more returning fire. There was nothing left but the smoldering shacks and vehicles, the muffled roaring of the final shack as it smoked into the sky.

Carl realized that he wasn't breathing. He didn't know how long he had been holding his breath. He was even afraid to try breathing, afraid nothing would happen when he needed to. His head was heavy, and he couldn't see clearly through the smoke. Then, as his automatic nervous system overcame his will, his mouth dropped open, and he gasped for air.

Lobo made some kind of sound. Carl turned toward him and tried to crawl over, but his legs collapsed and he sank to the ground. We're all dead, he thought. All of us died. Lobo's voice came weakly, stuttering, faltering, like a rush of unfocused air. Carl lay on his stomach near the hay bales and tried to pull himself to Lobo.

Lobo's fingers dug into the dirt. His legs lay twisted around one another.

Finally Carl understood the word Lobo repeated: "Medic, medic, medic . . ."

seventeen

The battle ended thirteen minutes after beginning. Even in the darkness, illuminated by the flickering fires, the debris was visible throughout the camp. Shell casings covered the ground like dead silver locusts following an aerial spraying. There was no place to step without hitting one of the empty shells. A pickup truck and two cars still smoldered, and occasionally parts of superheated metal snapped, making a sound like the quick crack of dry wood in a fireplace. Of the six shacks in camp, three were burning and a fourth had already collapsed onto itself in a smoldering heap of undistinguishable material. In the darkness and deep shadows around the fires, bodies had the characteristics of bulky lumps, maybe potato sacks, lying incongruously here and there. The dog looked like a cast-off fur coat.

Carl shook Claire into consciousness by pulling on her shoulders and repeatedly calling her name. There seemed to be no injuries other than the charred appearance of flash burns and the singed hair. Carl realized she must only have been knocked out by the concussion blast. Still, when she opened her eyes, they were empty and lifeless. Carl thought he could see right through them into the void behind. Claire looked at nothing beyond him. When he asked if she was all right, Claire stared at him and said nothing at all.

Carl could still hear Lobo's faint cries: "Medic . . . medic." It sounded as if some part of his brain called out instinctively; there was no urgency, no passion, no fear, not even pain in his voice. Carl pulled Claire to a sitting position, then told her he had to go help Lobo. When he left her, Claire got up and walked straight ahead toward the nearest burning shack.

With the stunned indifference of the survivor, Claire surveyed the aftermath with calm yet horrified disbelief. So much destruction. She took each step deliberately, cautiously, picking her way through chunks of burning wood and white-hot metal. She was surrounded by popping fires. There was nothing in her mind at that moment; no connections were being made between what she remembered and what she understood, what she witnessed. She felt a distinctive sense of belonging amid the debris of destruction; the smell of it thrilled her. She wove through the remains like a drunk lost on a familiar street.

A boy, no more than seventeen years old, was lying on his back in her path. His eyes and mouth were open. A lizard had stopped near the boy's head, and it watched Claire suspiciously, its tongue sending out a challenge. Claire kicked dirt at the lizard until it scurried off; then she crouched by the body. She thought maybe he was the boy who had come to the shed that afternoon intent on raping her. His hand had been shot off. His white T-shirt had been shredded, and where his stomach would have been, only a blackened mass remained.

Claire looked around the immediate area for the boy's hand, but it was gone. She would have liked to have put it with the body, his sad, lifeless body. She was fascinated with the boy, noticing the most inconsequential things: a mole on his right cheek, thick wax in one ear, a broken strap on one sandal, his hairless chest, dilated eyes, the mass inside his stomach that bubbled with pseudolife, the condensation mist, the steam rising from his stomach wound. She avoided the impulse to put her hands inside his stomach.

Fifty feet farther on, Claire found the body of a woman, old and heavy. Claire touched the body with a fingertip, the skin dry and cool. "Luz María," she said quietly. "Did *el Dios* save you after all?" Claire sat next to the body and wrapped her arms around her sides. The old woman lay facedown in the dirt; she did not have a back. Claire let her head fall back until she was looking up into the sky. "Did you go to heaven?" Claire laughed. The various columns of black smoke rose to 100 feet, where they blended into one gray-black umbrella cloud. It hovered over the camp like a blanket blocking the stars and moon. The horror of it all filled Claire with contentment; she wanted to sleep there. She shivered in the cool air and laughed to herself again.

Carl found the place where the 30.06 bullet had entered Lobo's lower chest and exited in the right side of his lower back. There was an astonishing amount of blood on the ground. Carl made a bandage for a second wound in Lobo's thigh to stop the gushing blood from a torn artery. Blood seeped through the bandage and onto the ground. Carl didn't have to know very much about bodies and wounds to see that Lobo was rapidly bleeding to death. The mass of blood on Lobo's chest had clotted, but the leg continued to spurt blood from around the bandage.

Carl started crying, unable to stop himself. The impotent frustration tore at him. He held Lobo's head in his hands and watched a tear fall onto Lobo's cheek, mixing with the blood spots there. He wiped it off with his hand and brushed Lobo's hair. "Tell me what to do?" he pleaded.

Lobo's eyelids blinked rapidly. "Medic," he whispered.

"For God's sake, tell me what to do?" Carl cried.

Lobo's eyes fell over until they were staring at Carl. He smiled in an ironic, pathetic way and whispered, "Some fucking mess this is."

"Yeah," Carl answered, smiling faintly. "Sure is. But you gotta tell me how to fix all this. Lobo?"

"Aw, fuck," Lobo breathed out in a single heavy exhale.

When Lobo's head fell to one side, Carl could see the bright red trail of blood dripping out of his ear. He could hear the blood gurgling in his lungs. Lobo had been dead for a minute before Carl realized it. The rolling motion in his chest settled into utter stillness, and Carl hugged Lobo's head. "Wake up, wake up," he begged, "don't do this to me."

When he finally believed that Lobo was actually dead, that he wasn't going to get up laughing at the fine joke, Carl eased himself away from the body and scooted back ten feet before he could turn around and stand up. They had to run. It felt as if they had been in the camp all night. Where were the police? Anybody? Couldn't the smoke be seen? Claire? He looked to the place where she had been. There was no sign of her anywhere. "Claire!" he screamed.

Claire felt as if she were in a void, neither here nor there, like being asleep, only still aware of her surroundings—as if reality existed only somewhere on the periphery of her consciousness. It was, though, a comforting, even familiar feeling for her.

In the dream, Carl was calling her name, but she couldn't see him. The cloud covered her like a ceiling, enclosing her in the morgue of the encampment.

She felt enlarged, flying, floating, sailing, blown-up. The weight of death had left her. She flew through the air, surveying the destruction. The thought that she had done all this was overwhelmingly powerful. The horror filled her with peace.

Carl stumbled through the smoking residue of the camp, screaming Claire's name. He couldn't see her anywhere. He passed three bodies. One without an arm. He tried to swallow the vomit. But he stumbled over the dead dog and threw up as he hit the ground. The nausea racked his abdomen and burned his nose and throat. The man's arm lay five feet in front of Carl's head. He screamed and rolled away from it.

When he was able to stand, he ran behind one of the cars and through a passage between two burning shacks. There he saw her, sitting on the ground next to a woman's body. Claire's head was tilted down, chin on her chest, as if she were sleeping. Her legs were crossed lotus-style. Carl ran over and jerked her up.

"Lobo's dead!" he screamed angrily into her face. He shook her so hard that her head flopped back and forth. "Look what we've done!"

Claire smiled, and Carl hit her. She fell backward and cowered to protect herself. Carl fell beside her and held her. "I'm sorry," he said over and over.

"That's all right," Claire answered, rubbing his hair. "It's okay, baby, I understand."

"We've got to get out of here," Carl said, panic in his voice. Claire looked at him curiously. She wanted to stay there forever. Carl was crying. "We've got to run," he said.

"All right," Claire said, getting to her feet.

Carl grabbed her arm and jerked her back through the rubble and over to Lobo's body. "See?" he ordered. "See, he's dead."

Claire looked at him, a sad expression on her face, then bent over to touch his cheek. "Thank you," she said. "I love it, too, Lobo, I love it, too."

"Everybody's dead," Carl cried.

"We aren't," Claire said quietly.

Carl pulled her toward the road at a jog. They made their way along the base of the ridgeline, the ridge they had climbed over to wait in ambush, then back through the brush until they were on the road into the camp. Carl remembered that he had dropped the M-16 next to Lobo's body and left it there. The open road terrified him. He took the forty-five automatic from his belt and held it in his right hand, pulling Claire along with his left. When they came around the first wide curve, they saw the burning hulk of the Ford. Carl pressed his body against the rock wall and pulled Claire next to him. They made their way slowly past the heat from the burning car until they had cleared the curve and could see the shadow of the Jeep ahead. Carl kept the automatic pointed at the Ford until they were by it. One black, charred rigid arm protruded from a side window, its fingers clinging permanently to the window frame. Smoke rose in curls from the hand as if a cigarette were burning there. When they were past the car, Carl ran full speed toward the Jeep, jerking Claire along with him.

When Carl was pushing Claire into the front seat, he noticed the smashed-out rear window.

"Susie!" He yelled her name, looking around the area. He knew when he saw the window that Susie must have been in the Ford when it hit the Claymores. But he called her name. "Susie! Where are you?"

"Fried," Claire said, as if any idiot could see that.

"She didn't even want to be here," Carl said when he got into the Jeep and started the engine.

"Ironic, isn't it?"

"What's wrong with you, Claire? What *are* you?"

"We got them all," she said, ignoring him. "Everybody's dead now."

Carl got the Jeep turned around and raced back down the road to the highway, hitting the bump at the pavement so fast that all four tires lifted off the ground. He spun sideways and headed east toward Flores Magón.

Behind them—Carl saw in a glance through the rear window—smoke climbed over the hills and into the night. Behind them lay the bodies of ten men and two women in the camp, four men and one woman in the Ford. And behind them Lobo dreamed permanently of the jungle.

Carl drove for five miles, then pulled off onto the shoulder. He ran to the rear and pulled everything out of the cargo compartment—tents, packs, clothes, weapons, leftover ammunition—and shoved it all into the ditch. He left his forty-five lying on the seat. When he got back inside, Claire held the pistol in her left hand, its barrel against her left temple, the hammer cocked.

"Claire!" Carl screamed, and lunged for her arm. As he knocked the pistol away, it fired, the bullet crashing through the upper paneling. The blast momentarily deafened Carl.

Claire turned and stared angrily at him. "Asshole." She spit out the word.

Everything had come unglued. Carl couldn't think clearly; his heart beat so urgently that he thought it would break out of his chest. He forced the pistol from her hand and threw it out the window.

"Why won't you accept the fact that you're the only one of us destined to come out of this?" Claire said.

"You are crazy!"

"So what else is new?"

"How can you sit there like that? How could you even . . . think?"

"Just drive the car and shut up."

"Promise me you'll never ever try anything like that again."

"You won't be around forever. I can wait."

"Claire . . ."

"There's a car coming."

Carl twisted his head and looked down the road. In the distance a pair of headlights grew larger.

"They'll be able to see the smoke when they get to here," Carl said, starting the engine and pulling back onto the road.

"And you, smartass, threw away all the guns, didn't you?"

"No more killing—ever," Carl said and picked up speed.

The approaching car did not slow as it passed them. From what Carl could make out in the darkness, it was some kind of old sedan. A cold wind whipped around the Jeep's interior from the broken rear window. When Lobo's image appeared, standing in the middle of the highway, Carl cried out and swerved the Jeep. Claire stared out the window with a silly smile on her face.

The silence kept Carl in a low-grade terror. Claire would not speak to him. She acted as if she had died at the camp, or on the road when he knocked the pistol away from her head, and he was only hauling her lifeless body away. It was getting colder inside the Jeep as they proceeded north to the border. Carl told Claire that they had to figure out something to do with the busted window. Claire looked at him as if she didn't know him.

Carl tried everything to keep from seeing the camp in his mind. He concentrated on remembering trivial incidents from his childhood. He thought of his opening day in college. He even went over the details of his visits with Claire when she was in Fairbrook. He needed some kind of explanation, some answer. He was crushed with responsibility. If he had not taken Claire out of Fairbrook, if he had not agreed to take her to Corpus Christi, if he had kept her away from the drugs, if he had not taken them himself . . . if, *if.* "Look at me!" he screamed at Claire. She did, and smiled sweetly. "God damn you!" Claire stared at the highway.

Carl had broken his wristwatch somewhere. The crystal was shattered, and the hands had stopped at 7:05. He had no idea what time it was after they went through El Sueco and turned north. There wasn't much traffic. Maybe a car or two every ten miles on the average. Tired from the constant pressure on the accelerator, Carl's knee began throbbing. He reached down to rub it, wincing at the sudden, sharp pain. He couldn't see his leg in the darkness, but his fingers felt the stickiness of blood. He had no memory of injuring himself.

In a few hours, maybe as few as three, they would be at the border. Carl had no idea how to get them across. Would the border patrols be alerted to what had happened at the camp by now? Regardless, what explanation would he use for the busted-out window, for the blood on his leg? Had he missed something when cleaning out the Jeep? Even one bullet? What would Lobo do? Lobo would have a plan. Is there some other way to cross the border without driving through one of the transit points? Should he leave the Jeep and take Claire across the river like a wetback? Is that possible? He could feel the panic rising in him again, after he had spent an hour trying to get rid of it.

Claire smoked incessantly and stared out the window. Sometimes his glance caught her smiling the way she had been off and on since they left the camp. So they did get across the border, then what? What was he going to do with her? About her? He looked over at her. She's crazy, he told himself, Claire is out of her mind. Maybe she always was. She set the fire, he told himself. She tried to kill me. She did kill Mother. Maybe she'll try again. He shook those thoughts from his mind and concentrated his attention again on the options for crossing the border. One thing at a time, he reminded himself. Take one step, then another step, then another. You can only do the best you can. He peptalked himself for fifty miles.

The abundance of his thoughts excited him. As they drove, his head seemed to clear, focus itself, and guide him. Lobo would be proud, he told himself. I can do it, he said to himself. He would wait near the border until there was a lot of traffic, as Lobo had, coming in. Then he would roll down all the windows, so the glassless one would not call attention to itself. Even in the lights at the station it would be dark beneath the dash where his leg would be hidden. And if they asked him to get out of the car, he would explain the knee as the result of a hiking accident. He regretted throwing away the packs. Oh, well. While waiting for the traffic, he would carefully inspect the Jeep for anything that would cause suspicion. Maybe he should buy some tourist things before crossing the border, so it would look as if they had been shopping. Would anybody return from Mexico without buying something? Of course not, he told himself. How much money did he have? He had left $1,000 at Lobo's apartment. But how much did he have with him? He couldn't remember. But any would do. And he knew there was some money in his wallet.

"Without any help from you," Carl said to Claire, "I have figured out how to get us back across the border." He waited for her to say something, and when she didn't, he continued. "You better get yourself together before we try it, too."

Claire looked at him and said, "I know a guy in Juárez who'll get some stuff for us before we get back into the old USA. It's a lot cheaper down here."

"Drugs? You want me to buy drugs for you, then take them across the border after what . . . we've done?"

"Sure."

"You are *crazy*."

"You keep saying that. Trying to convince me or you?"

"You."

"Don't bother. Look, I'll give you directions when we get into Juárez. The guy has a pharmacy near the market."

"Forget it."

Claire moved across the seat and put her arm around Carl, leaning her head on his shoulder. In a sweet, girlish voice she said, "I'm going to need it, Carlie. I can't be all sweetness and light at the border if I don't get myself right. Now consider that." She rubbed his thigh, and when her hand approached his knee, Carl pushed it away with a small cry.

"Are you hurt?" She sat up and tried to see his knee in the darkness below the dash. She sounded sincerely concerned.

"I think I must have cut my knee or something."

"Turn on the light, let me see."

"Lobo took out the bulb."

"Oh, yeah. Well, give me your lighter."

What a change, Carl thought. It seemed actually to matter to her that he was cut. He fished the lighter out of his pocket and handed it to her. Claire got down on the floorboard and inspected his leg in the flame from the Zippo. "Can I push up your jeans without it hurting?" she asked.

"I don't think so."

"You bled a lot, but it's all clotted now. I guess it's all right if it's quit bleeding." She raised up and stuck the lighter back into his pocket.

"How can you turn off and on like that?" Carl asked.

"That ability is why I'm *not* crazy," she said, patting his shoulder, then scooting back across the seat.

"There's more than one of you, Claire, and I think I know only one of them."

"Interesting," she answered. "Is that glow Juárez?" she asked, nodding toward the dim yellow haze on the horizon.

"How the hell would I know? I've never been here before."

"I'm sure it is."

"No drugs," Carl said.

"Okay. You deal with a wild woman trying to cross the border. Because let me tell you something, kiddo; I'm about to fly loose over here." When Carl didn't answer, Claire added, "Please?"

He decided to let her stew over it for a while, let her endure the silence. But he knew he would have to do it just one more time. But just once more.

At the central market in Juárez, Claire bought Carl a pair of slacks, a shirt, and picked up some bandages for his knee when she was conducting her other business in the pharmacy. She bought a bright full skirt for herself and a white scoop-neck blouse. She bought sandals for them both. They changed in the car, after Claire had dropped four whites down her throat. Carl asked for two and took them. Then, after they were dressed and the desert clothes had been stuffed in a garbage can at the entrance to the alley where they were parked, they went on a romp through the market. The amphetamines took Carl right off the ground and flung him through the market stalls like an erratic missile. He found himself wishing that everything about them were normal, that there were no past, so they could fly through the market like every tourist and buy anything pleasing to them. He wished for it so hard that he began to forget.

Claire had him buy two quarts of tequila. She said, "The border guards never believe anybody goes into Mexico and doesn't come back with cheap tequila. We get one bottle each without having to pay a duty."

So Carl carried the Cuervo in a sack along with a serape, a pair of carved donkeys that served as salt and pepper shakers, and a replica of a bowie knife. He had always wanted one of those. Claire carried the speed, wrapped in two plastic bags stuffed into the cups of her bra. They bought a sombrero because it was big and visible and would look normal lying in the back of the Jeep. Carl wanted to buy something to eat, but Claire wouldn't let him. Claire bought a flower pot.

Finally she told him they had enough. "Let's go. It's getting close to midnight on a Saturday night. We'll catch the crowds going home."

"I already thought of that," Carl said with disappointment. He wanted her to know that he could plan things himself.

And they passed through the border as easily as they had at noon that day. They had been in Mexico for just more than twelve hours.

"We did it," Claire said excitedly as they drove into downtown El Paso.

Carl pulled off at the curb, leaned out the door, and vomited.

eighteen

They headed for Corpus Christi to retrieve the money Carl had left there. The cars they passed on the farm roads that Sunday morning carried families to church. Carl would pull out to pass and look over to see them dressed in best clothes. Always the men drove. Sometimes there were no children; sometimes the car was full of them. The men had hard faces, lines grooved in their faces like tracks in mud. Their collars were too tight. They seemed to go for red ties. The children always looked back at the people in the Jeep. Sometimes they waved or made faces. A boy stuck out his tongue at Claire, and she gave him the finger. Carl could see the boy telling his father about it when he looked in the rearview mirror. The Jeep sped down the narrow two-lane back road, passing pickup trucks, Buicks, Pontiacs, and, it seemed, a million Chevrolets.

A norther blew in at dawn. The cold wind whipped through the broken window, and frost formed on the window ledge in spite of the heater's running full blast. Carl had thrown everything away. They had only the clothes they wore and what they had bought at the Juárez market. Claire covered herself in the serape. Carl stopped at a grocery store in Brackettville and found a cardboard box out back. He cut it to fit the window and taped it in place with a roll of electrical tape from the tool kit.

They rolled through the towns like an express Greyhound: Uvalde, Batesville, Big Wells, Catarina, Artesia Wells, down I-35 for a few miles until the turnoff at Encinal, then east to

Freer and Alice. Carl realized when they were on that short stretch of I-35 that if he turned around and drove for 1,300 or 1,400 miles, he would reach Minneapolis, home, where he could never go again.

They drove all day Sunday. They didn't eat. They seldom talked. Claire played the radio, twisting the dial, trying to keep a continual flow of music she liked. Carl didn't mind, there was nothing to say. She was a stranger anyway, just a rider. Or less. They had nothing to say. It was dark Sunday when they drove into Corpus Christi.

"How are we supposed to get in?" Carl asked when they pulled into the driveway at the apartment on Lobo Street.

"I know where the key is," Claire said as she got out of the Jeep and walked ahead of him.

Carl had a vision of the apartment's being filled with waiting police. The fact that there was nothing unusual around the building did nothing to destroy that image. Lobo's truck was parked in the driveway where they had left it. It made Carl feel even sicker than he had been when they turned onto the street and saw the sign: LOBO STREET. Lobo's face stayed with him. Certain words said in certain ways sounded like "medic" to Carl. When they passed a drugstore sign, the word "medicine" translated itself in Carl's brain to "medic." He knew that no matter how long he lived or what else happened, he would hear that word forever.

Claire unlocked the apartment and walked in. Carl, after looking up and down the hallway, followed her. He left the door open, and Claire went back to shut it.

"Leave it open," he told her. "We won't be here that long." He couldn't make himself look around the room.

"It is kind of spooky, isn't it?" Claire agreed.

Everything remained as they had left it on Friday. Carl noticed a pair of Lobo's boots lying by the couch, and he gasped to keep from crying. He turned away and walked directly into the kitchen. He took the money out of a lima bean box in the freezer and stuffed it into his pocket. They now had $1,000 plus the $40 or $50 he had left from the market in Juárez. Claire had gone into the bedroom. He could hear her opening drawers. Something about the feel of the money in his pocket, maybe, but he suddenly remembered that there had been more than $1,000 in Lobo's pockets.

"Come here," Claire called to him from the bedroom.

The money was cold against his leg. He didn't want to go into the bedroom.

"Carl? Come here."

"You come out here," he answered.

"Hey, I'm not going to carry these bags out by myself."

He had forgotten that their luggage was in there. Trying not to look at anything around him, Carl walked to the bedroom.

Claire had changed into jeans. She was standing at the foot of the bed, holding a piece of paper in her hands. Their luggage was where he left it, stacked on the bed.

"It's from Lobo," she said, holding the paper out to him like a dirty cloth. "Did you see him leave this?"

Carl shook his head. He didn't want to touch the paper, retreating from it like a viper.

"Here, take it. It's addressed to you." Claire grabbed Carl's hand and slapped the note into it. "Here, Ace," she said sarcastically.

Carl turned over the crumpled paper and started reading it. "Ace," it said at the top. Claire sat on the bed, watching him. Carl's hand trembled.

I knew you'd get back. Your kind survives, Ace. My kind? It doesn't matter. Listen, pal. Those girls are both crazy. Ditch them. Your sister's dangerous and she'll eat you alive if you let her.

Out back, in the tool shed behind old lady Manchester's garden, there's a metal box under a pile of burlap bags in the right hand corner. There are four cases of canning jars there. The box is in the bottom crate. It looks kind of like a safety deposit box. It's yours. It's nothing valuable or anything. Just some stuff you might like.

Well, stay low, Ace. Shit's gonna hit the fan real soon.

That was all. He had scrawled "LOBO" across the bottom.

Claire stood up and pulled on Carl's arm. "Are you fucking crying, or what?" she said.

Carl folded the paper and put it in the pocket of his jeans. His motions were careful, methodical, deliberate.

"Lobo was a sucker," Claire said.

Carl turned sharply toward her, but then his face calmed and he simply shrugged her hand off his shoulder. He said, "Claire, I love you. God help me, I love you. But I can't help you, and you do need to be helped. You aren't only crazy, you're evil. I'm going to take you back to Fairbrook . . ."

Claire jumped him like a wounded tiger, clawing her way over his body as she knocked him to the floor. Her fingernails dug into his face and cut him deeply before he could react. She cried out and tried to bite him. He could see the wild hatred in her eyes, the evil compulsion to kill him. She tore his cheeks to shreds before he could buck her off. She screamed obscenities into his face, her breath and spit hot in the wounds. Her screams were like some vicious thing shrieking in the night. He could see her only through one eye. The other had been cut by her fingernails. Carl tried to hold her down, but she squirmed beneath his weight like a dying snake. Blood from his face dripped onto her face. Her screams degenerated into incoherent noises.

Then she stopped. Stopped everything as quickly and suddenly as if she had died. But her eyes were open and looking at him. Carl felt the tension in her muscles relax.

"Oh, Carl," she whispered. "Oh, look at your face. I hurt you."

Carl released his hold but stayed on top of her. For an instant he felt the impulse to smash her head into the floor. Killing autobreeds, he thought. Killing once leaves it as an option forever. His body trembled, but he was losing the will to fight with her. She looked so sad and troubled.

"Carl, Carl, Carl," she repeated his name. "I don't know why I hurt you. Am I really sick? I didn't mean to hurt you, Carl. Do you forgive me, darling?"

She tried to lift her head, to bring their faces closer together. It looked as if she wanted him to kiss her. Her cheeks were pockmarked with the drippings of blood from his face. They looked like freckles. She started crying, and unable to help himself, Carl sobbed over her, his tears falling into her face and smearing spots of his blood.

Through her tears, Claire said, "We only have each other, Carl. We can't ever leave one another. We would die without each other. I will die without you. Please don't ever talk about leaving me."

"Claire . . ." But he didn't know what else to say.

Claire reached up and pulled him down to her. He lay on top of her, feeling the slight movement in her hips. She put her lips against his ear and whispered, "I love you, I love you. Please make love to me. I need you. I need you, Carl."

She pulled his hand up and put it on her breast. She licked the inside of his ear, breathing heavily into it. And he needed her. He had needed her every moment of his life.

Claire turned her face and licked the blood from his wounds, the saltiness of her tongue stinging as it slid over the cuts. "Let me taste your blood," she whispered, and licked around his lips. Carl winced but could not move away from her. She pushed her tongue into his mouth and moved her hips against him. His erection pushed into her jeans.

Claire moved one arm down his side and slipped it beneath her. She tried to get her hand into her back pocket. All the time saying to him, "We have to be together always. I know you won't let me go back there, not away from you forever. I know you love me as much as I love you." She got her hand into her pocket and touched the metal. Her free hand pushed itself between them and rubbed his erection. "We will always be together, always, just the two of us now." The other hand began withdrawing the Buck folding knife.

Carl thought she was trying to push down her pants. I can't do this, he told himself. I can't let this happen. But he could feel her, taste her, smell her. She was his Claire. Maybe he could help her. Maybe if they were alone together, if they could have the time to work through the problems . . . "Mayday, Mayday!" his brain screamed.

Claire pulled her hand from between their crotches and reached behind his back to join the hand holding the knife. Quietly she unfolded the blade. Carl did not hear the click. Claire withdrew her tongue from his mouth and moved her head to the side so she could see the arm with the knife poised over his back. She raised it as high as possible over the middle of his back, the handle held tightly in both hands.

Her eyes were on his when her arms dropped. She wanted to see, face-to-face, what death looked like. It looked surprised. That's all. The blade penetrated an inch before she felt an obstruction, maybe a rib. She jammed her arms down, pulled the blade forward as if its point were directed at her own heart, and buried it until her hands met his back. The weight of Carl on her increased 100 pounds, or so it felt. The look of surprise was still in his eyes when his head dropped down, bumping her temple with his forehead and nearly knocking her out. He never made a sound. He just exhaled. She could feel the warmth of his blood dripping over her sides.

It took her remaining strength to push out from under him. She knew he was dead without touching him again. The knife handle looked like a black stick in his back. Its blade tip had penetrated half an inch into his heart.

Claire scooted away from Carl's body and stared at the knife handle. It looked like a bodily defect, but one that had always been there. She hesitated to pull it out. She reached over and pushed his hair out of his eyes and back over his ear. He could have been soundly sleeping. Lobo's crumpled note protruded from Carl's pocket, and Claire pulled it out with two fingers. "Crazy?" she said to the note. "Oh, yeah? Crazy like a fox." She pulled the blanket from the bed and gently draped it over Carl's body, the knife handle holding it up like a tent pole. It didn't look proper to her. She reached under the blanket without uncovering the body and withdrew the knife, surprisingly easily. Then she let the blanket fall back. That's better, she thought. She laid the knife beside the body and, with the note in her hand, went outside to the tool shed. She went into the musty darkness of the place and had to use a cigarette lighter to see. After finding the burlap, she lifted off the top three cases and pulled open the flaps of the fourth. There was nothing in it but the metal box. It was lighter than she thought it would be. She carefully reclosed the tool shed and took the box back into the apartment, back into the bedroom where Carl lay beneath the blanket. "Well," she said to the hump on the floor, "let's see what Lobo had in here." It wasn't locked.

On top was a piece of official paper trifolded with the name showing: James Earl Marlar. So that's his name, Claire thought. No wonder he preferred Lobo. It was his GI insurance, with his mother listed as beneficiary. Claire pulled out an envelope in which there were three photographs. One was a portrait shot of Lobo in his army uniform, and she thought he looked extraordinarily handsome without the beard and scraggly hair, even if a little odd. He wore the rank of Sergeant First Class, the shoulder patch of the 82nd Airborne Division, and the Ranger crest. On his chest were three rows of ribbons, a Combat Infantryman's Badge, and silver senior parachutist wings. The other two photographs showed Lobo in jungle gear posed along a road between two rice paddies, and Lobo and two other soldiers in face paint sitting outside a bunker. That was the Lobo she recognized. She put the photographs on the bed and inspected the velvet boxes stacked in the bottom. Each held a medal: Silver Star, Bronze Star with clusters, Vietnam Campaign Citation, the Combat Infantryman's Badge, and two she didn't recognize. The three-row rack of ribbons lay in the bottom.

"God," Claire said, "why would anybody keep shit like this?"

She noticed that a blood trail was running out one side of the blanket.

"Well, Carl, what would you have done with all this shit?"

She pulled the blanket away with a single jerk and knelt beside Carl's body. "Want to be a hero, kiddo?" she said. Then she took each of the medals and pinned them to his shirt. They looked pretty all lined up in a row across his chest. "You are so cute," she said to the body.

She started to re-cover the body but changed her mind. He looked nice lying there with all those ribbons and medals stuck on his shirt. It would be a shame to spoil the effect.

"I think I'm going to miss you a lot, kiddo," she said to the body. "You probably think now that I don't love you, but I do. I really, really do. I've always loved you, and only you. Now, you see, there's nobody for me to love. But I knew it would end up like this. I never was supposed to have anybody to love or to love me. That's just the way it was always supposed to be. I think I'm sad."

*   *   *

Don Merritt

It took her a half hour of searching to round up four candles, a Bible, some weeds from Mrs. Manchester's garden, and set them up just the way she wanted it to look. She spread her altar on the bedroom floor next to Carl's body. Candlelight bounced off the medals on Carl's shirt. It looked like sparks.

The Bible had been Rabbit's. It was red, stolen from a motel room, and hollowed out to carry a packet of heroin. She placed it on the floor between the bed and the body, with a candle just off each corner. Two of the candles were incense. The thick, sticky smell floated through the room. She made a wreath around the Bible with the weeds. She took the Buck knife off the bed and, without cleaning its blade, put it ɔn top of the Bible. She liked the way the black handle looked against the red plastic on the Bible cover.

"Nobody can say we Grant women don't know how to mourn," she told Carl. She tried to prop open his eyelids so he could watch, but they wouldn't stay up.

She sat there for ten minutes, staring into the candlelight, trying to think of something to say. The medals on Carl's chest looked so pretty with the light dancing on them. She sat with her legs crossed, nude, her fingertip stroking the shiny black Buck handle.

Finally Claire picked up the knife and held it out over the Bible, where light from all four shrinking candles leaped off the bright blade. The weeds began smoldering, thin wisps of smoke curling up into the air and mingling with the raw incense. Claire touched the knife point to the taut skin on the rise of her right breast and made the first cut.